LOWBOY

'Brilliantly imagined . . . An unusually vivid portrait of a young man about to be overwhelmed by his psychotic imagination. It's very well done and has been rapturously received by critics on both sides of the Atlantic.' *Literary Review*

'America's most original young writer has given us a book for the ages. Compelling, compassionate, and deeply unsettling, *Lowboy* introduces us to the brilliant sixteen-year-old Will Heller, a Holden Caulfield for our troubled times.' GARY SHTEYNGART, author of *Absurdistan*

'A breathtaking journey.' O, *The Oprah Magazine*

'The novel has a thriller-like pace and Wray keeps us riveted. The opening pages recall Salinger, but the denouement and haunting aftertaste may make the stunned reader whisper "Dostoevsky". Yes, it really is that good.' *Kirkus*

'A suspenseful story by one of *Granta*'s Best Young American novelists.' *Dazed and Confused*

'Sucks you into the tunnels under New York and doesn't let you go until its perfect ending. Wray effortlessly portrays the cracked and distorted mind of his teenage hero. What a beguiling novel.' TIM PEARS, author of *In the Place of Fallen Leaves*

'A dizzying, assured novel which flirts with tough subject matter.' *Waterstone's Books Quarterly*

'John Wray invests his anti-hero's skewed perspective with empathy and complexity, as well as offering up a finely detailed portrait of multicultural New York that makes it easy to see why he was named one of the US's best young writers by *Granta* magazine.' *Metro*

JOHN WRAY is the author of *The Right Hand of Sleep*, which won a Whiting Writers' Award, and *Canaan's Tongue*. He was chosen as one of *Granta*'s Best Young American Novelists in 2007. Born in 1971, he lives in Brooklyn, New York.

Also by John Wray

Canaan's Tongue
The Right Hand of Sleep

LOWBOY

JOHN WRAY

CANONGATE
Edinburgh · London · New York · Melbourne

This paperback edition published in 2010 by Canongate Books

Published in Great Britain in 2009
by Canongate Books Ltd,
14 High Street, Edinburgh, EH1 1TE

First published in the United States in 2009
by Farrar, Straus and Giroux
18 West 18th Street, New York 10011

1

Copyright © John Wray, 2009

The moral right of the author has been asserted

British Library Cataloguing-in-Publication Data
A catalogue record for this book is available on
request from the British Library

ISBN 978 1 84767 152 3

Design by Cassandra J. Pappas

Printed and bound in Great Britain by Clays Ltd, St Ives plc

www.meetatthegate.net

TOWER HAMLETS
LIBRARIES

91000000503870

Bertrams	06/08/2010
AF	£7.99
THISCA	TH10001395

For Violet

LOWBOY

On November 11 Lowboy ran to catch a train. People were in his way but he was careful not to touch them. He ran up the platform's corrugated yellow lip and kept his eyes on the train's cab, commanding it to wait. The doors had closed already but they opened when he kicked them. He couldn't help but take that as a sign.

He got on board the train and laughed. Signs and tells were all around him. The floor was shivering and ticking beneath his feet and the bricktiled arches above the train beat the murmurings of the crowd into copper and aluminum foil. Every seat in the car had a person in it. Notes of music rang out as the doors closed behind him: C# first, then A. Sharp against both ears, like the tip of a pencil. He turned and pressed his face against the glass.

Skull & Bones, his state-appointed enemies, were forcing their way headfirst up the platform. Skull was a skinny milkfaced man, not much to look at, but Bones was the size of a MetroCard booth. They moved like policemen in a silent movie, as though their shoes were too big for their feet. No one stood aside for them. Lowboy smiled as he watched them stumbling toward him: he felt his fear falling away with each ridiculous step they took. I'll have to think of something else to call them now, he thought. Short & Sweet. Before & After. Bridge & Tunnel.

Bones saw him first and started pounding on the doors. Spit flew noiselessly from his mouth against the scuffed and greasy glass. The train lurched then stopped then lurched forward again. Lowboy gave Bones his village idiot smile, puckering his lips and blinking, and solemnly held up his middle finger. Skull was running now, struggling to keep even with the doors, moving his arms in slow emphatic circles. Bones was shouting something at the conductor. Lowboy whistled the door-closing theme at them and shrugged. C# to A, C# to A. The simplest, sweetest melody in the world.

Everyone in the car would later agree that the boy seemed in very high spirits. He was late for something, by the look of him, but he carried himself with authority and calm. He was making an effort to seem older than he was. His clothes fit him badly, hanging apologetically from his body, but because he was blue-eyed and unassuming he caused nobody concern. They watched him for a while, glancing at him whenever his back was turned, the way people look at one another on the subway. What's a boy like that doing, a few of them wondered, dressed in such hideous clothes?

The train fit into the tunnel perfectly. It slipped into the tunnel like a hand into a pocket and closed over Lowboy's body and held him still. He kept his right cheek pressed against the glass and felt the air and guttered bedrock passing. I'm on a train, he thought. Skull & Bones aren't on it. I'm taking the local uptown.

The climate in the car was temperate as always, hovering comfortably between 62 and 68 degrees. Its vulcanized rubber doorjambs allowed no draft to enter. Its suspension system, ribbonpressed butterfly shocks manufactured in St. Louis, Missouri, kept the pitching and the jarring to a minimum. Lowboy listened to the sound of the wheels, to the squealing of the housings at the railheads and the bends, to the train's manifold and particulate elements functioning effortlessly in concert. Welcoming, familiar, almost sentimental sounds. His thoughts fell slackly into place. Even his cramped and claustrophobic brain felt a measure of affection for the tunnel. It was his skull that held him captive, after all, not the tunnel or the passengers or the train. I'm a prisoner of my own brainpan, he thought. Hostage of my limbic system. There's no way out for me but through my nose.

I can make jokes again, Lowboy thought. Stupid jokes but never mind. I never could have made jokes yesterday.

Lowboy was five foot ten and weighed 150 pounds exactly. His hair was parted on the left. Most things that happened didn't bother him at all, but others got inside of him and stuck: nothing to do then but cough them up. He had a list of favorite things that he took out whenever there was a setback, ticking them off in order like charms on a bracelet. He recited the first eight from memory:

Obelisks.
Invisible ink.
Violet Heller.
Snowboarding.

The Brooklyn Botanic Garden.
Jacques Cousteau.
Bix Beiderbecke.
The tunnel.

His father had taken him snowboarding once, in the Poconos. The Poconos and the beach at Breezy Point were items nine and ten. His skin turned dark brown in the summer, like an Indian's or a surfer's, but now it was white as a dead body's from all the time he'd spent away.

Lowboy stared down at his deadlooking arms. He pressed his right palm hard against the glass. He came from a long line of soldiers, and was secretly a soldier himself, but he'd sworn on his father's grave that he would never go to war. Once he'd almost killed someone with just his two bare hands.

The tunnel straightened itself without any sign of effort and the rails and wheels and couplings went quiet. Lowboy decided to think about his mother. His mother was blond, like a girl on a billboard, but she was already over thirty-eight years old. She painted eyes and lips on mannequins for Saks and Bergdorf Goodman. She painted things on mannequins no one would ever see. Once he'd asked about the nipples and she'd laughed into her fist and changed the subject. On April 15 she would turn thirty-nine unless the rules changed or he'd miscounted or she died. He was closer to her house now than he'd been in eighteen months. He had these directions: transfer at Columbus Circle, wait, then six stops close together on the C. That's all it was. But he would never see his mother's house again.

. . .

Slowly and carefully, with studied precision, he shifted his attention toward the train. Trains were easier to consider. There were thousands of them in the tunnel, pushing ghost trains of compressed air ahead of them, and every single one of them had a purpose. The train he was on was bound for Bedford Park Boulevard. Its coat-of-arms was a B in Helvetica type, rampant against a bright orange escutcheon. The train to his grandfather's house had that same color: the color of wax fruit, of sunsets painted on velvet, of light through half-closed eyelids at the beach. William of Orange, he thought, giving himself over to the dream of it. William of Orange is my name. He closed his eyes and passed a hand over his face and pictured himself strolling the grounds of Windsor Castle. It was pleasantly cool there under the boxcut trees. He saw dark, paneled corridors and dust-covered paintings, high ruffled collars and canopied beds. He saw a portrait of himself in a mink pillbox hat. He saw his mother in the kitchen, frying onions and garlic in butter. Her face was the color of soap. He bit down hard on his lip and forced his eyes back open.

A self-conscious silence prevailed in the car. Lowboy noticed it at once. The passengers were studying him closely, taking note of his scuffed Velcro sneakers, his corduroy pants, his misbuttoned shirt, and his immaculately parted yellow hair. In the glass he saw their puzzled looks reflected. They think I'm on a date, he thought. They think I'm on a field trip. If they only knew.

"I'm William of Orange," said Lowboy. He turned around so he could see them better. "Has anybody got a cigarette?"

The silence got thicker. Lowboy wondered whether anyone had heard him. Sometimes it happened that he spoke perfectly clearly, taking pains with each word, and no one paid him any mind at all. In fact it happened often. But on that day, on that particular morning, he was undeniable. On that particular morning he was at his best.

· · ·

A man to his left sat up and cleared his throat. "Truant," the man said, as if in answer to a question.

"Excuse me?" said Lowboy.

"You're a truant?" the man said. He spoke the sentence like a piece of music.

Lowboy squinted at him. A dignified man with an elegant wedge-shaped beard and polished shoes. His face and his beard were exactly the same color. He sat very correctly, with his knees pressed together and his hands in his lap. His pants were white and sharply creased and his green leather jacket had a row of tiny footballs where its buttons should have been. His hair was bound up in an orange turban. He looked stately and unflappable and wise.

"I can't be a truant," said Lowboy. "They've already kicked me out of school."

"Is that so," the man said severely. "What for?"

Lowboy took his time answering. "It was a special sort of school," he said finally. "Progressive. They sent me home for good behavior."

"I can't hear you," said the man. He shook his head thoughtfully, letting his thin mouth hang open, then patted the seat next to him. "What did you say?"

Lowboy stared down at the empty seat. It had happened again, he decided. He'd been moving his lips without actually speaking. He stepped forward and repeated himself.

"Is that so," said the man. He heaved a gracious sigh. "You aren't coming out of prison?"

"You're a Sikh," Lowboy said.

The man's eyes opened wide, as though the Sikhs were a forgotten race. "It must be a *very* good school, to teach you that!"

Lowboy took hold of the crosspole and let himself hang forward. There was something melodramatic about the Sikh. Something contrived. His skin lightened slightly where his face met his turban, and the hair behind his ears was platinum blond. "I read about you in the library," Lowboy said. "I know all about you Sikhs."

They were coming up to the next station. First came the slight falling back of the tunnel, then the lights, then the noise, then the change in his body. His left side got light and his right side got heavy and he had to hold on to the pole with all his strength. The fact that he'd met a Sikh first, out of everyone in the tunnel, signified something without question but its meaning refused to come clear to him. I'll think about him when we stop, Lowboy said to himself. In a little while I'll think about him. Then I'll know.

The platform when it came was narrow and neglected-looking and much less crowded than the one before had been. He'd expected to find everyone waiting for him—his mother, Dr. Kopeck, Dr. Prekopp, Skull & Bones—but there was no one on the platform that he knew. The doors slid open and closed on nothing.

"The capital of the Sikhs is the city of Amritsar," Lowboy said as the C# and A sounded. His head was clear again but he still wanted to smoke. "Amritsar is in Punjab. Sikhs believe in reincarnation, like Hindus, but in a single god, like Muslims. A baptized Sikh never cuts his hair or beard."

"A fine school." The Sikh smiled and nodded. "An extraordinary school."

"I need a cigarette. Let me have a cigarette, please."

The Sikh shook his brown face merrily.

"The hell with this," said Lowboy.

The train gave a lazy twitch and started rolling. Both seats on the Sikh's right side were empty. Lowboy sat down in the farther one, mindful of the Sikh's bony elbow and his legs in their pressed linen pants. He took a deep breath. It was reckless to get close to another body just then, when everything was so new and overwhelming, but the empty seat between them made it possible. It was all right to sit down and have a talk.

He checked to see who else was listening. No one was.

．　．　．

"The Sikh religion is less than seventy years old," Lowboy said. His words fluttered before him in the air.

The Sikh pursed his lips and bunched his face together. "That is not so," he said, enunciating each word very clearly. "That is not so. I'm sorry."

Lowboy put his hand on the seat between them, where the Sikh's hand had just been. It was still slightly warm. "Can you say definitely that it's older than that?" he said. He drummed against the plastic with his fingers. "You're not seventy years old."

"I can say so," the Sikh said. "I can say so absolutely."

Why does he have to say everything twice, thought Lowboy. I'm not deaf. It was enough to put him in mind of the school. The way the Sikh was looking at him now, trying hard not to seem too curious, was exactly the way the doctors did it there. He forced his eyes away, fighting back his disappointment, and found himself staring down at the Sikh's feet. They were the smallest feet he'd ever seen on a grown man. Those look like shoes a doll would wear, he thought. Sikhs are supposed to be the tallest men in Asia. He looked from the shoes to the Sikh's face, flat and pleasant and unnatural as a cake. As he did so he began to have his doubts.

Here they come, Lowboy thought, forcing his mouth and eyes shut. His throat went dry the way it always did when the first doubts hit. The train braked hard and shuddered through a junction. The air grew warmer by exactly six degrees.

"All right, then," he said cheerfully. But it wasn't all right. His voice sounded wrong to him, precious and stilted, the voice of a spoiled English lord.

"All right," he said, feeling his skin start to prickle. "It's perfectly all right, you see."

．　．　．

When he let his eyes open they were back inside the tunnel. There was only one tunnel in the city but it was wound and snarled together like telephone wire, threaded back on itself so it seemed to have no beginning and no end. Ouroboros was the name of the dragon that ate its own tail and the tunnel was Ouroboros also. He called it that. It seemed self-contained, a closed system, but in fact it was the opposite of closed. There were openings spaced out along its length like gills along the body of an eel, just big enough for a person to slip through. Right now the train was under Fifty-third Street. You could get off at the next station, ease your body through the turnstile, and the tunnel would carry on exactly as before. The trains would run without a single person in them.

Two men got off at the next station, glancing back over their shoulders, and a third man moved ahead to the next car. Lowboy could see the man in question through the pockmarked junction doors, a middle-aged commuter in a rumpled madras jacket, Jewish or possibly Lebanese, flipping nervously through a giltedged leather datebook. Soon the Sikh would switch cars too and that was perfectly all right. That was how you managed in the tunnel. That was how you got by. You came and sat in a row and touched arms and knees and shoes and held your breath and after a few minutes, half an hour at the most, you separated from each other for all time. It would be a mistake to take that as an insult. He'd done the same a thousand times himself.

Lowboy patted himself on the knee and reminded himself that he hadn't gotten on the train to talk to little grandfatherly men about religion. He'd gotten on the train for a reason and he knew in his heart that his reason was the best one that anyone could have. He'd been given a calling: that was what it was called. It was a matter of consequence, a matter of urgency, a matter possibly of life and death. It was as sharp and light and transparent as a syringe. If he got careless now he might lose track of his calling or confuse it with something else or even forget his calling altogether. Worst of all he might begin to have his doubts.

He turned toward the Sikh and nodded sadly.

"I get off at the next stop," he said. He coughed into his sleeve and looked around him until the people who'd been watching looked away. "Next stop!" he repeated, for the benefit of all present.

"So soon?" said the Sikh. "I haven't even asked—"

"William," said Lowboy. He gave him his bankteller's smile. "William Amritsar."

"William?" the Sikh said quaveringly. He pronounced it *Well-yoom*.

"But people call me Lowboy. They prefer it."

A long moment went by. "Pleased to meet you, William. My name is—"

"Because I get moody," Lowboy said, raising his voice. "Also because I like trains."

The Sikh said nothing. He looked Lowboy over and ran two bird-like fingers through his beard. Trying to make sense of me, Lowboy decided. The idea made him feel like a hermit at the top of a cliff.

"Underground trains," he said. "Subways. Low in the ground." He felt his voice go quiet. "Does that make sense to you?"

The train started braking and Lowboy got to his feet, still keeping his eyes on the Sikh. The Sikh kept motionless, propped up straight in his seat like a nearsighted little old lady on a bus.

"You're not a doctor, are you?" Lowboy said, squinting down at him. "An MD? A PhD? A DDS?"

The Sikh looked surprised. "A doctor, William? Why on earth—"

"Can you prove to me that you're not with the school?"

The Sikh gave a dry laugh. "I'm past eighty, William. I once was an electrical engineer."

"Bullshit," Lowboy said, shaking his head. "Balls."

Everyone in the car was looking at him now. There were times when he was practically invisible, monochrome and flat, and there were others when he gave off a faint greenish glow, like teeth held up to a blacklight. When that happened his voice got very loud very fast and the only thing he could do was keep his mouth shut. The air outside the glass got darker. There were things he wanted to explain to the Sikh, to apprise him of, but he held his breath and pressed his lips together. He could keep himself from talking when he had to. It was one of the first things that he'd learned to do at school.

"Who was that chasing you?" said the Sikh, propping his elbows on his beautiful sticklike legs. "Were they truancy officers?"

Lowboy shook his head fiercely. "Not sent by the school. Sent by—" He caught himself at the last moment. "By a *federal agency*. To frighten me. To try and make me follow their itinerary." He looked at the place on his wrist where his watch should have been, but there was nothing there, not even a paleness. He wondered if he'd ever had a watch.

"You'll have to excuse me," he said. He turned measuredly around to face the doors. It was too warm in the car for sudden movements.

The train seemed to hesitate as it came into the light. Its ventilators went quiet and its mercury striplights flickered and it rolled into the station at a crawl. The station was a main junction: six lines came together there. Its tiles were square and unbeveled, lacquered and white, like the tiles on a urinal wall. The only person on the platform was a transit guard who looked ready to fall down and die of boredom any minute. Lowboy frowned and bit down on the knuckle of his thumb. There was no good reason for the platform to be empty at 8:30 on a Tuesday morning.

. . .

The guard watched the train pull in out of his left eyecorner, careful not to seem too interested. The old school trick. Lowboy thought of the last glimpse he'd had of Bones, pounding on the glass and shouting at the conductor. He thought about Skull running alongside the train and making panicked circles with his arms. He looked at the transit guard again. Something was clipped to the inside of his collar and he held his head cocked toward it, moving his lips absently, like someone reading from a complicated book. Watching him made Lowboy want to lie down on the floor.

"I made a mistake," he said, turning back to the Sikh. "This isn't my stop."

The Sikh seemed happy to hear it. "I suppose, then, that you ought to take a seat."

"I'll tell you why they expelled me," Lowboy said, sitting back down. "Do you want to know?"

"Here comes the policeman," said the Sikh.

Lowboy turned his head and saw the transit guard hauling himself up the platform and glancing sideways into each car and mumbling into his collar. The doors remained open. No announcement was given. If the guard looked bored it was only because he knew about each event before it happened. Lowboy let his head rest against the window for a moment, gathering his strength, then eased his body sideways until his cheek touched the Sikh's shoulder. The collar of the Sikh's shirt smelled faintly of anise. Lowboy's eyes started to water.

"Can I borrow your turban?" he whispered.

"You should go back to school," the Sikh said through his teeth.

"I wish I could," said Lowboy. His left hand gave a jerk. The rest of the car was looking from the transit guard to Lowboy to the Sikh. Some of them were starting to get restless.

"Do you have a family?" the Sikh said. He shifted in his seat. "Do you have anyone—"

"Give me a hug," said Lowboy. He took the Sikh's arm and ducked underneath it. He'd seen the trick in the movies but he had no way of knowing if it worked. The anise smell got stronger. He saw the transit guard reflected in the windows and in the doors and in every set of eyeballs on the train. He buried his face in the Sikh's leather jacket. The Sikh sucked in a breath but that was all.

"Hello, Officer," said the Sikh.

As soon as the guard was gone Lowboy retched and leaned forward. The Sikh pulled his arm free as matter-of-factly as a nurse and smoothed out a crease in his pantleg. "I have a grandson in Lahore, in Pakistan," he said. "You put me in mind of that boy."

"Was he a truant?"

The Sikh smiled and nodded. "His name is Sateesh. A bad boy like you are. When he was sixteen—"

"I'm not ready yet," Lowboy said, tapping out a rhythm against his chest. "They never should have kicked me out of school."

The train began rolling and the niceties of life resumed, the breathing and the coughing and the whispering and the singing out of key. The singing especially seemed strange to him after the long awful silence but he was overjoyed to hear it. He hummed to himself for a little while, grateful for the rocking of the train, then took a breath and made his face go flat. What he had to say next was solemn and imperative and meant for the Sikh's ears alone. He had nothing else to offer, either as a gesture or a covenant or a gift: only his one small discovery. But lesser gifts than that had saved men's lives.

"Your religion values sacrifice above all things," he said. He caught his breath and held it. "Sacrifice is important. Am I right?"

The Sikh didn't answer. Lowboy had expected him to react in some way, to cry out or throw up his hands or give a laugh, but instead he kept his sallow face composed. He wasn't looking at Lowboy anymore but at a girl across the aisle who was fussing with a pair of silver headphones. He no longer seemed wise or elegant or even clever. The longer Lowboy stared at him the more lifeless he became. It was like watching a piece of bread dry out and become inedible.

"You're drying out," said Lowboy. "Are you listening?"

It's because of the heat, Lowboy thought. We're all baking in it. The Sikh stared straight ahead like someone sitting for a portrait. He's preparing himself, Lowboy thought. Mustering his resources. The Sikh would get out at the next station and move to another car, or transfer to a different train, or call the police, or even send a message to the school: Lowboy knew he'd do one of these things. But it was terrible that the Sikh would act in ignorance, without waiting until he'd received his gift. A worse setback could not have been imagined.

All at once, without moving, without turning his head or taking in a breath, the Sikh said quietly and clearly: "What is your reason, William?"

"My reason?" Lowboy said. He could hardly believe it. "My reason for running away, you mean?"

The Sikh blinked his eyes idly, like a kitten sitting in a patch of sun.

"I'll tell you why," Lowboy said. "Since you ask." He leaned over. "The world won't make it past this afternoon."

. . .

The Sikh turned his head and regarded him now, though only his watery close-set eyes had life. Lowboy couldn't be sure that he was listening, since he hadn't yet said a word, but it seemed extremely likely that he was. The moment of revelation made a leisurely circuit of the car, glittering dimly in the air, then passed away without the slightest sound. Lowboy paid it no mind. The Sikh sat bent stiffly forward, bobbing his head impatiently, digging the heels of his pennyloafers into the floor. Fidgeting like the girl across the aisle. Why was everybody so impatient? It was true of course that time was running out. There were two transfers at the next station: an orange and a blue. Choices would have to be made. They were being made already.

A hissing came off the rails as the train crossed a switch and the noise cut straight up through the car, hanging in sheets down the length of the aisle, as if to offer them a kind of shelter. Lowboy blinked and took a breath and said it.

"The world's going to die in ten hours," he said. He shoved his fist against this teeth so he could finish. "Ten hours *exactly*, Grandfather. By fire."

The look on the Sikh's face was impossible to make sense of. His body was the body of a somnambulist or a corpse. Lowboy closed his mouth and crossed his arms and nodded. It was difficult, even painful, to keep his eyes on the Sikh, to sit there and wait for the least show of feeling, to smile and keep nodding and hope for the one true reply. He decided to look at the girl with the headphones instead.

She was sitting straight up in her seat, the perfect mirror image of the Sikh, as poised and geometric as a painting. The longer Lowboy looked at her the less he understood. His take on the girl, on the Sikh, on everything in the car refused to hold still any longer. His thoughts slid like mercury from one possibility to another. The spaces between events got even wider. They were empty and white. He forced himself to focus on the surface of things and on the surface only. There's more than enough there, he said to himself. He let his eyes rest flatly on the girl.

The girl's hair was colored a dull shade of red, the shade dyed-black hair turns in the summer. It was cut in a way he'd never seen before, with long feathered bangs hanging over her eyes. When she leaned forward her face disappeared completely. Lowboy pictured a city of identical girls, all of their faces hidden, silver headphones plugging up their ears. He'd been a cosmonaut for eighteen months, a castaway, an amnesiac, the veteran of an arbitrary war. The world had gotten older while he'd been away. Away at school, regressing. He studied the girl's hands, cupped protectively in her lap, hiding whatever the headphones were attached to. She seemed ashamed of her hands, of her lap, of her intentionally torn crocheted stockings. She'd hide her whole body if she could, he thought. He felt a rush of recognition. So would I.

Her hands were chapped and pink, with short, ungraceful fingers, but there was something about her fingers that he liked. Only when she brought one to her mouth did he notice that the nails were bitten down to the cuticles, torn and unpainted, the nails of a girl half her age. Something worked itself loose in his memory. I've seen hands like that before, he thought. A backlit picture came to him then, a body reclining in midair, a sound that wasn't quite a woman's name. A few seconds more and he'd have remembered the name, even said it out loud, but before that could happen he made a discovery. The name and the backlit picture fell away.

The girl across the aisle was smiling. She was smiling without question, blushing and parting her bangs, but the meaning of her smile kept itself hidden. "It's the music," Lowboy murmured to the Sikh. "There's music in those headphones that she likes." But even as the Sikh nodded back—blankly, disaffectedly—Lowboy saw he was wrong. The girl's smile wasn't private; it was unabashed and open. And she was smiling it at nobody but him.

That made Lowboy remember why he'd left the school.

Cautiously, as an experiment, he tried to smile back at the girl. He kept his eyes wide open and made sure to show her his teeth. The strangeness of what he was attempting made the roof of his mouth go numb. There'd been no girls at the school, at least not in his wing, and he hadn't cared about girls before he'd been enrolled. But now he did care about them. Now they made him feel wide awake.

"Don't leer at her that way," said the Sikh.

"I'm not leering," Lowboy said. "I'm being sexy."

"You're frightening her, William."

Lowboy waved at the girl and opened his eyes wider and pointed at his mouth. Her smile went blank and stiffened at its corners and he adjusted his own smile accordingly. The girl jerked her backpack open and tilted her face forward, lowering her bangs like a shutter across a storefront. She gaped down into her backpack like a baby looking into a well.

"Why won't she take those fucking headphones off? I want to tell her something. I'll *sing* it to her if she wants. I want to—"

"The world will end?" the Sikh said. "Why is that?"

Lowboy stopped smiling at once. What magnetism he might have had was neatly and resourcefully sucked away. The question had been meant as a distraction, nothing more: to keep him from establishing contact. To disarm him. The girl with the backpack receded and the Sikh slid quietly forward to take her place. He wasn't the man that he had been before. The rest of the car went dark as though the Sikh were in a spotlight. There was no curiosity in his expression, no humanity, no love. He spoke in a completely different voice.

"Your voice has changed," said Lowboy. "I don't think I can hear you anymore."

"Don't trouble that poor girl any longer, William." Behind his sparse discolored beard the Sikh was grinning. He raised his head and coughed and gave a wink. "Why not trouble me instead?"

It was then that Lowboy saw the danger clearly. The fact of it hit him in the middle of his chest and spread out in all directions like a cramp. "No trouble," he said. He said it effortfully and slowly, biting his breath back after every word. "No trouble at all, Grandfather. Go away."

The Sikh flashed his teeth again. "Grandfather?" he said at the top of his voice. He said it to the rest of the car, not to Lowboy. He was making a public announcement. He looked up and down the car, the consummate entertainer, and brought a shriveled hand to rest on Lowboy's shoulder. "If I was *your* grandfather, boy—"

His voice was still booming up and down the car like the voice of a master of ceremonies as Lowboy slid his hands under the Sikh's beard and pushed. The Sikh lifted out of his seat like a windtossed paper bag. Who'd have guessed he was as light as that, thought Lowboy. The Sikh arched his back as he fell and opened his mouth in a garish slackjawed parody of surprise. A standpole caught him just below the shoulder and spun him counterclockwise toward the door. The booming was coming not from the Sikh anymore but from an intercom in the middle of the ceiling. "Columbus Circle," Lowboy shouted. "Transfer to the A, C, D, 1, and 9." No jokes anymore, he thought, laughing. No part of this is funny. A woman halfway down the car stood gasping in the middle of the aisle. He turned to face her and she shut her mouth.

"Boy," the Sikh said breathlessly. He was sputtering like the intercom above him. *"Boy—"*

Lowboy got down on his knees next to the Sikh. "Sacrifice makes sense," he said. "Would you agree with that?"

The Sikh flashed his teeth and made thin meaningless noises and brought his hands together at his throat.

"You're worried about me," Lowboy said. He shook his head. "Don't worry about me, Doctor. Worry about the world."

The Sikh slid gradually backward until his head came to rest against the graphite-colored crease between the doors. His eyes transcribed a lazy mournful circle. His turban sat next to his elbow like an ornamental basket, still immaculately wrapped and cinched and folded. So that's how they do it, Lowboy said to himself. They put it on and take it off just like a hat.

"Boy," the Sikh said again, forcing the word out with his tongue. It seemed to be the only word he knew.

Lowboy bent down and took hold of the Sikh's jacket. He could feel the little footballs grind together under his fingers. "It's all right, Grandfather," he said. "I've got something in mind."

Detective Ali Lateef—born Rufus Lamarck White—enjoyed anagrams, acrostic poems, palindromic brainteasers, and any cipher that could be broken with basic algebra. When casework was slow he amused himself by inventing simple alphabets, usually of the phonogrammic type, and using them to post compromising anecdotes from the life of Lieutenant Bjornstrand, his immediate supervisor, on the Missing Persons Progress Panel above his desk:

KJJH54DSG QWEJDJ88 65XPTH. GHY69DD HN53T UGH8?
GH77!

These notes were Lateef's only eccentricity. In every other respect he was straightforward and obliging, and no one had ever, in that office where abuse was the only reliable sign of friendship, questioned his abilities on the job. His clothes, his race, even his lack of a wife were brought up almost daily, but his casework was never once made mention of. His case reports were passed around like textbooks. This was a source of deep and abiding satisfaction for Lateef, though he wouldn't have admitted it to a single living soul.

His embarrassment at his name was another thing Lateef kept to himself. No person, living or dead, had ever been made a party to it: not his colleagues, not his occasional drinking partners, and certainly not anyone in his family. His father, an MTA motorman known for most of his life as Jebby White, had rechristened all of his children on January 1, 1969, after changing his own name to Muhammad Jeroboam in front of the King's County clerk. It had taken Rufus the better part of a year to pronounce his new name properly, and the sound of it still felt foreign in his mouth. Had he been old enough to decide for himself—had he been consulted in any way whatsoever—the change might have excited him, possibly even become a source of pride; as it was, he'd tried to come to terms with it for more than forty years.

What bothered him most was the fact that his father was the least political man he knew. When the Motormen's Local had struck in 1976, he'd returned to work after only two days, shambling and apologetic, a week before the official strike was ended; it had been easier for him to change his surname than to demand a living wage. Lateef's father saw no contradiction in this, but he himself couldn't think about it without taking something in his hands—a doorknob, a paperweight, the cast epoxy butt of his pistol—and gripping it until the memory subsided. He was a churchgoing man but forgiveness came slowly to him.

His anger and his reticence made Lateef a man of solitary pleasures. His tastes ran to 78-rpm records, statesmen's autobiographies, and single malt Scotch, preferably from the Highlands; the women he knew referred to him, sometimes dismissively, sometimes wistfully, as Old Professor White. He lived in a roomy but charmless walkup on the affordable side of Prospect Park, across from the stucco ramparts of the Brooklyn Botanic Garden. His father and mother were both still living—improbably enough, with each other—on the opposite side of his block; when they left their windows open he could hear their threadbare squabbles word for word. Like his co-workers, his parents virtually never made reference to his work: he might have been a hit man, from the elaborate care they took, or a soldier in some unmentionable jihad. He might have been making people disappear instead of finding them.

"Special Category Missing" was Lateef's area of expertise. It wasn't a coveted field, as such: usually the SCM was found dead, in which case Homicide stepped in, or wasn't found at all, and after a demoralizing, fruitless search the bureaucrats in Cold Case took it over. Seventy percent of SCMs went either terminal or cold, but for reasons obscure even to himself Lateef took comfort of a kind in that statistic. He liked the invisibility of Missing work: the invisibility of the SCM, the invisibility of the crime, even the invisibility, to a certain degree, of the investigator himself. If a file went cold—receding silently to a place where, in all probability, its invisibility would become permanent—he never failed to feel a touch of vertigo. The fact that he enjoyed this sensation was something he thought about on certain evenings, sipping Scotch in his patent-leather armchair in the dark. But not very often.

From his first SCM, Lateef had shown a talent for the work—Bjornstrand liked to call it "disappearance envy"—and over the years his talent had been distilled into a kind of virtuosity. Even the dreaded Notification Call played to his strengths: patience, politeness, and a slight but unmistakable distance from the present moment. At such times he was able to think of himself, without the slightest embarrassment, as a perfectly fashioned instrument of God's will. Even his own name seemed to represent him.

The morning of the eleventh could easily have been such a time. Lateef sat straightbacked at his desk, humming to himself unmusically, thumbing briskly through a stack of photocopies. From time to time he closed his eyes, raised a sheet to his face, and basked in the aroma of fresh toner. There were days when he hated the smell, when he scrubbed his hands and shirtsleeves to get rid of it, but that morning it acted on him like a drug. An SCM had come in that promised not to bore him, depress him, or make him feel like a proxy for Homicide. It was unusual in that it was structured, in that it had a clearly defined and symmetrical shape; it was unusual in that its shape had not been given to it after the fact, by the investigating officer, but before the fact, by the SCM himself. And it was unusual in that it involved a cipher.

It would have been a perfect morning, one of the best of his career, if the mother had been willing to sit down. There was always a mother, of course, or a boyfriend or a roommate or a wife: typically they either sulked or panicked. But this particular mother had been stationed outside his office for the last three quarters of an hour, ignoring the NO SMOKING posters, talking to herself in a steady unembarrassed monotone and blocking both the elevator and the stairs. Lateef went stealthily to his door, parted the black-, red-, and green-striped Venetian blinds—a Kwanzaa present from his father—and looked out at her.

It was obvious that she came from another country. She stood with her feet pointed inward, like a peasant in a painting by some old master, and let her ash drop innocently to the floor. She had none of the defensiveness of the other complainants, none of their deference, none of their incredulity or shame. When they brushed past her she looked at them with a kind of affectionate surprise, smiling and blinking, then back down at her orthopedic-looking shoes. The kind of shoes a nurse would wear, Lateef said to himself. But the woman outside his office door could never have been a nurse. The shoes had been chosen to make her look less graceful—they must have been— but somehow they had the opposite effect. There was something involuntary, even feral, about the way she held herself. The beautiful woman's indifference to everything around her. She seemed to have no idea of the inconvenience she was causing. She held her cigarette between her thumb and ring finger, a little distastefully, like a twig that she'd just pulled out of her hair.

Lateef pushed his door open—ignoring Bjornstrand, who was leering at the woman and fluttering his eyelids—and waited for her to acknowledge him. "We don't smoke in the waiting area, Mrs. Heller. You can smoke inside my office if you want."

If he hadn't already known she was the mother, he'd have known it from the look she gave him then. "Not in the waiting area," she repeated, as though reciting a lesson. She glanced around her calmly, apparently for an ashtray, then stepped past him with the cigarette still lit. By the time he'd gotten to his desk she'd stubbed it out—On what? he wondered—and was watching him without the slightest sign of interest.

"Please sit down, Mrs. Heller."

She stayed as she was. "Don't worry, Detective," she said pleasantly. "My son will not be breaking any laws."

"He already has," said Lateef. "He's stopped taking his medication, condition one of his release. And he's assaulted a passenger on the uptown B."

Her arm moved toward the stool but never reached it. Her face had the same chalkish, spiritless blankness now that each of them came to wear without exception. Her cropped blond hair seemed indecorous somehow, out of keeping with her grief. It ought to be dyed black, Lateef found himself thinking. Either that or shorn off altogether.

"What I mean to say, Detective, is that there's no cause for alarm. No need to get out the cutlery."

He raised his eyebrows at this, anticipating a smile, but her expression stayed fixed. "To call out the cavalry, I think you mean," he said finally.

She blushed very subtly and Lateef watched her blushing. It was at that moment, waiting for her to recover her composure, that he had the day's first unprofessional thought. He brought his fingertips together and suppressed it.

"You'll find him today," she said. "Tonight at the latest. He'll come along without making any trouble."

"What if we don't find him till tomorrow, Mrs. Heller?" He glanced down at the stack of photocopies. "What if we don't find him until Thursday?"

Again she avoided his question. "How long will it take to catch him, do you think? How many hours?"

"If he stays on the subway, then we ought to find him soon. If, on the other hand, he decides to head up to the street—"

"He'll stay on the subway. He'll stay there until he gets caught."

There was a quality to her voice now that could almost have passed for pride. Lateef squinted at her. "Mrs. Heller—"

"*Miss* Heller," she said. There was nothing flirtatious about her. She was still standing next to the seat she'd been offered. She seemed to want nothing to do with it.

"Your son is in serious trouble, Miss Heller. He's run away from his escorts, not only causing the staff at Bellavista Clinic distress, but also requiring both the NYPD and the MTA to mount a difficult, hazardous, and potentially very expensive search. He's threatened a number of passengers, behaved recklessly on the platform at Rockefeller Center, and already committed one assault that we know of." Lateef heaved the sigh—professional, regretful, boundlessly patient—that he kept in reserve for complainants of a certain category. "All of this in the first hour after his release." He let that hang between them in the air. "The first *hour*, Miss Heller."

Now she sat down. "I'm sorry that he's done that."

"So are we." He said nothing for nearly a minute, watching as she considered her position. He passed the time by trying to place her accent. European: he was certain of that much. A northern country. Denmark, possibly.

"Can we continue, Miss Heller?"

"Of course we can." Her accent was harsher, more foreignsounding than before. "Why couldn't we?"

"No reason at all. Let's make a list, together, of any reasons your son might have had—"

"Have you ever taken Clozapine, Detective?"

He coughed and passed a hand over his face. "I can't say I have," he said. "I can't say that I've ever felt the need."

"My son says it's like being pressed under glass."

"Under glass. All right."

"Having been told that, and having seen what it does to him, I can understand . . ." She hesitated. "I can't *understand*, maybe, but I can certainly appreciate—"

"What can you appreciate, Miss Heller?" Lateef said, raising his eyebrows. What he was going to say next was uncharitable, even cruel, but he made no attempt to temper it. "Is there a better drug for your son than Clozapine? A more effective one, maybe, with fewer side effects? Something you haven't yet had the chance to try?"

She stared back at him dully, folding and unfolding her arms. It was a long while before she gave him an answer.

"There is nothing, Detective, that we haven't tried. Not a thing. I have no doubt that it says so in your file."

"I'm not interested in my file just now, Miss Heller. It's important to me that we get this clear." He slid the photocopies to one side and returned her dull-eyed look. "Was your son right to do what he did this morning?"

Her mouth opened slightly but no sound came out of it. An argument of some kind had started out in the hall—Bjornstrand and a voice he couldn't place—and he listened to it absentmindedly. When she finally spoke her voice was so inflectionless, so slight, that it was hard to understand her. But he'd known from the beginning what she'd say.

"No, Detective. I don't believe my son was right."

She said no more than that, only sat with her head slightly bowed, keeping her palms pressed flat against her knees. There was no sense of urgency about her, no hostility, no alarm. She seemed in no great hurry to recover her son. She wasn't bewildered by what had happened, or in shock: shock was more immediate, less controlled. As Lateef took her measure, trying—as he often did during questioning—to picture her on an uneventful day, he came to understand that he was witnessing the end of a long and unbroken arc of daily suffering. Not its beginning but its end.

"Miss Heller," he said.

She surprised him by sitting up at once. There was color to her face now, even a kind of sharpness. He found himself oddly flustered by her look. As though I've been caught eavesdropping, he thought.

"How are you going to find my son, Detective?"

His eyes fell automatically to the file. "Most kids who run, Miss Heller, run to get away from something. They'll take off in whatever direction's easiest, and nine times out of ten they don't get far. But your son seems to have a definite goal in mind." He waited for her nod before he continued. "I want to learn as much as I can about his reasons for running. Then, hopefully, you and I can make a guess— an educated guess—as to what his goal might be."

She sat back and gave him a tentative smile. "People don't often look for reasons when it comes to Will."

"I have a way of working, Miss Heller, that I like. I think of things in terms of cause and effect."

She nodded at him, still smiling. "Thank you for that."

He pulled a drawer open and took out a short yellow pencil, the sort that banks and public libraries keep at their counters, and tested its point with his thumb. "Is there a reason for what your son did today?"

"There's always a reason."

He unwrapped a packet of index cards, set the cards down parallel to the folder, then arranged them into seven equal piles. "A reason you could put into words for me?"

She looked at him as though he'd just betrayed her confidence. When she spoke again her voice was as smooth and formal as a clerk's. Her accent seemed English now, possibly Scottish. "You mentioned a letter, Detective, when you rang."

"More of a note, really." He pushed the drawer shut. "On hospital stationery. Folded into quarters and set on the lintel of the door to your son's cell." He paused a moment. "His room, that is to say. At the clinic."

"The lintel?" she said, frowning.

"The little wooden ledge above the door. No one thought to give the room a once-over, apparently, since your son was being discharged that same morning. The note was addressed to 'Violet.'" He tapped the pencil end soundlessly against the desktop. "Tucked into the note were seven days' worth of Zyprexa tablets, crushed into a powder, and five hundred milligrams of Depakote. He'd been so good about taking his meds for the past six months, and had shown so much insight into his, ah, disorder"—he was reading from the file directly now—"that the staff had cut back on their supervision." He put the folder aside. "Their hunch is that he kept the pills under his tongue until he was able to hide them. A small amount of the medication was ingested that way, but not much."

"He knew that he was getting out," she said evenly. "That's why he stopped."

"What do you mean?"

"He took his meds to keep the doctors happy. He planned to stop taking them as soon as he could." She smiled again, more crookedly this time. "He told me so."

Lateef looked away from her at once, focusing on a waterstain in the ceiling's farthest corner, then began rummaging through his casework with as much effrontery as he could muster. He let thirty seconds go by, then an entire minute. She seemed perfectly satisfied to sit mutely across from him for as long as he chose to ignore her.

"I guess this comes as no surprise to you, then," he said finally. "Your sitting here in my office, my asking you these questions, the NYPD manhunt for your son."

"It doesn't."

He almost swore at her. "Do you mind if I ask you something, ma'am? Why didn't you just ask the state of New York to hold on to your boy for another eighteen months?"

"I did."

He'd already taken in breath to speak, already composed his reply, so that now as he sat back in his chair the air slid out superfluously through his teeth. The room was silent for an instant, suspended in a perfect vacuum; then the everyday noises resumed. The photocopiers sputtered, Bjornstrand's donkeylike laughter carried in through the vent, and in one of the neighboring offices a man cursed the Department of Motor Vehicles in Yiddish. She was sitting as she'd been from the beginning, hands braced against her knees as if to keep herself upright, looking past him out the soot-encrusted window. For the second time it occurred to Lateef that he was witnessing the end of something, but this time he had no idea what it could be.

"May I see the note, Detective?"

He'd made a number of mistakes with her already: he saw that clearly as he looked at her. He'd overestimated her tiredness, extended her more sympathy than she'd expected, and she'd responded by wasting half an hour of his time. Without meaning to, without being aware of it herself, she was frustrating him at each and every turn. For a few fleeting seconds, when she'd shown signs of anger or dismay, he'd come close to feeling that he understood her; the rest of the time she'd given him nothing he could use. He resolved, for the sake of expediency, to put it down to her foreignness. They take things differently in Denmark, he decided.

"*Violet,*" he said, unfolding the note and pushing it across the desk. "Do you know anybody by that name?"

She nodded absently, spreading the paper out flat. "Will's nickname for me. My favorite color."

"But your given name is Yda? *Y-D-A?*"

"That's right."

"And Heller is your maiden name?"

Most women would have felt the need to clarify—to explain, for example, that they'd elected not to change their name, or mentioned the father, even in passing—but she did nothing of the kind. She held the note a hairsbreadth from her face and stared at it, then reached down for the cigarette and pressed it to her mouth. Again he felt that he was spying on her.

"Why did you request that your son remain at Bellavista past the date of his release?"

But the note took up the whole of her attention. "I can't read this," she murmured. "He's made a scramble of it." She held the paper at arm's length now, shaking her head, as though it had been given her in error. It was with something close to gratitude that he saw it quivering slightly in her fingers.

"It's been translated into code." He took the note back reverently, touching it only with his fingertips: he was on solid ground again. The text, which apparently meant nothing to her, was as clear to him as his own handwriting. "A cipher, technically speaking."

She was sitting forward now, staring furiously at the paper. She was suddenly much easier to make sense of. "You can understand this thing?"

"Nobody can do that, Miss Heller, without the key." He laid the note between them on the desktop, sideways, so they both could read it:

LEVP UCKGER. YKS BVUE RBE JVHE KT V TGKWEP VJL
C LKJR. C LKJR BVUE RBE JVHE KT V TGKWEP UCKGER
WBY CQ RBVR?

C TEEG VGG PCABR KGL UCKGER ISR RBE WKPGL CQ
AERRCJA BKRREP. EUEPY IKLY FJKWQ RBCQ. EUEPLY
IKLY FJKWQ RBCQ VJL MPEREJLQ BE/QBE LKEQJR RBE
WVY MEKMGE LCL WCRB HE WBEJ C WVQ QCOF. LK
YKS PEHEHIEP UCKGER? APVJLVL OKSQCJQ REVOBEPQ?
RBE WVY RBEY LCL WCRB HE VR RBE IEACJJCJA.

RBE WKPGL CQ AERRCJA BKRREP EUEPY LVY. WBEJ
MEKMGE QRVPR RK RVGF VIKSR CR RBE PEVGCRY
GEVUEQ RBECP HKSRBQ. KQDY C OVJ QEE RBCQ
UCKGER MKQQCIGY IEOVSQE CUE IEEJ QCOF.
MKQQCIGY IEOVSQE CUE IEEJ VWVY QK GKJA JKW
RBVR C OKHE IVOF C OVJ QEE CR.

RBE WKPGL CQ AERRCJA BKRREP JKR QGKW VJL
QREVLY ISR GCFE V QJKWIVGG (JKR V DKFE) KP V
IKSGLEP AERRCJA TVQREP VGG RBE RCHE. RBCQ CQ

JKR HY KWJ CJUEJRCKJ UCKGER IEOVSQE C PEVL CR
VJL C QVW CR KJ RBE JEWQ.

C WVJR RK KMEJ GCFE V TGKWEP UCKGER. GCFE V
TGKWEP LKEQ CJ MKERPY. C RBCJF RVBR HCABR
BEGM VQ RBE WKPGL CQ CJQCLE KT HE VJL RBVR
WCGG/HCABR BEGM RK OKKG RBE WKPGL. MKQQCIGY.
IKLCEQ WCGG BVUE RK AER OKGL JKW UCKGER. HVJY
IKLCEQ. VJYRBCJA EGQE CJ RBE WKPGL YKS OKSGL
BEGM HE WCRB ISR JKR WCRB RBCQ. CH QSPE YKS
FJKW RBVR UCKGER.

VGQK YKS HCABR REGG.

"It's a substitution cipher," Lateef explained. "Each letter in the
source message has been exchanged for another letter of the regular
alphabet, according to a key. The key can be any word: let's say 'cat,'
for example. If 'cat' is the keyword, then the cipher alphabet—the alphabet here in the note—would start with the letters C, A, T, instead
of A, B, C. The rest would follow normally."

She hesitated, but only for an instant. "The whole alphabet gets
shifted by three places?"

"In the system that your son is using, yes. Minus C, A, and T.
They'd come only at the beginning."

She ran a finger slowly down the page. "You'd still need to know
what word he's picked," she said.

"That's right. Both the sender and the receiver need to know the
keyword for the cipher to work." He sat back in his armchair, aware
that he was pausing for effect. "Which sometimes makes it possible
to guess."

"You've figured it out, haven't you."

He felt a rush of helpless pride. "Ciphers happen to be a hobby of
mine. Though I have to tell you, Miss Heller, I've never actually
come across—"

"What's the keyword?"

He pushed a pad of legal paper toward her. "The term of endearment your son uses for you. *Violet*."

DEAR VIOLET. YOU HAVE THE NAME OF A FLOWER
AND I DONT. I DONT HAVE THE NAME OF A FLOWER
VIOLET WHY IS THAT?

I FEEL ALL RIGHT OLD VIOLET BUT THE WORLD IS
GETTING HOTTER. EVERY BODY KNOWS THIS. EVERY
BODY KNOWS THIS AND PRETENDS HE/SHE DOESNT
THE WAY PEOPLE DID WITH ME WHEN I WAS SICK. DO
YOU REMEMBER VIOLET? GRANDDAD COUSINS
TEACHERS? THE WAY THEY DID WITH ME AT THE
BEGINNING.

THE WORLD IS GETTING HOTTER EVERY DAY. WHEN
PEOPLE START TO TALK ABOUT IT THE REALITY LEAVES
THEIR MOUTHS. ONLY I CAN SEE THIS VIOLET
POSSIBLY BECAUSE IVE BEEN SICK. POSSIBLY BECAUSE
IVE BEEN AWAY SO LONG NOW THAT I COME BACK I
CAN SEE IT.

THE WORLD IS GETTING HOTTER NOT SLOW AND
STEADY BUT LIKE A SNOWBALL (NOT A JOKE) OR A
MUDSLIDE GETTING FASTER ALL TIME. THIS IS NOT
MY OWN INVENTION VIOLET BECAUSE I READ IT AND I
SAW IT ON THE NEWS.

I WANT TO OPEN LIKE A FLOWER VIOLET. LIKE A
FLOWER DOES IN POETRY. I THINK THAT MIGHT HELP
AS THE WORLD IS INSIDE OF ME AND THAT WILL/
MIGHT HELP TO COOL THE WORLD. POSSIBLY.
BODIES WILL HAVE TO GET COLD NOW VIOLET. MANY

BODIES. ANYTHING ELSE IN THE WORLD YOU COULD
HELP ME WITH BUT NOT WITH THIS. IM SURE YOU
KNOW THAT VIOLET.

ALSO YOU MIGHT TELL.

When she'd finished she said nothing for a time. Then all at once
she sat up straight and gave a girlish laugh. "My son isn't going to
kill anybody, Detective."

Lateef watched her carefully. "I don't recall suggesting that he was."

Reluctantly she glanced down at the note. "Why a code, though?
He never used a code with me before." She shook her head. "It's really only nonsense either way."

"He must have wanted the nonsense to stay secret."

"But why?" She shook her head. "Because he wants to open like
a flower? Is that why? What could possibly be the harm—"

"Your son does suffer from paranoid schizophrenia, Miss Heller,"
Lateef said as tactfully as he could. The words left an odd taste behind,
like aspirin mixed with tap water. He put the note back in his file.

"It's funny, actually." She covered her mouth with her hand. "To
have to come to a police station, at eight thirty in the morning, to
find out that he's worried about the weather!"

"Can you explain what you mean, Miss Heller? I'm not sure—"

"Will's not going to kill anybody, Detective," she said, and laughed
again. But he no longer saw any reason to believe her.

After the noise of the train had faded Lowboy sat for a long time with his hands covering his eyes, the way he'd learned to do at school, and waited for the Sikh to leave his thoughts. He shut his mouth and bent his knees and braced his head against the wall behind him. The bench he sat on was heavy and unwelcoming, designed to discourage panhandlers and drunks, but he was grateful that he had a bench at all. He counted his breaths, the way Sikh warriors do on the morning of a battle, and let the counting fill his head completely. He counted from one to seven, held his breath for a moment, then counted back from seven down to one.

It was hard work and it made him very tired. Certain things the Sikh had said did not go quietly. *You're frightening her, William*, for example. And *If I was your grandfather, boy*. And *That is not so*. They turned shrill before they left, shrill and urgent and unkind, and behind or below them was a much larger sound, a droning like that of turbines or high-tension wires that no amount of counting could dispel. Lowboy was well acquainted with the sound. It was as familiar to him as the noises of the tunnel and the trains but it had no place among them. He himself had brought it with him underground.

As always when he was frightened the image of Violet came to him, flickering on the backs of his closed eyes like light from an electric candle. Sometimes it was Violet's ghost that visited him, sometimes only a picture, but always she was bright and full of love and terrifying. Now he saw her sitting straightbacked in a chair, smoothing out the wrinkles in her skirt the way she did when she was worried, her blond hair sticking straight up like a boy's. She'd heard about his escape by now, been called by the police or by the school, most likely even seen the note he'd left. He wondered whether she had understood it. He hoped that she had, and that she was proud of him—secretly and defiantly, the way a mother should be of her son— but by the look of her ghost she wasn't proud at all. Her ghost looked sad and desperate and pale.

A long time gone, almost too long to think about, there had been a gargantuan bed. His father and mother had slept in it. The bed was square and high up off the floor and patterned in rustcolored flowers. Her hippie sheets, Violet had called them. What he'd liked best was to crawl to the bottom, in the early morning when they were both still asleep, to that tight and airless hollow where their four feet came together. The cotton had been rough against his face, like the sail of a ship, and the smell of his parents had made the air turn colors. Red for the father, green for the son. Violet for Violet. She wore a nightshirt that said FLATBUSH IS FOR LOVERS across the back and his father wore madras pajamas. One time the pajamas had come undone, and his father had said something under his breath, and Violet had laughed and slid her hand inside them. When he thought of it now his tongue stuck to his mouth and he felt so much love that he had to spit part of it out. Everything had happened easily back then, in such a simple ordinary way. The world hadn't yet even dreamed of ending.

But that had been once, and today was November 11. Today he was sitting on a bench in a subway station, counting from one up to seven, lonelier than any prophet in the desert.

• • •

The name of the station was MUSEUM OF NATURAL HISTORY. He'd passed through it times without number on his way to the park, strolling with Violet past the dog runs and the ballfields and the chainlink fence around the reservoir, his arm in her arm back at the beginning, later her arm confidingly in his. A man stood on the opposite platform now, shoulders hunched and buckled, face turned toward the corner like a dunce. He wavered and sidestepped like somebody on a train. Between the man's head and Lowboy's there was nothing but air and humidity and the steady clicking of the argon lights.

Lowboy looked up the platform, remembering. Set into the tiled wall—lined up in a row, like headstones in a mausoleum—were sixteen skeletons cast in matted bronze. He turned his back on them indifferently. The skeletons belonged to animals long since vanished from the world: it was plain to see that they had been mistakes. He covered his eyes and tried to forget them and after a while he succeeded. When they were finally gone he took his hand away and made sure that the Sikh's voice had quieted. Then he looked at the platform again.

As soon as his eyes came open he regretted it. The objects around him flickered for an instant before coming clear, as though he'd caught them by surprise, and their outlines began to twitch and run together. Oh no, he thought. The argon lights were stuttering like pigeons. There was some kind of intelligence behind them. He tried to convince himself that what he saw made no difference, that it was none of his business, but it was too late to convince himself of anything. He clutched at the bench, breathing in little sucks, and forced himself to look things in the eye. The bench was smooth, the wall was bright, the skeletons were as dull and dead as ever. Everything was as it should have been, inanimate and still. Even the people waiting for the train seemed perfectly assembled and composed; but that was wrong again. It was as though he'd caught a glimpse behind the curtain in a theater, behind the canvas backdrop and the props, and though the play was a good one he couldn't forget about the ropes and pulleys. You should have expected this to happen, he said to himself. You did expect it. But the truth was that he hadn't expected it so soon, not yet, and he felt hollow and incapable and sick.

A cigarette wrapper skittered up the platform, dancing past the bench coquettishly: a bashful totem. A harbinger. He pressed his face against his legs and panted.

To keep himself calm he considered his coming surrender. There were moments when he doubted that he'd be able, in the end, to answer his calling, when the thought of a naked body was enough to make him retch, and there were other moments when there was nothing else he wanted. Who will I find? he thought, touching his skull to his knees. Who will I find around here? He thought of the girl on the train with the Sikh, the music lover, and remembered the way she'd turned to him and smiled. Her long bangs, her distractedness, her beautiful nailbitten fingers. He stared out between his legs toward the dark neglected terminus of the platform, where the dunce had been standing, and wondered whether it could happen there. If I found somebody crazy, he thought, and nearly laughed out loud. If I found somebody crazy enough it could.

Already he felt the wave of doubt receding. Sometimes it passed through him hurriedly, haughty and careless, as if to show how little he was worth. Other times it capsized him completely. Not today however. His eyes followed the tracks into the dark. The empty water-flecked channel where only the trains resided. The acidic yellow of the safety stripe. Behind the third rail a rat was lying splayed on its belly, twitching contentedly, drinking coffee out of a battered paper cup.

"Here's to a wonderful night together," Lowboy said, raising an imaginary glass.

As he sat there with his head tipped low, watching the rat watching him, sounds carried diffusely up the platform. Two pairs of footsteps or one pair reflected. Voices rushed in behind: silvery voices with no feeling in them. Voices like static on an old TV set.

"Smells like *bodies* down here."

"Smells like people, actually. Maybe you've never met any."

"Do me a favor." A loose drawn-out sigh. "Next time I talk you out of a cab, just set me on fire and walk away. Will you do that?"

No sound after that but the chirping of the automatic turnstiles. The footsteps had stopped a few feet from his bench. He wouldn't have raised his head for anything in the world. The voices sounded just like Skull & Bones.

"How was London, by the way? I've never been."

"London was fine. We went to this one place. You know the place." A pause. "The *Tower*." Another pause, more lazy than the first. "There really are a lot of people there."

Lowboy made disgusted faces at the floor. Skull & Bones had never been to London: he knew that for a fact. He became aware of a muffled hacking sound, like a kitten gagging on a burl of fur. The voices had dimmed now, turned soft and discreet, as though they were discussing matters of the heart.

"*Indians* in London, am I right?"

"Indians and Pakistanis. But it's cleaner, believe it or not. Less panhandlers."

"Panhandlers." Another pause. "They think this city *belongs* to them."

"I'd always thought it did."

"It doesn't, actually. It belongs to me."

I'll hop the tracks, thought Lowboy, biting down on the knuckle of his thumb. If they don't shut up I'll hop them. I'll go now.

Just then the uptown B arrived and saved him. Its ghost blew into the station first, a tunnelshaped clot of air the exact length of the train behind it, hot from its own great compression and speed, whipping the litter up into a cloud. He opened his mouth to taste it on the air. The cigarette wrapper spiraled upward, fluttering like a startled bird, and for the first time he noticed the zebra-striped sign mounted over his bench. He knew what the sign was for and he said its name proudly: *the indication board*. His voice was clear in his ears now, serene and assured, because he knew what was going to happen next.

The train came in as hard as the ghost train before it, knocking the wind flat and paving it over with sound. First the hissing of the current, then the shrieking of the wheelheads, then the champing of the brakepads in their sockets. There was no hearing anything else. If objects on the platform were trembling now it was with the force of the slackening cars, not because of the falseness of the world. Lowboy bent forward to watch for the conductor's booth, still clutching at the bench with all his fingers. He saw the conductor from a long way off, a heavyset man with a longsuffering face, goggles flickering like strobelights as he came. His booth eased to a stop across from Lowboy's bench with all the symmetry of prophecy fulfilled. He glanced at Lowboy obliquely, pressing the goggles to his face, then rolled his dim eyes up to check the board. When he'd satisfied himself that all was in alignment, he made a small grudging movement with his elbow and the doors came open. They stayed open for ten seconds, the prescribed minimum. The conductor's lips flapped slackly as he counted. Lowboy watched his every move, enraptured.

"Getting on?" said the conductor.

Lowboy shook his head shyly. "I'm waiting for the C."

"See that posting?" The conductor's face jerked toward the wall. "C's not running right today. Best be getting on with me."

"That's all right," said Lowboy, shivering with pleasure. "I don't mind."

"You hearing me, son? I just told you the C—"

"Your ten seconds are up," said Lowboy. "Shut the doors."

The conductor lifted his goggles and pinched the bridge of his nose for a moment and replaced them with exaggerated care. Other than that he gave no evidence of surprise. He let the C# and A ring out, ticked his head from right to left, then shot back into his cubby like a cockroach. Lowboy closed his eyes and waited for the signal— two long buzzes, close together—that gave the motorman the go- ahead. When he opened them the train was long gone, the platform was empty, and the cigarette wrapper lay nestled in his lap. Only then did he remember about the voices. He looked around him cir- cumspectly, careful not to draw attention, but Skull & Bones had dis- appeared without a trace. The rat was still there but the cup was missing. No one else on either platform. An arm's length from the bench, halfway to the nearest column, lay a crisply folded twenty- dollar bill.

Lowboy stared down at the money and tried to explain it. An acci- dent, he decided. Out of somebody's pocket. The explanation was plausible and clean, an educated guess, the kind that they approved of at the school. A Clozaril-flavored answer, he said to himself. Clozaril with Thorazine on top.

He braced his head against the wall and did nothing. It was hard to imagine getting up from the bench and putting the twenty into his pocket. He hadn't touched money in a year and a half, not since get- ting enrolled, and the tunnel was no place for accidents. On the other hand he was starting to get hungry. There was nothing in his pockets, not even a napkin or a matchbook or a pencil. Not even a pill. "On the other hand," he said out loud, listening for the echo off the tiles. Accidents will happen, he reminded himself. Accidents will happen all the time.

The face on the bill, of a thin schoolteacherly man with pistachio-colored hair, reminded him of someone that he knew. His father possibly. But he knew the name of the schoolteacher well enough. "Jackson," he said, pointing down at the money. "Andrew Jackson, Indian killer."

Jackson smiled up at him with green patrician lips. I'd gladly trade you, Lowboy thought, for a Swiss cheese omelet and a side of fries.

"That's right, little boss! *Intimidate* the money. Don't just put it in your pocket like a fool."

Lowboy raised his head slowly. The woman who'd spoken was straightbacked and enormous and stood with her feet wide apart, like a boxer or a circus acrobat. She could have been any race in the world, from Sikh to Sudanese to Cherokee. She could even have been white. She wore plastic shopping bags inside her sneakers and frowned at him as though he was hard to see.

"It's counterfeit," said Lowboy. "It's not right."

"Counterfeit," said the woman. "Is that so." She pinched her chin between two yellowed knuckles. "What if I was to pick it up anyways, and put it into my portmanteau?"

"In your what?"

"'Portmanteau,'" the woman said, lowering her voice, "is a word from the French. Meaning wallet."

"I know that," said Lowboy. He thought for a moment. "You could do that," he said finally. "That might work."

"Might it now," said the woman. She inspected the money closely, turning it clockwise with her foot, then sighed and shuffled off behind the columns. Time went by. Lowboy leaned forward and touched his middle finger to the bill. A current shot up from his palm to his shoulder, locking his jawbone and making his teeth knock together. He pulled back and the feeling stopped at once.

"I thought you said that bill was *counterfeit*, little boss," the woman hissed, stepping out from behind the nearest column. She held a small blue suitcase tightly in both hands, the way a baby clutches at a blanket. Her hands were too small for the rest of her. She moved her body modestly, taking tiny bashful steps, considering every move before she made it. Her dark eyes never wavered from the bill.

"How much does a twenty buy these days?" Lowboy said, making room beside him on the bench.

"Don't you know about money?"

He shook his head. "I've been away."

The suitcase jangled as she set it down, as though it were filled with champagne flutes or Christmas lights, or possibly empty bottles of perfume. They sat for a while with the suitcase between them, watching people come and go across the tracks. An express train came and went, and for an instant Lowboy worried about the money, but the money stayed exactly where it was. It didn't even flutter. Finally the woman cleared her throat and nodded and smoothed her eyebrows down with her two thumbs.

"$20," she said, "don't buy too much of nothing, on the floor."

Lowboy grinned at her and shrugged his shoulders. "What's your name?"

"Heather," said the woman. She drew herself up smartly. "Heather Covington."

"Heather Covington," he repeated. He looked the woman over. She was adjusting the plastic lining of her shoes.

"You don't look like a Heather," he said.

She gave him a wink, as though he'd played into her hands, then opened her suitcase and brought out a battered blue passport.

"What's this for?" said Lowboy.

"Introductions."

He took the passport and flipped through it. Except for a faint yellow stamp from Fort Erie, Canada, all of its pages were blank. The issue date was 4/2007. "Heather Dakota Covington," he read out. "Hair Auburn. Eyes Green. Weight eighty-seven pounds." He paused. "Born Vienna, Virginia, 11/13/1998."

She smiled sweetly at that, still averting her eyes, then tucked the passport back inside her coat. He looked at her closely. The smile sat tightly on her face, sliding sideways a little, as though it was hard work to keep it there. She turned toward him expectantly, pointing at her mouth, and for a moment he thought she was doing some sort of impression. Then he recognized the smile. It belonged to the girl in the passport.

A train came in across the tracks, a downtown express, full of people staring dully into space. "November thirteenth," Lowboy said finally, for the sake of being friendly. "What's today?"

"The eleventh."

"Then the day after tomorrow is your birthday."

"Goddamn fucking right it is."

"You should take the money, then. Many happy returns."

She yawned at him. "It's not my birthday yet."

He sat up straight and tried to make a joke. "You should celebrate your birthday early this year. I recommend it."

"How come?"

"We might be dead tomorrow, Miss Covington."

"Call me Heather." She smoothed her eyebrows down again, more precisely than before. "I already *took* the money, little boss."

Lowboy looked down and made his Philip Marlowe face. She took the passport out again and held it open. The bill was tucked between its last two pages.

He opened his mouth and closed it. Heather Covington only smiled. Her wide brown features seemed suddenly like a landscape that he knew. Another dimly recollected picture. Three years gone, he told himself, remembering. Violet had borrowed a car and they'd driven to the Pennsylvania hills. Let's go someplace empty, she'd said. Just us two. Which had made him laugh because who else would have come. The hills had looked wrinkled and brown, like a sad old man's neck, and it had been hot in the car. You're my hero, she'd told him. My little professor. I can't wait to see what you'll become some day.

That was the first day that he'd heard the turbines.

"What are you giggling over, little boss?" Heather Covington said. Her voice buzzed in his ear like a mosquito.

Slowly and regretfully he let his eyes open. "Why do you keep calling me that?"

She kicked her legs out and inspected the toes of her shoes. "You don't look like a regular boss to me. That's why."

"I'm not any kind of boss," he said. "Not yet."

"I guess that's right," she said. "Boss wouldn't leave no twenty on the floor."

"I don't care about the money, Miss Covington."

"Why don't you care about it?" She narrowed her eyes. "You a celebrity, little boss?"

"Call me Lowboy," he said. "I prefer it."

"Shit," said Heather Covington. He felt her disapproval like a hand against his face. A breeze was building in the tunnel, humble but determined, the advance guard of a great mustering army. Near the turnstiles two fat college girls were holding hands and crying and touching their foreheads together. Beyond them a maintenance crew in orange vests stood propped together in a kind of huddle.

"You ought to be a celebrity," Heather Covington said. "There's money in it. All you do is put on underpants and pout."

"What are you going to spend that twenty on?" Lowboy said. "A Swiss cheese omelet?"

She laughed at that. "Last time I paid for my breakfast, I was—"

She frowned. "I was still—" She patted the side of her suitcase. "Don't you worry about me."

"Where do you go to eat?"

"I used to go to the kitchens," she said. "They had organic greens. Street Life Ministries was my favorite." She batted her eyes at the memory. "They have a kind of a vehicle takes lunch around. Old creamy kind of a truck. You know the color. Ham sandwiches, turkey sandwiches, coleslaw. Coleslaw is my personal reason to believe in God." She held up a finger. "With pepper."

"Pepper's good on coleslaw," Lowboy said. "When I was little—"

"It's easy for me to put food in my mouth. I have no need of the clergy." She ran her tongue along her bottom teeth. "The clergy runs the kitchens. They make the food and give you it for nothing. Then they teach the parents how to fuck the children."

"All right," said Lowboy, watching her features give way. "All right." The fact that he couldn't understand her didn't bother him at all. It made him feel alive and restless and unmedicated. He'd had the same feeling at school, listening to the new arrivals shudder and shriek, lit up like fireworks by the ideas inside them.

I could give my body to her, he thought suddenly. She might take it.

"I want to tell you something," Lowboy said, fighting to keep the excitement out of his voice. "I want to tell you something about the world."

"Not interested," said Heather Covington.

"Everyone knows what's happening to the air—what we're *doing* to the air, I mean. The air is changing every single minute. It's thickening and flattening and building up speed. The air is getting hotter every day." He ducked his head and looked her in the face. "Is that correct?"

"*Uhhh,*" said Heather Covington.

"But not everybody knows it's not happening on a straight line— not at all. The air is getting hotter on a curve."

He bit down on his wrist—to check himself, to keep himself from stuttering—and watched her. There was no way of knowing whether or not she understood him. Her eyes were clenched shut and her mouth was quivering.

"The line is curved, Miss Covington," he said, taking her unprotesting hand in his. "The change gets faster every single second. It's like squaring a number." He laughed. "It *is* squaring a number." He dug his fist into her hand to rouse her. "There's almost no way of stopping it once it starts."

"Sounds like a credit card," said Heather Covington. She seemed to be saying it to someone on the ceiling.

"But there's a way I found. I invented it myself." He was whispering now. "It has to do with what's inside my body."

"Stop it," Heather Covington mumbled, looking straight above her.

"The world's inside of me," said Lowboy. "Just like I'm inside the world. Religions teach that. Buddhism." He rested his free hand against her cheek. "Are you listening, Miss Covington? I read it in *National Geographic.*"

Heather Covington didn't answer.

"To cool down the air, I have to cool myself down first." He cupped her face in his palms like a Hollywood lover. "I'm going to open like a flower, Miss Covington."

"*Stop* it!" she shouted, pushing her head back against the tiles. "Because I *said* to stop!" Her arms flailed out in all directions, at the maintenance workers and the MetroCard dispenser and the coeds. The coeds turned and gaped at her but the rest paid no attention. "Stop it!" she said again, spitting the words out like a judgment. She gave a hacking brokenhearted laugh.

"The train is coming," Lowboy said, patting her on the shoulder. But it didn't seem to do her any good.

Tell me about your son's illness," said Detective Lateef.

Violet sat crookedly on the little roundbacked stool. Her panic at Will's letter had quieted and she felt more tired than she could ever remember feeling. She was grateful for the detective's question, grateful to be asked something that she could answer. It was the first of all his questions that she was grateful for.

"Can you be more specific, Detective? You're asking me to describe the last four years of my life."

Already he seemed impatient with her: he passed a hand roughly over his face, as though it cost him strength to keep awake. But in spite of this she knew that he was not unkind. He's a bachelor, she thought, watching him shuffle his papers. Desperate women put him off his stride.

He made a mark of some kind on one of the photocopies. "How old was your son when he had his first break?"

"Twelve." She waited while he made another mark. "It was in the garden of his grandfather's house, in Brooklyn. Richard—my husband's father—was still alive back then. It was the year before Will started gymnasium."

"Gymnasium?" Lateef said, frowning slightly.

She felt her face go hot at once. "I'm sorry, Detective—high school. We call high school 'gymnasium' in Austria."

"In Austria," he said slowly. "Is that right." For a moment he avoided looking at her; then he smiled, shook his head, and made a quick lateral mark in his notes. Crossing something out, she guessed. Where on earth had he imagined she was from?

"I don't know why I said that," she heard herself stammer. "I've been in this country sixteen years—seventeen in December—but still, certain things—"

"That's perfectly all right, Miss Heller. Please go on."

His face grew set and she saw that it was time to give her answer. She allowed herself a few more seconds, examining the memory before giving voice to it, holding it painstakingly up to the light. But there was no need to examine it. It played out photographically before her, each instant distinct from those before and after, like exposures on an unspooled reel of film. She could go back and forth in the events of that day as often and as carefully as she liked.

"The garden had a low brick wall around it, about Will's height if he stood up straight." She cleared her throat. "Richard spent most of his time out there, hunting for weeds. He was a hard man to talk to, very strict, but he was wonderfully patient with Will. There was so much compost in his garden that he'd had to build steps to get up to his vegetables. His tomatoes had won some sort of neighborhood prize, a medal he kept in the kitchen." She shook her head slowly, remembering. "He had four rows of them that took up half the garden— you know how small those Park Slope backyards are—and past that was a little patch of lawn, with a cast-iron table and a chair that only Will ever sat in. The tomatoes made a kind of barrier there, a screen that hid the table from the house. That was Will's favorite place." She hesitated a moment. "I'm not sure you need to be writing all this down, Detective. Richard's been dead for almost three years now."

"It helps me to pay attention, Miss Heller." He glanced up at her. "Does it make you self-conscious?"

She shrugged, and he went back to his scribbling. There was a matter-of-factness to his voice now that made her feel that she was giving him what he wanted. The filmreel was unspooling more quickly than before and she found that she had to hurry to keep up.

"It happened on a Sunday. I was making breadcrumb dumplings in Richard's kitchen, something old-fashioned and Austrian, feeling about seventy-five years old"—she gave a dry little laugh—"and Will and his grandfather were fixing a trellis in the basement. I wanted Will to taste something, a sauce I was making, and I called down for him to come upstairs. But Richard told me Will was in the garden."

"Did your son have any close friends at this time?"

"No," she said quickly. I sound so defensive, she thought. But her voice when she spoke next was even sharper. "He spent most of his time by himself or with Richard, puttering around in the garden."

He nodded curtly at that, as though she'd given him the answer he'd expected. Everything I've said might be redundant, she thought. I wonder whether he would stop me if it was.

"Go on, Miss Heller."

She took a breath. "I went to the garden door and looked outside. I couldn't see Will, but that didn't surprise me: I expected him to be at the table, out of sight. He used to spend whole afternoons wedged into that little chair, reading his comic books and doodling. He was making up the wildest things—mostly superhero stories—and drawing funny pictures to go with them. I was in some of the stories, usually as the villian. I was called The Final Solution and I wore a black rubber cape." She smiled crookedly. "If you were a therapist you'd start listening closely now."

"I *am* listening closely, Miss Heller."

"I know that." She felt awkward now, unsympathetic, like someone auditioning badly for a role. "I had a spoonful of sauce in my hand and dinner cooking on the stove. The easiest thing would have been to call Will's name, but I never thought of that. I was careful to be quiet, I remember, when I pushed the back door open." She sat gingerly forward on the stool, her eyes half closed, listening to it squeak under her weight. "As though I expected to catch him at something. But I expected to find him drawing his little comics, nothing else. That was all he ever did back there."

"What did you find this time?"

"This time?" she said. For a moment nothing came to her. "This time I went to the back of the garden—it was only a dozen steps—and found him lying facedown in the grass."

Lateef was studying the ceiling tiles and chewing on the blunt end of his pencil. She could only assume he was listening. "Go on, Miss Heller."

"I crouched down next to Will and turned him over. All of this happened very quietly, I remember. His eyes were open, but they were . . ." She hesitated, waiting for the proper word to come. "Unconvincing somehow, like the eyes of an expensive doll. I remembered something I'd heard about sleepwalkers—that it's dangerous to wake them—but Will sat up as soon as I touched him. His eyes came into focus and he got to his feet and let me lead him back into the house. Then Richard and I put him to bed."

She noticed that Lateef had put his pencil aside, and she looked questioningly at him, but he motioned to her to go on.

"Will was an unusual boy, always off in some corner, but this was nothing like that. He barely seemed to recognize the house. I knew right away that he was sick." She laughed. "I'm a morbid person, Detective—I'm not proud of that. But my worst ideas always come true. What other kind of person could I be?"

After what seemed a very long time, a slow dull spell of wasted quiet, he nodded once and coughed into his sleeve. "What was your father-in-law's reaction to the change?"

"He told me I was being hysterical. He called me an overprotective little fool." She held her breath a moment. "Worse than that, actually. Finally I admitted that I might have jumped to conclusions, if only to stop him from talking. I was terrified Will would overhear us, but we checked on him and he was fast asleep." She searched her pockets one after the other and eventually dug out a broken cigarette. "Even now he looks perfectly normal when his eyes are closed."

Lateef produced a lighter from some hidden precinct of his desk and slid it hospitably across the desktop. So he smokes, she thought. Not cigarettes, I'll bet. She pictured an enameled meerschaum pipe.

"How long was it until his next break?"

She didn't answer until the cigarette was lit and she'd taken a long and brazen drag from it, pinching it together in the middle. She exhaled and sat back and watched him wait for her to go on talking, doing his best to master his impatience, his yellow bankteller's pencil hovering above the desktop like a wasp. His interest in what had happened seemed suspect to her now, almost spiteful, as though he was secretly on the payroll of the *Post*. She imagined Will's picture on the front page with a suitable caption beside it:

TEEN FIEND LOOSE IN TUNNELS

or something even more cataclysmic, something deliberately free of thought or sympathy. Headlines from the trial came back to her but she suppressed them. Talking about Will seemed reckless to her suddenly, even mercenary. But not to talk about him made it seem as if he were dead.

"Is there a bathroom on this floor, Detective?"

He looked surprised. "Of course, Miss Heller. Just follow the hallway left until it ends."

She gave him an apologetic smile and stood up at once, leaving her coat and handbag on the stool. She glanced back at him as she pushed the door shut, but he was busy with his cards and photocopies. What a kind face he has, she thought. How considerate he looks when no one's watching. Maybe I should tell him everything.

She closed the door behind her as gently as possible, guiding it shut with her fingertips, like a governess leaving a nursery. The hallway was full of the same stricken faces she'd seen when she arrived: old men with blank expressions, bewildered-looking women, teenagers

who shrank from her as she went by. She moved past them as unob-
trusively as she could, filled with a revulsion she could neither account for nor dispel. The few who met her eyes did so resignedly,
expecting nothing from her and receiving nothing. There wasn't a
thing on earth that she could do to help them.

The hallway was long and dropceilinged and ruthlessly bright,
plastered in gray-green linoleum: the most bureaucratic hallway she
had ever seen. A masterpiece, she said to herself. Someone should
charge admission. The first third of the corridor was carpeted in coffee-
colored shag, the rest in blanched, discolored pile. It ended without
fanfare at an ancient tinted window, open just wide enough to be used
as an ashtray. On any other day she'd have asked herself why in
God's name the window had been tinted, even laughed out loud at
the bleakness of the place; instead she touched her forehead to the
glass. After a brief spell of quiet, once she was sure she was alone,
she brought out the idea of Will and let it hang above her in the air.

"Do not die," she said matter-of-factly, just loud enough to feel it
in her throat. "Do not die. Do not die. Do not die." Her upper lip
brushed the pane of the window as she spoke. She could feel the
bucking of the wind on the far side of the glass and a fluttering line
of cold across her thighs. She recited the phrase under her breath
like a nursery rhyme, letting the words run together as she'd done
countless times in the past, mixing English and German until the
thing she was pleading for and the syllables themselves lost their
meaning and she was left with nothing but the sound of her own
voice. After a time even that fell away and she felt husked-out and
contented. She took her first steady breath since she'd entered the
building, ran a hand through her hair, stared down at the pudding-
colored carpet and wondered how she would manage to go back. To
go back would mean to keep talking, to answer when the detective
spoke to her, to tell the story all the way to its end. Try as she might
she couldn't picture it.

Less than a minute later she was perched on her fiberglass stool,
waiting on his convenience, watching him shuffling his photocopies

as if she'd never left the room. She felt a surge of affection for him then that she could in no way justify. Proof of my perversity, she thought, and had to cover her mouth to keep from laughing.

"Detective Lateef," she said finally. "There's something that I want to say to you."

He raised his head politely. "What is it, Miss Heller?"

"You're a decent man, Detective. I see that. I want you to know that I'm thankful for your trouble and your time—" He began to interrupt her but she held up her hands. "Please let me finish." She let out a breath. "I'm not usually so difficult. I guess you'll have to take my word for that."

He nodded amiably, saying nothing. What's he waiting for? she thought, smiling back at him as best she could. Is there some other compliment I haven't thought of?

"I'd appreciate it, Detective, if you'd explain to me how I can be more—"

"What happened after your son's first episode?"

She said nothing for a moment, taken aback by his formality. Then she took up the story exactly where she'd left it.

"We spent the night at Richard's. I was afraid to wake Will up, and Richard insisted that sleep was all he needed." She shook her head. "It wasn't, of course. At three o'clock that morning I fell out of my bed as though someone had tipped it over. The house was rattling like a subway station. It took me a while to understand what was happening: the stereo downstairs was playing at full blast, distorting terribly. The music was something Richard liked to play, Bix Beiderbecke with some orchestra or other, a big-band record with lots of strings and trumpets. I hadn't thought of Will yet, hadn't connected him to what was going on. Then my foot came down on something cold and wet. It was a little heap—maybe a handful's worth—of broken tomatoes out of Richard's garden."

"Tomatoes?" Lateef said, frowning. "The ones he'd won his prize for?"

She gave a stupid laugh. "Isn't that like the punchline to a joke?"

"What do you mean by 'broken,' exactly? Crushed in the hands?"

"With the feet, I think." She hesitated a moment, then nodded. "He put them on the floor and stepped on them."

Lateef tapped the pencil end against his teeth. "What did you do then?"

"I went out into the hall. Richard was already down in the living room. He was fighting with Will, shouting as loudly as he could, but I couldn't make out a word. I hung back on the landing, not knowing what to do, telling myself I'd go downstairs when the music stopped." She pressed her hands together. "I didn't want to go downstairs. It's Richard's house, I told myself: Richard's stereo, Richard's music. Go back to bed. And then I was in the living room with Richard screaming at the top of his lungs and Will rolling around between us on the floor."

"Was the music still playing?"

She nodded.

"Why hadn't your father-in-law turned it off?"

"I have no idea."

"That would have been the thing to do. Don't you agree?"

She shifted away from the desk, confused by the simplicity of his question. As usual his expression told her nothing: his face was flat and abstracted, almost sullen. She was used to telling Will's story a certain way, without any interruptions, but he seemed to be set on asking things at random. A trick of the trade, she decided. He was trying to force her story off its rails.

"I guess Richard had forgotten about the music," she said finally. "He was yelling at Will, using every kind of threat, but he couldn't seem to bring himself to touch him. There was an odd smell in the air, metallic and sweet, like almonds roasting in an oven. Some part of the stereo overheating, I guess. Richard hadn't even noticed me."

The reel was running faster still and she held back as long as she could, trying with all her might to slow it down. "The music was so loud that I could feel it in my teeth. Will was lying on the floor with his arms against his sides, giggling and singing. He looked like someone in a state of bliss. The louder Richard cursed the happier he got. It made me weak in the legs to look at him. His hands and lips were slathered in tomato juice and he was singing the same two words over and over." She stopped to catch her breath. "I got down on my knees to try to make it out. For some reason a line from a play came to me, one of the favorites of Will's father: *Let's reason with the worst that may befall*. I heard that line clearly, heard it in my husband's voice, but it only made me feel more desperate." She sat up straight again. "What do you think about that, Detective? Could it be a sign of shock?"

Lateef blinked at her but said nothing. Apparently she was meant to go on talking.

"I took Will by the shoulders and held him close to me, partly to quiet him, but also to keep from having to look him in the face. It seemed ridiculous to me even as I did it, like boxers hugging one another to keep from getting hit: it's always bothered me when they do that." She closed her eyes. "Richard was still on his feet, but by now he was listening too. With Will's head next to mine I could finally make out what he was singing. It was 'Kill me.'"

"'Kill me'?" Lateef said. He said it very smoothly and politely.

She nodded. "Flatly, in a monotone, the way that people sing when they're in church."

Lateef made a small mark—an *X*, she thought—at the bottom of an index card and set it aside. She couldn't help but wonder what it meant.

"Was this phrase something that your son repeated later?"

She shook her head. "I got up to turn off the music but I could barely keep my balance. I couldn't seem to make my eyes stay open. I'd shut them, open them just enough to see, then take a step and let them shut again. I couldn't imagine what would happen when the music finally stopped. Richard scared me almost more than Will did, I remember: he seemed totally out of control. I had to remind myself that he was eighty-four."

She was surprised at how patient he was when she fell silent again: it obviously cost him effort not to press her. Finally he coughed into his fist. "Please go on, Miss Heller."

"I will, Detective. If you could give me just a minute—"

"Of course I can. Would you like a drink of water? Would you like to have a smoke?"

She stood up from the stool as he said this, nodding reasonably, but sat down again right away. "What I'd like is to get this over with."

How eager I am to make the right impression, she thought, feeling her face settle into her most childish smile. He must be wondering what the hell I'm smiling at. She took a handkerchief from her coat and held it up to her mouth, for no other reason than to hide her face behind it.

"We can take another break if you need to, Miss Heller. Do you want to take another break?"

He talks like an anchorman, she found herself thinking. Not a trace of an accent. His parents must be educated people.

"There's not much more to tell, Detective. I'm okay."

"All right, then. Let's get this finished, shall we?"

She put the handkerchief away and nodded.

"What happened when you turned the music off?"

"The telephone started ringing in the kitchen: someone calling to complain about the noise." The stool groaned under her as she sat forward. "Richard looked at me for the first time since I'd come into the room, opened his mouth to say something, then went out to get the phone without a word. Will was still lying curled up on the floor. I whispered to him that I knew how he was feeling, that I knew he was in pain, though of course I knew no such thing. How could I have had a clue what he was feeling? 'We'll get help for you, Will,' I said. 'We'll get you a doctor.' He looked at me as though I was talking in a made-up language. After a while he said, 'What's different, Violet?'"

"What did you say to that?"

"I told him the truth: that I thought he was sick. 'Maybe, Violet,' he said. 'That might possibly be true.' He was still on the floor, still rocking himself backwards and forwards. I was overjoyed to hear him making sense. I thanked luck and chance and providence and everything else I could think of. I might even have given thanks for Richard. Then Will sat up and said, 'You're a piece of old bread, Violet. A piece of dead music.'"

She watched him scrawling dutifully in his notepad. She hadn't realized she'd stopped until he raised his eyes.

"What then?"

"That was too much somehow, that sudden disappointment. I took hold of him by the shirt and begged him to tell me what was happening. He bit his lip for a few seconds—I remember that clearly—and looked at me as if I was in his way. 'Nothing's happening, Violet,' he said. 'Now get the fuck out of here before I kill you.' Then he rolled over on his side and went to sleep."

She sat for a time with her head tipped to one side, not looking at anything. The noises from the hallway came and went. "That's it," she said at last. "That's all of it."

"All right." He sat back heavily in his chair. "Thank you, Miss Heller."

She leaned toward him stiffly and laughed for no reason and watched him consider her story. It was a relief to watch him. Nothing she'd said had taken him aback or gratified him in secret, the way some of Will's doctors had been gratified, or disgusted him, the way everyone else she knew had been disgusted. Not anything Will had said or done, not his grandfather's senile vindictiveness, not even her own bad judgment or stupidity. It was a great thing to be listened to with such businesslike calm, to be listened to and allowed to tell things simply. It's his job to make me feel this way, she reminded herself, but the knowledge was a tiny thing compared to her relief. He's good at his work, she thought. So much the better.

"Ali Lateef," she heard herself murmur.

His head jerked up at once. "What did you say?"

"Ali Lateef," she repeated, talking quickly to cover her embarrassment. "That's a beautiful name. Is it Moroccan?"

His face lost its abstracted look immediately and he laid both hands down flat against the desk, as if to brace himself for something. "Thank you, Miss Heller," he said after a pause. "My given name was actually Rufus White."

I've offended him, she thought. How did I manage to offend him?

"You were right to change it," she said cautiously. "Ali is more dignified than Rufus."

He held up a hand—a conductor signaling for quiet in a crowded theater—and stared down at the file in front of him. There was an impatience to his movements now that she could not explain. She held her breath and waited for his next question. She expected it to be unpleasant and it was.

"There's something you haven't told me yet, Miss Heller. Something you're keeping from me. Would you like to tell me now?"

She forced herself to look him in the eye. "I'm not sure I know what you mean."

"Are your son's episodes always violent?"

The breath she let out barely made a noise. I'll tell him soon, she said to herself. Soon but not yet. When she answered him her voice was clear and steady.

"Will's 'episodes,' as you call them, are never violent, Detective. Not in the way that you mean."

"I don't agree. Just now you described your son as threatening to do you harm." He smiled at her regretfully. "I'm committed to recovering him for you, Miss Heller. Shouldn't that be reason enough to trust me?"

She was being manipulated now, led in circles like a child, but she managed to keep her outward manner civil. "It's a question of accuracy, Detective, not of trust. Will's said all sorts of things—terrible things, I admit—but he's never actually done me harm." She hesitated. "Or done anyone else harm, in any significant way—"

"In any *significant* way?" Lateef said, cutting her short. All at once he reminded her of Will's doctors. "We seem to have different definitions of that word."

She found herself staring sullenly at the floor, the way Will himself did whenever he felt cornered. "I know he's cut himself from time to time, in small ways, and jumped—or fallen, possibly—from a second-story—"

"You know exactly what I'm referring to, Miss Heller." His voice was even harsher than she'd expected. "It wasn't about violence to *himself* that I was speaking." He brushed the cards aside—as though they'd never been of the slightest consequence, as though they'd been a ruse to coax the story out of her, nothing more—and produced an enormous yellow folder from a drawer of his desk. The sight made her weak. He's been saving it, she thought. Keeping it in reserve. She knew exactly what the folder held. She watched him as if through a half-open door, as if from the hallway outside, suddenly as obsolete as all the others. The story she'd told was an appendix to that folder, possibly even less. The folder itself was the only thing he needed.

Lateef put a finger to his temple—every gesture he made was a performance put on for her benefit, she saw that clearly now—and made a show of leafing casually through the file. It was ridiculously thick, overdone and amateurish, a hurriedly assembled prop. Who'd have thought Will was so important to them, she thought. Then another idea struck her, with such unexpected severity that she almost cried out loud: He's not important to them. They're not afraid for Will at all. It's everybody else that they're afraid for.

Lateef laid the folder down and cleared his throat. "There seems to be nothing I can do to convince you not to waste my time, Miss Heller. So what I'm going to do is this: I'm going to read you the details of your son's original offense."

"Please don't," she said woodenly. "I know perfectly well—"

"On Monday, March fifth, 2008, at one forty-five p.m., William Heller, age fourteen, and Emily Wallace, age fifteen, entered the Fourteenth Street subway station at the southwest corner of Union Square. They were seen by the station attendant, Lawrence Grayson, who notified the truancy officer on duty, Robert T. Sullivan. Officer Sullivan located both children on the downtown 6 platform. He approached with circumspection, as Emily Wallace was, in Officer Sullivan's opinion, 'in hazardous proximity to the tracks.' William Heller appeared agitated. He was moving in what the officer described as a 'spiral-type pattern,' talking animatedly to Emily Wallace, who was standing still. After approximately one minute Emily Wallace took hold of William Heller by the shoulders and embraced him. Officer Sullivan did not interpret this as a sexual gesture."

He paused there—there, of all places—and coughed into his fist. For dramatic effect, Violet thought, and the knowledge made her mouth go dry with hate. When he spoke again she closed her eyes and shivered.

"William Heller freed himself from Emily Wallace and pushed her onto the tracks."

Blood was rushing to Lowboy's head like steam from a boiler as he let himself be dragged into the dark. Heather Covington was a few steps ahead of him, whispering to herself affection-ately, moving carefully along the tunnel's concrete seam. The last feeble light lapped against her. He could just make out her feet in their cellophane leggings, rustling with each step she took, as though she were picking her way through fallen leaves.

The tunnel was wide and straight and the lights of the A took a long time to fade. It got warmer and damper and soon it got too warm to breathe. The world is inside me, Lowboy said to himself, and I am inside the world. He opened his mouth but no air entered it. Every so often Heather Covington would reach back and pull on his shirt, hissing at him to hurry, but he refused to be rushed. What he was about to do was no small or trivial thing. He kept his eyes on the back of her head, cropped and burly as a man's, and let his shoulder brush against the bowed concrete. A song came to him as he watched her: "Toddlin' Blues" by Bix Beiderbecke. Richard used to play that song and he would dance to it. Also "Fidgety Feet." Heather

Covington had feet like that. He wondered when the next A train was coming.

Every half-dozen steps the wall fell back into a mansized socket. Lowboy had seen them often enough from the train, even once seen a person inside: a frightened-looking woman in a wrinkled orange jumpsuit, holding a wrench across her body like a soldier at a drill. Richard had told him that the woman lived in the tunnel, that she'd never once seen daylight, and he'd still been too young to know better. He'd lain awake that night shivering with envy, picturing catacombs and petrified forests and houses built on phosphorescent lakes. And Richard had sat at his bedside, more patient than he ever was by day, and had run his fingers through his hair to calm him.

A river cut across Manhattan once, Richard had said. Split the city in half, about where Broadway is now. You still awake, Will?

Yes, Richard, he'd answered. I'm awake.

The Quiet River, the Indians used to call it. Musaquontas. You can't get rid of a river, you know. You can only dig it under. They've had to close whole stations down because of it. The truth of the matter is, that's why there's no Second Avenue line. The old Musaquontas is still in the way.

From that night on he'd thought of the sad little streams that trickled between the subway tracks as the sidearms and tributaries of the Musaquontas. Headwaters of the Quiet River. He'd imagined himself following them out to the sea.

"Almost there," said Heather Covington. Her fist closed around his bloodless hand. His hand seemed miniature compared to hers, tiny and white, a bird's egg cradled in a wooden spoon. Her palm was rougher than the wall behind her. She was moving quickly now, taking impatient strides, not stopping to look where she put her feet. She didn't seem frightened or angry anymore. She didn't seem sick. He could tell by the way she moved that she was happy. I've made her that way, he thought suddenly. Just by saying what I wanted. I helped her remember something that she likes.

Soon they came to a place where there was no light left. She stopped him there and went on alone, not saying a word, as though talk was out of keeping with the quiet. Somewhere a pipe or a weep-hole was dripping. Lowboy stood with his arms held out like a sleep-walker, keeping perfectly still, listening to the fallen-leaf sound getting fainter and fainter. He wondered how far underground he was. The heat he was feeling was the heat of the earth's molten core: what else could it have been. He kept his eyes wide open, expecting the blackness to yield, but it only pushed itself farther into his ears and his nose and his mouth. Water was running close by, and the rumble of traffic carried up through his feet, as though the city had somehow gotten underneath him. That's not Manhattan, he thought. It's New Delhi or Perth or Beijing. He listened for wind or a train or the chittering of rats but there seemed to be nothing to hear. Nothing was moving anywhere but water.

It's too dark for rats down here, Lowboy said to himself. Too dark for everything. Or maybe there just isn't enough air.

Then Heather Covington was next to him with her heavy square palm covering his mouth. She lowered it to his back and pushed him forward. Why didn't I hear her coming? Lowboy wondered. Did I fall asleep?

After less than a minute she steered him sharply to the left and the hum of the city got louder. He was in a low, close-walled passage, ten or fifteen feet long, with a flickering wash of light at its far turning. The light got sharper as she shepherded him forward until he had to shade his eyes to take a step. She was behind him now, breathing in tight hurried sucks. He remembered a joke about what cavemen did when they got lonely. Except that she's the caveman, he reminded himself. I'm the knocked-out monkey. He smiled and let her usher him into the brightness and the airiness and the sudden cold, covering his eyes with all ten of his fingers.

When he took his hands away he saw an L-shaped room with rust-streaked walls lit by four high quadrangles of daylight. Heather Covington had let him go and was using her feet to clear a path across the littercluttered floor. Her shoes were set neatly side by side in the room's farthest corner and the bags were just behind them, laid out on a checkered sweatstained quilt. Her suitcase stood open against the lefthand wall. He stepped dazedly forward, dabbing at his watering eyes, careful not to stray off the path. When he came to the quilt he stopped and turned and looked up. Set into the ceiling were four metal grates, perfectly square and black, and on the far side of the grates was the city. People passed over the grates in clumsy arabesques, waddling like flightless birds, and pigeons and clouds and helicopters passed over the people. He sat down Indian-style on the quilt and kept looking. How funny people look from underneath, he thought. Especially the girls. The strangeness of it all made him swallow his breath.

"Where are we?"

"Eighty-fourth and Columbus," said Heather Covington. She sat down close beside him.

"Can they see us?"

"They could if they looked down." She made a sound that could have been a laugh. "Mostly they don't."

Lowboy wiped his eyes. "Why don't they?"

"Shhh," said Heather Covington. She ran two knuckles up the back of his skull until he looked at her. Her other hand was moving down the front of her shirt, pulling it open in unhurried twists. His own hands were dead but she seemed not to care. The look in her eyes wasn't urgent at all, only quiet and sure. Her breath smelled like butter and clove cigarettes and beer. She leaned forward and breathed into his ear, saying two small words no one had ever said to him before. Her chapped lips rasped like twigs against his skin. The light began to dance across her face, keeping him from seeing what she wanted. Her hands were at the buckle of his belt. The light made them look oversized and thick, like gloved hands in a black-and-white cartoon. I'm being raped by Minnie Mouse, he thought.

"Does that tickle?" she asked him. Her hands never slowed.

"No," said Lowboy. "It's all right." He looked up at the grates. "Say those two words again."

"Sure," she said. "Look here at me." But instead of saying anything she took his hand by the wrist and put it inside her shirt. There were more underneath, two or possibly three, but she bunched them up and pressed his hand against her. She let out a breath when his knuckles met her ribs and he saw it billowing above him in the air. It's cold in here, he thought. Close to freezing. But it was just a thought and had no weight at all.

"Now, then," said Heather Covington. "Let's see how our boy's feeling."

To distract her Lowboy slid her shirt up higher and took one of her nipples in his fingers. "Ouch!" she said softly. But that didn't stop her.

"I guess he's all right," she said after a while, looking him over. She seemed taller than before. She was growing toward the sunlight like a clambering vine. "He's doing good," she said. "But let's make him do better." She caught the tip of her tongue between her teeth. "Let's give him some of the knowledge of the world."

"No," Lowboy said thickly. "You lie back." The room was getting colder and he knew it had to happen soon or never. He brought his face close to hers, then closer still, until she had to take her hands away. "Get down on the quilt," he told her. He'd intended his voice to sound patient and deep, like the voice of a soldier, but instead it rattled like a broken hinge. He put his hands on her shoulders and began to push. He'd expected her to be surprised at the change in him, suspicious of it, but he saw no trace of surprise in her at all.

Her face slid sleepily back out of the light. Her lacquered black eyes ticked from one side to the other. Try as he might he found no recognition there. Her hands were still at his hips but they were pulling her own jeans open now, not his. The rush of the street was still booming behind him but it was less important than the booming in his body. Her jeans came open and she pushed them down in three impatient jerks. "Help me with this," she said girlishly, digging a fingernail into his hip.

He took hold of her damp greasy cuffs and pulled them toward him. He'd helped Richard the same way, he remembered, on days when he'd come in tired from the yard. The thought of those white meatless legs compared to Heather Covington's almost made him laugh out loud. She was lying with her elbows tucked behind her and her shirts bunched up above her belly and her trunklike legs on either side of him. She seemed even bigger than she'd seemed before. She didn't sigh or blink or make a sound. His corduroys were around his ankles too, like the pants of a toddler waiting for a change of clothes, and he stared down at his indecisive body. There wasn't much of him compared to her.

"Now?" he said, inching himself forward. "Is it now?"

She closed her eyes and opened her legs wider. He looked away for the length of a breath, then leaned forward until he could feel the warmth of her bare skin against his face. The smell forced his mouth and eyes shut. He thought about the inside of his body: how cold and shutaway it was, like a doll forgotten in an empty house. He thought about the end of the world, about the people above the grates, about the tunnel, about MUSEUM OF NATURAL HISTORY. The sparkling tiles, the unforgiving benches. The dinosaurs set like urns into the wall. He pictured his own skeleton there, then Heather Covington's, then Violet's. What he needed to do was as clear as if it had been burned into him with electric wire. He needed to break the membrane that had held him all his life, to slip out into the putrefying world. He had to put himself into another body. He had to bite down on his tongue and push.

Above the grates someone was laughing softly.

"I can't do it," he gasped, gagging on his own breath. "It's gone to sleep, Miss Covington. Take a look."

She pushed herself up. She didn't seem suprised or angry. "Too young," she said, brushing the hair back from his face. "Too childish."

"It's my meds," he said. "They take away your juices."

"Never took mine," she said. "Just the opposite." She looked down at him. "You almost *there*, little boss. You don't think if I—"

"No," he said, pushing her hand away. "Don't touch it."

"All right," she murmured, bringing her legs together. "All right." She looked down at herself for a moment. "Pass me my effects."

"Your what?"

"My *effects*, boy. My clothes." She reached past him and picked up her jeans and worked her legs back into them. He was curious to see the expression on her face but he couldn't bring himself to look at her. If their eyes met it was possible that he'd vanish in a puff of yellow smoke. Yellow for cowardice, Lowboy thought, staring down into his lap. Yellow for disease.

"What they got you on?" Heather Covington said after a time.

He lifted his shoulders and let them fall. His arms felt like pieces of dough. "Zyprexa, Depakote—"

She puckered her lips. "Zyprexa!" she said. "I remember that one. Zyprexa make me twitch."

"Zyprexa wouldn't do that." His voice was barely loud enough to hear. "Zyprexa's a second-generation antipsychotic. Those don't give you the shakes."

She leered at him. "Listen to the little boss. Rex fucking Morgan, MD."

Lowboy said nothing.

"They had me on Prolixin," she said after a while. "Maybe it was that."

"Prolixin would do it."

She slid closer. "What about Zyprexa? You say Zyprexa take away your juices?"

"Depakote does," he said, running his hand over the quilt. "It makes you not want to do it. That's why I stopped." He hated the way his voice sounded, explaining about meds like a middle-aged RN. He cleared his throat. "Depakote's fat-based. They all are. To get past the blood-brain barrier." He looked at her now. "The blood-brain barrier is made out of fat, actually."

"The blood-brain barrier," she said politely. "Good enough."

"Your brain's floating in jelly, Miss Covington. Fatty jelly." He smiled at her. "Sort of like a French pâté."

"That would explain it," she said, buttoning up her shirt.

"But the rest of your body has a hard time with fat. So it stays in your blood—"

"Where you scrape this shit up at, little boss?" She leaned over and poked him in the ribs. "I bet the skullfuckers told you."

"Nobody told me." He passed a hand over his face. "They had a book about it at the library."

She whistled through her teeth. "No kind of library where *I* got sent."

He lay back on the quilt. The light was paler now, less cutting, and he could stare at it for a long time without having to blink. "The library was two blocks from my house, on the corner of Seventh and Greenwich. I went there when they told me I was sick."

She cleared her throat and spat onto the floor. "And you believed them, hey? You believed the skullfuckers?"

He focused on the clouds above the grates. He waited for them to move but they kept still. "I'm sick, Miss Covington. You know I am."

"I'll tell you what I know." She shook her head. "I know I'm down here and they're not. I know I got no kind of meds in me. I know—" She hesitated. "I know that I've got *ideas.*"

"I have them too," he said. "I wish I didn't."

"You don't have my ideas, you little cracker. Nobody got my ideas but me." She stared at him fiercely, working her jaws in a slow circle, as though she were sharpening her teeth.

"I don't want them."

He expected her to hit him but she didn't. She sat up very straight, heaved an unamused sigh, then pulled his jeans back up and zipped them closed. She did it roughly, matter-of-factly, the way that Violet would have done it. It was enough to make him wonder.

"Do you have kids, Miss Covington?"

For the space of a breath she stared wide-eyed at him, sucking in her cheeks. Then her face went slack. "If you so sick, Rex Morgan, what you messing with me for? Why not go home and get your diapers on?"

"I told you why." He took a breath. "The air is getting—"

"Hotter," she said flatly. "I remember." She brought a wrist to her nose and sniffed at it thoughtfully, like someone standing at a perfume counter. "I tell you what. If I was a skullfucker, I might say that all this foolishness about the air—"

"Thank you, Miss Covington," Lowboy said, getting to his feet. "Thank you very much. That's all for now."

She laughed and hooked a finger through his belt. "Where you running off to, little boss? Hang around a little. I'll be good."

He was full in the light now, squinting down into the corner, and the hand she held him with looked disembodied. People were walking across the grates in twos and threes, innocent and self-assured as children. Watching them he began to feel the cold.

"You'll shut up?" he said, shifting from one foot to the other. "You'll mind your own business? You'll put a sock in it? You'll say it with flowers?"

She said nothing to that, only pulled him back down, and he shook his head but let himself be pulled. It was warmer beside her. Their feet were in the sunlight but their bodies were sequestered and secure. He looked down at his dirty Velcro sneakers. They looked ridiculous in the brightness, oversized and crude, surplus footwear from a failed moon landing. He yawned and laid his head back on the quilt.

"I want to stay here forever," he said. "I don't ever want to go back up."

"You and everybody else," Heather Covington said. "Everybody want to be the Dutchman."

"The who?"

"Dutchman," she sighed. "Like the opera. Like the play. Dutchman been riding the 6 train for seventeen years. He ain't crossed a turnstile since 2002."

"How does he stay alive?" Lowboy said. He propped himself up on his elbows. "What does he find to eat?"

"Don't know as he eats anything," she said indifferently. She pulled her suitcase toward her and began to rummage through it. Something inside made a clinical sound, brittle and sharp, like beakers in a high school science kit. "Maybe he eats candybars from the kiosks. Maybe he fries chickens on the rail." She winked at him. "Maybe he eats horny little boys."

The sunlight lost its color suddenly. Lowboy hummed to himself and laid his head down again and waited for her to keep talking. He wanted to believe her very much. What mattered most about the Dutchman was that the Dutchman was impossible. If the Dutchman existed then other impossible things could exist, like the Loch Ness monster or Ouroboros or the devil. The thought of it made Lowboy's teeth start to chatter and the hair on the back of his neck stand on end. If the Dutchman existed you couldn't be sure about anything. Half the books in the library would have to be rewritten. People would start walking backward down the street. He almost laughed out loud at that. If the Dutchman existed the world might not actually end.

He rocked himself gently and watched Heather Covington fussing. She was mumbling to herself now, hunched over the suitcase like a jeweler, putting some small thing together slowly. She seemed to have forgotten that he was waiting. He hummed to himself and tapped his feet against the channeled concrete floor. The idea of the Dutchman got bigger as he waited and began to throw off white and green and coppercolored sparks. Something was going to happen. The kingdom of the impossible stood glittering over his left shoulder, waiting quietly to admit him. All he had to do was turn his head.

"How old is the Dutchman?" he said. His voice sounded clumsy. "What does he look like?"

"White," said Heather Covington. "He don't smell right. Most times he's got a whole car to himself."

The way she said it told him not to press her. He rolled onto his stomach and pushed his face into the quilt, breathing the sourness in, trying to keep his excitement to himself. The Dutchman is real, he thought. He's an actual living person and she knows him. Maybe she's even brought him to this room.

"Why only the 6 train?" he said. "Why just that line?"

"Hhff," said Heather Covington. Something was in her mouth now: something brittle. Her left arm jerked upward and he heard a sucking. The air smelled like butane for a moment, then like roasted almonds, then like sweat.

"Miss Covington?" he said.

"Shut your mouth," she whispered, lowering her head until it vanished. With her head gone she looked like a monster on some ancient map of the world. She made a sucking sound through her teeth and kept her body absolutely still. "Little baby," she said, bracing her left hand against the floor. She coughed without covering her mouth. "Little baby," she said. "Little dollar bill."

The air was full of smoke now and the smell slid down his windpipe like an eel. He put a hand over his mouth, then over his eyes, then over the whole of his face. When he took it away Heather Covington was lying splayed out with her arms bent behind her, breathing in a soft contented stutter. Her right eye was open but her left eye was closed. A thimblesized glass bowl lay sideways in the hollow of her chest, rolling like a buoy with each breath. The smoke led up toward the city like a ladder.

"I'll tell you something," she said. "I never expected you to get on me."

He bit down on his lip and looked at her. "How come?"

"I'm ugly as a bitch."

He kept his eyes on the bowl, thinking of a way to answer her. Finally he propped himself up and looked at her closely and saw she was right. Her face was as flat and lifeless as a skillet.

She coughed. "I wasn't always ugly, though. I use to be a little blue-eyed girl."

"I know that," Lowboy said. "I saw your passport."

"Ever heard of Dr. Z?" She sighed and began rolling up her sleeves. "*Zizmor*, I mean. Jonathan Zizmor, MD. That Jew skin doctor on Third Avenue."

"I've seen his ads," said Lowboy. He grinned at her. "I like the one that says BLEMISHES?—BLOTCHES?—BUMPS? in purple letters."

"That's him," she said. "That's the one." She held a gray forearm toward him, running two fingers along its skin, then brought both hands up gravely to her face. There was no light in her black eyes any longer. They looked like two holes punched into a piece of paper.

"Jonathan Zizmor did this to me," she said.

Just then a noise fell down on them like a hammer against a nail and the darkness folded over into nothing. A man in a uniform was squatting above them, unhooking something heavy from his belt. "That you, Rafa?" the man said, shining a light down into the smoke. His voice sounded agreeable and mild.

"Heather Covington, Officer Martinez." She was wide awake again and her body was as solid as an arch. She put her right hand on the back of Lowboy's neck and leaned forward to keep him out of sight. He couldn't see the policeman but he could hear him drop to his knees against the grate. Heather Covington's head was trembling slightly, like an old woman's or an alcoholic's, but her eyes were hard and clear and full of hate. Lowboy braced his back against the wall.

"Smells like good times down there, Rafa," the officer said. "Smells like you've been doing yourself some cooking."

"Smoking crack, Officer Martinez," Heather Covington said brightly. "Trying to make the time go by."

The policeman heaved a sigh. "Thank you, Rafa. Thanks for including me in your life." The stillness between his breaths was absolute. "What are you doing over there in the corner? Why not turn around and talk to me?"

Heather Covington shut her eyes and took the tip of her tongue between her teeth. "Can't," she said finally. "Can't do it, Officer. I'm not *presentable*."

For a moment the officer made no sound at all. When he spoke again his voice was free of all emotion, even and smooth, the voice of a surgeon asking for a sterile cloth. "Who's that with you, Rafa?"

As she turned her head to answer Lowboy kicked against the wall and slid out between her spread legs like a baby. The roar of the street shook the room like a matchbox and the officer was banging with his flashlight against the grate but by then he was already back inside the tunnel. He'd have run straight out onto the tracks but the sound of the water saved him and he caught himself on the crimped edge of the seam. He teetered and bobbed like a drunk at the end of a pier. He waited there as long as he could stand it. Nobody followed him.

Maybe he arrested her, Lowboy thought. Maybe he shot her. Maybe they're smoking crack together. He opened his eyes wide, then shut them, then opened them again, straining to make out a difference in the blackness. Twice he heard the sound of rustling leaves. He counted from one to one hundred, took a few deep breaths, then counted from one hundred down to one. When he was done he went to the next station.

A breeze was building in the tunnel as he started walking. Uptown train coming, he said to himself, and it helped to take his mind off what had happened. Express, he decided, feeling the air against his open fingers. The through train to the Bronx. The uptown D. He quickened his steps as the sound overtook him. He felt clearheaded and relieved to be alone. He was hidden again, as safe as he'd ever be, down in the lightless, airless bowels of the world. The hum all around was a sweet thing to hear, gathering as the wind gathered, and it seemed as though it had something to tell him. He laid his head against the tunnel wall and listened.

Years later, in the rarefied seclusion that most of his life had been a dress rehearsal for, Lateef would claim that he'd recognized Violet Heller's significance right away. If he hadn't, he'd have sent her home at once: she wasn't telling him enough to indulge her. "I had a feeling about Violet, right from the beginning," he'd say quietly, then withdraw behind his famous blank-eyed smile.

The truth was that he kept her in his office because she looked like a portrait by Brueghel, awkward and immaculate at once, and because there was nothing to do for the moment but wait. She was eccentric, of course, and stubborn—it was impossible, thank God, to imagine her in hysterics—but unlike most of the mothers who put themselves in the way of his paycheck, she refused to be parted from her self-control. She doesn't want to give me that satisfaction, Lateef thought, and the idea held his interest. But never for a moment did he suspect that she had any real part to play, either within the Special Category Missing or outside of it. Not until the call came in.

Her reaction to her son's case report had been predictable enough: she'd gone absolutely still, as though he'd propositioned her, and had stared at him in a way that he'd been acquainted with since his first day on the job. If she'd kept quiet it was only because her mouth had gone too dry with rage to speak. He'd returned her look calmly, even encouragingly: his misgivings had subsided as he watched her. Her own attitude, after all, had forced his hand.

"Obstruction of justice seems to come naturally to you, Miss Heller." He let the file fall theatrically closed. "I'd almost think you had a history yourself."

"You're a born policeman, Detective," she said, looking past him out the window. "Every little old lady is a mafioso."

"Listen to me, please. Everything I've learned about your son leads me to believe that time is very tight. His medication is at a negligible level, he's in a hazardous environment, and his psychoses tend to be violent." He sat back a moment and let that register. "In my opinion, there's a good chance that a crime will be committed: a serious crime, Miss Heller. A felony. It could very well be happening as we speak."

"Then why aren't you out looking for him, Detective?" she said, rising mechanically to her feet. "Why are you sitting here doing absolutely fucking nothing, shuffling cards like we have all the tea in China?"

She was standing an arm's length from him now, legs set hard against the desk, opening and closing her fists like someone at the onset of a seizure. If I laugh now, he thought, I'll have lost her completely. She looks as though she might actually take a swing.

"All the time in the world, I think you mean."

Her palms came down on his desk with such force that a drawer clattered open. "*Answer* me, Detective! What the hell are we still doing here?"

Her accent's stronger now, Lateef thought, composing himself before he gave his answer. She sounds like a Hollywood Nazi. "We're waiting for the phone to ring, Miss Heller. That's all we *can* do, I'm sorry to say. Unless you have some ideas about your son that you'd be willing to share with this department."

"I do have some ideas, in fact." She sucked in a breath. "I wonder why you didn't ask before."

He permitted himself a smile. "You don't seem very shy with your opinions."

"You're manipulating me now, Detective." She turned away from him tiredly. "If I thought you were acting out of a genuine desire—"

The buzzing of his deskline interrupted her. She stopped herself at once, her mouth hanging open like a sleeper's, and stared at the receiver with a look of simple dread. He paused a moment before answering, watching the fact of the call sink into her. There was no trace of relief in her expression.

"Excuse me just a minute, Miss Heller."

She gave no sign of having understood him.

The conversation was brief—a minute at the most—and for his part Lateef said almost nothing. When he set down the receiver Violet slumped slightly forward, making a small defeated sound, as though her worst fears had already been confirmed. Any doubt he might have had that she believed her son was violent vanished in that instant. She'll work with me now, he thought. No more putting on airs. She knows there's no more sense in wasting time.

"A traffic cop working the intersection of Eighty-fourth and Columbus spotted your son through a grate. This was about twenty minutes ago, at ten forty-five. According to the officer, he appeared unharmed."

"Through a grate?" she murmured. "Under the sidewalk?"

He nodded. "He's still in the MTA network."

She was already standing. "I told you he'd stay underground. In the last note he sent—"

"Slow down just a little, Miss Heller. I wouldn't mind keeping you company."

· · · ·

There was somehow no question, Lateef would say later, of leaving her at the Department. She took it as a given that he'd bring her. It's certainly not unheard-of, he reminded himself, following her almost bashfully into the hall. She might easily prove useful, if only to make a positive ID. But what struck him most, both then and afterward, was that the agreement was entirely unspoken: it was as natural a thing as turning off the light. He'd no more have thought of stopping her than of leaving his wallet or his .38 behind.

She led the way downstairs and out of the building, not once looking back to see if he was following, and crossed Centre Street without a moment's hesitation, stopping only at the entrance to the lot. He didn't ask how she'd known where his car would be: he no longer expected her to act like a complainant. He was gratified, how-ever—even slightly relieved—when she swept confidently past his car.

"Just missed me, Miss Heller. Behind you on the left."

She'd chosen a patrol car at random and was standing at the driver-side door, her arms crossed at her waist as though she ex-pected to be cuffed. "That one?" she said, with obvious disappoint-ment. "The little green hatchback?"

"The little green sport utility sedan."

"Does it even have a siren?"

"Excellent mileage." He unlocked the passenger-side door for her. "A pleasure to park."

She kept quiet until they were on the West Side Highway. "You're not a family man, apparently."

"Why do you say that, Miss Heller?"

"This car of yours. It's spotless."

He said nothing to that, only smiled and shrugged his shoulders, and she seemed appreciative of the silence. She tilted her seat back and closed her eyes. He felt the urge to watch her but resisted it. At the stoplight at Thirty-fourth Street she sat up with a start, as though her name had been called, and fixed her gray eyes wonderingly on his.

"That sticker on your bumper. Is it true?"

He squinted at the stoplight. "What sticker would that be, Miss Heller?"

"Does this thing really run on soybean oil?"

He caressed the dashboard lovingly.

"Will would admire you for that."

"Would he? Why?"

"Global warming is his allconsuming passion. That's how the world is going to end, you know."

"No argument there," Lateef said, switching lanes.

She opened the glove compartment and saw the gun inside and pushed the compartment shut. "I'm surprised you didn't know that, come to think of it. You must not have read Will's case file very closely."

She was looking away from him as she spoke, watching the numbered cross streets arcing past. She was milder now, less strident, more composed. The arrogance had been leached out of her voice. Because she's been asleep, he decided. She'll be arrogant again soon enough. But he found himself telling her the truth regardless.

"I have no access to your son's case history, Miss Heller. The files on all minors are sealed at sentencing. I'd have to call in all my favors just to see it." He sighed. "To be honest, I doubt whether I have that much pull."

For the better part of a minute she said nothing. Lateef kept his eyes on the road, feigning indifference, but even so he could tell that he'd astonished her. Finally she took hold of the rearview mirror and tipped it until their eyes met. "What the fuck did you have in that folder?"

"A clipping from the New York *Daily News.*"

"But how?" She shook her head in disbelief. "If you weren't allowed—"

"I happened to remember your son's case. It's part of my job to read the paper, ridiculous as that may sound."

Fifteen minutes earlier she'd have risen to the occasion, made some joke about not seeing him do much else, but this time she said nothing. They were coming to the intersection of Amsterdam and Seventy-second. She waited until he'd made the turn onto Amsterdam, then said in a disinterested voice: "You'd have more luck with your witnesses, Detective, if you stopped treating them like political prisoners."

He let his eyes rest on the city bus in front of them. "You're not a witness, Miss Heller. You're a complainant. And I treat everyone who lies to me the same way."

She blinked at him. "What do you mean by that?"

"You told me that your son had no friends but his grandfather, no interest in anything but comic books. When obviously he was spending time with that girl."

She tilted her head out of view.

"Why didn't you mention the girl to me, Miss Heller?"

"I didn't think she was important."

"I'd have to disagree. I think she is."

She started to answer him, then stopped herself. When she spoke again her voice was strangely muffled. "Will's not a murderer, Detective. Will is a boy with an illness."

He frowned at her. "I wasn't aware the girl was killed, Miss Heller."

"She wasn't killed," she said quickly. "Emily is fine." Both her arms were braced against the dashboard. "Could you slow down, Detective? We're practically up that bus's muffler."

"We don't have all the tea in China," Lateef said gravely, but she didn't seem to hear.

"It's incredible that Emily wasn't killed," she said after a time. "Her head came down an inch from the third rail. The 6 was less than a stop away, just a few hundred yards uptown, but they managed to get the signals switched somehow." A taxi rolled past them and she watched it pass. "By the time they took Will away she was already in a bed at City Hospital."

"Did she testify at your son's trial?"

"She refused to testify. She told everyone she'd jumped of her own volition." Violet shook her head. "No one believed her, of course."

She leaned forward and rested her head against the dash. Lateef kept quiet for the length of four full blocks, determined not to rush her. He knew the rest was coming and it was.

"Try to imagine, Detective, what it's like to have a child—" She stopped in mid-sentence and straightened in her seat. "What it's like to have a child, only one, and to feed that child all of your own old ambitions. It's wrong for other parents, of course, but you feel different, free to indulge yourself, because your child is very close to perfect." She arranged her hands more precisely in her lap. "It isn't only because you love him that you think of him this way. He's gentler than most other children are, more self-contained, more independent. As far as anyone can tell—teachers, neighbors, even other children— he's also a good deal smarter. He takes your life over completely."

They were coming up to Eighty-second Street, just three blocks from the sighting, but Lateef made a slow right and lifted his foot off the gas. She seemed neither to notice nor to care.

"Then picture what came next," she said. "Picture everything I've told you happening."

After that she stopped talking and dug the heels of her palms into her eyes. He circled the block at a leisurely pace and brought them back to Amsterdam without a word. Her crying didn't alarm him; just the opposite. It was proof that something had fallen away between them. A barrier had been removed, not through anything he'd said or done, but simply because her son had been sighted alive. She's saving her strength now, Lateef thought. Saving it for what's coming. She knows better than to waste it all on me.

"Emily was a remarkable girl," she said when she was done. "She was taller than Will, the way girls that age often are, and she had lovely dark hair that always hung straight down into her eyes. A tomboy, I suppose you'd say. I never understood what brought the two of them together: it's so odd for a fourteen-year-old girl to give a younger boy the time of day." She smiled to herself. "Will had begun to be handsome, but it wasn't just that. There was something between them."

Lateef pulled up at Eighty-fourth and Columbus and let the motor idle. "Did your son think of her as his girlfriend?"

"I asked him the same question. It got me grounded for a week."

"Had Emily been told about his illness?"

"She knew about it." She tapped a fingernail against the dashboard. "Everybody knew by then."

He considered that for a moment. "And it made no difference to her?"

"It didn't bother her at all. She made a point of telling me." She drew in a deep breath and made a face. "I suppose she must have thought it was romantic."

"I'm guessing that you didn't like her much."

She smiled at him. "You should ask Will's therapist about that, Detective. Ulysses S. Kopeck, MD. He'll tell you about my unfortunate fixation on my son."

"I don't get along with that kind of doctor," Lateef said, killing the engine. "They always seem to think I'm paranoid."

"Do they really?"

He nodded resignedly. "Apparently I view everyone as a suspect."

She gave a laugh, then stopped herself, as if at a sudden memory. "Kopeck was right about me, though, in spite of everything. I've always asked more of Will than I should have."

"All mothers ask things of their sons."

"I asked more."

Something in her answer made him uneasy. "What sort of things, Miss Heller?"

"You have to understand that I came to this country more or less by accident, from one day to the next. Aside from Will's father, I didn't have a friend in the world. I had nothing." She shifted slightly in her seat. "You're wondering what this has to do with Will."

Lateef didn't answer.

"I hadn't planned to have a child—Alex had three kids already, with his first wife—but when Will was born I became a different person." She hesitated. "Does that make sense?"

"Different in what way?"

She brought her knees together. "I'd expected to need Alex more once the baby was born, but the truth was I needed him less. I felt like a dead body brought back to life, and it was Will who had done that, not Alex. I had everything suddenly instead of nothing." She shook her head slowly. "From the day he was born I told him every thought that flitted through my head: I talked to him for hours on end. It never occurred to me to keep the least thing from him. I needed a friend—an equal, an adult—and I brought Will up to play that role for me." She let her eyes rest on Lateef. "Will had no say in any of this, of course. It never would have occurred to him to object. That's what I mean, Detective, when I tell you that I asked too much of him."

Lateef said nothing for a moment. "It must have been hard for you when Emily came along."

"It was very hard for me."

"What did you think of her?"

She stared out at the curb. "I didn't know what to do with Emily. She confused me. I treated her the way you treat your complainants."

"Poor Emily."

"The first time Will brought her over, I thought she'd been sent by the school to make sure he got home. She was terribly excited to be mixed up in something so serious." She bit her lip for a while. "Will was still functioning then, still able to go to school most of the time. He left the two of us in the kitchen and went straight to his room and shut the door. I didn't know what to think. I was about to thank Emily for escorting him home when she smiled at me, like any other girl with a crush would do, and told me that she'd met Will on the train. She was a perfectly normal-seeming teenager, polite and well-spoken, but there was something desperate in the way she looked at me. What could this girl want from us? I thought. I asked her what Will had done, still thinking that something must have happened, but she just looked down at the floor and said, 'He didn't have to do anything, really.' I don't know which of us was more embarrassed." She took another deep breath. "She ended up staying the night."

Lateef raised his eyebrows. "In your son's room?"

She smiled. "You're forgetting my possessiveness, Detective. I made a bed for her out on the couch."

"What about the girl's parents?"

"I called them, of course. Emily asked me not to but I insisted. I was expecting trouble—a few awkward questions, at least—but her father couldn't have cared less. He told me that it happened all the time."

"Not the possessive type, apparently."

"Not so much," said Violet. "Shouldn't we be getting out?"

"Of course," he said, fumbling with his seatbelt. "After you, Miss Heller."

She waited for a bike to pass, a model citizen, then opened her door and eased out gracefully. Lateef stayed in the car a moment longer, frowning at his reflection in the driver-side mirror. You're flirting with her, he said to himself. The idea depressed him. He often joked with his complainants, especially the difficult ones, but in this case it brought no advantage. Watch yourself, Professor White, he thought. You've already made at least one joke too many.

It turned out he needn't have worried. She was standing on the curb with her arms crossed against the cold, oblivious to the looks of passersby, waiting impatiently for him to join her. The women looked her over as they passed, letting their eyes linger on her loose and charmless clothes; the men simply stared at her face. When he finally followed her out of the car, he realized that she'd been trying to speak to him.

"What was that, Miss Heller?"

"I don't want you to misunderstand what I've told you, that's all." She turned away from him as she spoke, glancing down into a grate beside her feet. "I may have aggravated my son's illness—I won't deny that—but I didn't cause it."

"It's my understanding that schizophrenia is caused by genetics," Lateef said carefully.

"They don't have a clue what it's caused by," she said, hunching over. "They don't know a goddamn thing."

"That's not true, Miss Heller." He coughed into his fist. "They've done tests that show an electrical difference in the brain. And they have medication to treat it, like any other illness of the body. The Thorazine, for example, that your son was taking—"

"Thorazine!" she said fiercely. Her back was turned on him now but he could picture her contemptuous smile regardless. "Do you know how they discovered Thorazine, Detective? By mistake. They were using it as a tranquilizer in surgery." She nodded to herself. "They have no idea why Thorazine works, or Clozapine, or any of their other silver bullets. Schizophrenia might as well come from eating powdered sugar."

"It isn't caused by needy mothers, though. No one's made that claim for years."

She looked at him now. "I aggravated my son's condition, Detective Lateef."

He didn't know what to say to that. He looked around vainly for Officer Leo Martinez, Twenty-third Precinct, who was supposedly working the corner. Violet had already turned back to the grate. He felt awkward behind her, stifflimbed and useless, a feeling he generally reserved for his days off. One of the benefits of his work was that it made no allowance for awkwardness: awkwardness was an Upper East Side luxury. His father had told him that once, and he'd laughed at his father, but the idea had stuck. And now he'd been reduced to the role of observer—worse than that, of witness—and his work had failed to offer him protection. The moment passed quickly, but it left him bewildered. His irritation at Martinez mounted. I'll make that boy hop when he gets here, he thought, and the idea brought him comfort of a kind.

"Is this the grate?" Violet said suddenly. "This one here?"

"I'm not sure, to tell you the truth. The on-duty officer—"

"There's a room down there," she said.

"What do you mean?"

She bent down and brought her face close to the grate. "A bed with some clothes on it. A little blue suitcase."

Lateef squatted next to her. "I wouldn't call that a bed," he said, feeling more ineffectual than ever. "A comforter, that's all, or some kind of—"

"This is it," she said, touching the grate with her fingers. "This is where Will was seen."

Just then a boy in a uniform appeared around the corner, tearing a packet of Dutch Masters open with his teeth. The uniform seemed too big for him, cut for someone less dainty, and in spite of his painstakingly nurtured mustache he barely looked old enough to smoke. He grinned when he saw them and held out a hand to Lateef. "Detective!" he said, looking past him at Violet. "Very nice to meet you. Thanks for coming."

"Officer Martinez?" Lateef said, keeping his hands in his pockets.

"Right," Martinez said, tipping his hat to Violet. "And this lady is . . . ?"

"Yda Heller," said Violet.

"Nice to meet you, Miss Heller. I hope you don't mind—"

"What have you got for us, Officer?" Lateef cut in.

Martinez cleared his throat. "Well, sir. Not so much. I saw the boy."

"What boy?"

"Sorry, Detective," Martinez said indulgently. "I saw *a* boy. Fitting the description you sent out."

"Where was this?"

Martinez glanced over his shoulder, as if confiding a secret, then pointed at the grate under their feet.

Lateef looked at Violet, but she was on her knees already, craning her neck to see into the shaftway. He beckoned Martinez closer. "I have no doubt, Officer Martinez, that this is more fun for you than standing in front of Dunkin' Donuts pretending to be a traffic light, but Miss Heller and I are a little pressed for time. Where—where exactly—did you see the boy?"

"Right in there," Martinez said, sticking out his lower lip. "Right where she's looking at."

"You're sure it was him?" Violet said without turning. "Did he tell you his name?"

Martinez smiled again. "Ain't too many blond kids screwing around down there, Miss Heller."

"Someone was with him?" Lateef said. "A woman?"

Martinez nodded. "She run away, though. Both of them did. Back into the tunnel."

Violet looked at him over her shoulder. "How long ago was that?"

"Quarter to eleven."

"Half an hour," she said, sitting back on her heels.

"Thirty-seven minutes," Martinez corrected her, looking at his watch. "Thirty-eight, actually."

Lateef shook his head. "And these grates don't open?"

"Not for us, sir," Martinez said brightly. "You got to call MTA central for the key. They don't even have it at the station."

"And you did that, I assume?" Lateef said, bringing his hands together in an attitude of prayer.

"Did what?"

"Called the MTA. Put in a key request."

Martinez coughed and looked down at his belt.

"All right," said Lateef. He took in a slow and charitable breath. "All right, Martinez. Go ahead and place that call."

"He's long gone," Violet murmured.

"Martinez," Lateef said, keeping his voice level, "go down into that station—go right now, do you hear me?—and put in that request."

Martinez grinned at Violet. "I got to tell you, Detective—"

Lateef spun on his heels and raised his eyebrows at Martinez. Martinez sidled off, muttering to himself, running a thumb over his mustache as if to reassure himself that it was still in place.

A long and uneventful moment passed. Violet seemed to have forgotten why they'd come. "Thirty-eight minutes," she said, staring off into the traffic. "He could be in Sheepshead Bay by now."

"He could be," said a small voice. "But he not."

Slowly, deliberately, with no outward sign of surprise, Violet brought her face down to the grate. "Have you seen my son?"

A laugh. "I more than *seen* him, Lady Bird."

Lateef was crouched next to Violet now, shielding his eyes from the glare off the street. In the halflight underneath the grate an up-turned face looked toward them, as flat and empty as a cardboard box. The face seemed to be smiling.

The doors came together and the C started rolling and Lowboy made himself invisible. He'd come out onto the platform ahead of the train and he didn't think the motorman had seen him. On the other hand there was no sure way of telling. His eyes were dazzled by the tubelights and his legs were weak from running and his head was alive with what the wall had told him. I'll get off at the next stop, he thought, checking his pantlegs for soot. I'll switch to the downtown local. He kept his breath steady and tried not to seem too excited.

For once no one was watching him. Two middle-aged women in biker jackets were having a fight across the aisle and nobody seemed to have noticed him sit down. He waited a moment longer, watching the women sneer and poke at each other with their short ungraceful fingers, then decided it was safe to close his eyes. Things got quiet right away. He thought about what had happened with Heather Covington, how his body had stopped listening to his brain, and decided that he felt all right about it. There were reasons why it didn't work, he thought. It was cold for one thing. And anyone could have seen us. And she smelled like she was 1,000,000,000 years old.

Her name wasn't even Heather Covington, he said to himself. I can't believe I ever thought it was.

He could tell by the shifting of his body against the seat that the train was coming into a station. The airbrakes kicked in and people stumbled to their feet but he was having too many thoughts to switch trains now. Sourceless revelations sparked and spun behind his eyelids and memories flashed like stoplights in between. He drew himself up and made his Sherlock Holmes face and tried to have just one thought at a time. Rafa, he thought. That's what the officer called her. Smells like good times down there, Rafa. He stared at the pocked brown floor between his shoes. "Rafa," he said quietly, feeling the sound climb out of his throat. It sounded like a Mexican curseword.

The brakes kicked in harder and the train came up short. He sat forward when the C# and A sounded and discovered that the car was almost empty. The women with the men's haircuts were outside now, laughing and nodding and rolling their eyes at each other. The few people left were sitting alone doing nothing. He let his eyes close again.

The problem was this, he thought. I didn't know her. No one does it that way. They find somebody they know to do it with. That makes it private: a confidential matter. That makes it safe. They do it in the comfort of their homes.

Either that or they pay for it, he thought.

"I wonder how much it would cost," Lowboy said out loud. He remembered the money he'd found and how Heather Covington had picked it up and kept it. More than twenty, he thought. It would cost more than that. Unless you had a girlfriend. He smiled stupidly into the crook of his bent arm. If you had a girlfriend maybe twenty would be enough.

An idea came to him then. Like all good ideas it was so obvious and straightforward that it seemed ridiculous at first. But the more he thought about the idea the bigger and more beautiful it grew, spreading out in all directions like a stain, until it was the only one he had. Before the train pulled out again he knew where he was going next and why.

I'll go to *her*, he thought. She wanted to do it: she told me herself. She told me on the stairs at Union Square. It's got to happen sometime, Will, she said. It happens to every person in the world.

I'll do it to you right now, if you want me to. He let his eyes open. She told me that.

I'll do it to you, Will. And then you can do it to me. Just put both of your arms around me like this.

He made two fists and took a breath and held it. She was hard to think about, harder even than Violet, but he could do it if he thought of her as nameless. Her name was off-limits to him, strictly prohibited. I know her name anyway, he said to himself. I know what she was called. But when he tried to say the word he made no sound at all.

Her face was easier to think about, less of a risk, but try as he might he couldn't get it clear. He dug his thumbs into his skull and tried again. Her pale smooth face that had always been so friendly. At school he'd tried to draw it in a book, once they'd let him have a book, but each picture he'd drawn had been less true. On the first page there had been a slight resemblance, just enough to place her, but by the middle she could have been any girl at all. As the weeks passed he found himself copying details from one sketch to another instead of trying to find her likeness in his memory. Her decaying longsuffering likeness. On the last day he'd drawn a circle with two slanting lines on top of it, a little round house without any openings. After that he'd put the book away.

That was when everything went flat, like cutouts in a children's pop-up book, and he decided not to get up out of bed. The school turned itself into a cutout, sharpedged and glossy as a postcard, and he kept low to keep from punching holes in it. But in spite of his best efforts holes were made. He forgot about her then, forgot about everyone but Violet, and swallowed every last thing he was fed.

Meds were slid between his teeth like change into a meter. Time went by.

I wonder where she's living now, he thought. I wonder whether she still goes to Crowley. He thought it over for a while, weighing the pros and the cons, then finally decided that she did. Of course she still goes to Crowley, he said to himself. She was on the waitlist for Crowley before her parents even met. He thought about her father, huge and righteous in his terrycloth robe, reading *The Economist* out loud at the kitchen counter. The most fatherish father there had ever been. He would never take his daughter out of Crowley.

The train pulled into the next station and the car began to fill with halfdead people. That's the tiredness, thought Lowboy. They want to curl up on the ground and go to sleep. He yawned at them as they came in, showing them his teeth, and some of them yawned back. The little whitehaired woman next to him was wearing a mink pillbox hat. Jehovah's Witness, he decided. She was eating nuts out of a napkin and muttering to herself, and as he watched her it occurred to him that he was starving. That's something else that I need money for, he thought. Homefries and bacon. Honeydipped nuts. He pointed at his mouth but she ignored him.

The doors closed after exactly ten seconds and the station fell resignedly away. He'd seen the sleight of hand a thousand times before—the room whose doors close on one place and open, after a few minutes of darkness, on another—but today he was seeing the world with different eyes. The walls of the car, for example, which had always seemed so solid, were actually as hollow as an egg. A hole had been cut into the bottom of his seat and behind it was a dusky fibrous vacuum. The pencaps and candywrappers stuffed into the opening only made the hole seem emptier. Another stageset, Lowboy thought, and bit down on his sleeve to keep from laughing. Unreality broke over him again, stronger and more emphatic than before, but this time he was able to endure it. It's a wave, that's all, he told himself. A wave like any other. You can ride it like a surfer if you want to.

In the furrows between crests of the wave he saw things very sharply, the way the air comes clear after a rain. He saw the inside of the car for what it was: a controlled environment, a staging area, planned down to the last detail by people he would never know or see. No surprises in here, Lowboy said to himself. No accidents. He studied each element of the car with his new eyes, imagining it as a kind of blueprint:

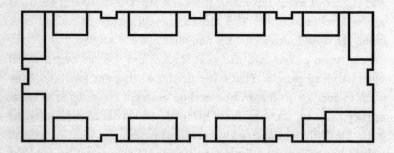

He would never meet the people who'd drawn the blueprint, never have a chance to question them, but he could learn things just by looking at the car. You could see, for example, that they were fearful men. The pattern on the walls, which he'd always taken to be meaningless, was actually made up of thousands of miniature coats of arms, symbols of the authority of the state. The interior of the car was waterproof, the better to be hosed down in case of bloodshed. And the seats were arranged not for maximum efficiency, not to seat the greatest number of people comfortably and safely, but to express the designers' fear with perfect clarity. No one sat with their back turned to anyone else.

He decided to get out at Columbus Circle. To his surprise it happened very simply. He stood up and guided himself into the funnel of exiting bodies, feeling the space around him compress like air sucked into a jet, and let himself be spat onto the platform. The people around him never pitched or stumbled. It's only when you think about things that they get hard to do, he thought. A Bronx-bound D pulled up across the platform and the crush of bodies grew more intricate. How easy this is, Lowboy said to himself, letting the crowd spin him clockwise. So much easier than standing still. Whole families pushed past him as if he were nothing but a misplaced turnstile. After a quarter of an hour, like tidewater playing with a cigarette filter, the current had brought him full circle. But as soon as he thought about what he was doing he froze in his tracks like a deer.

He might have stayed there forever if the tunnel had let him: he might even have forgotten his calling. But from one moment to the next the crowd was blown away like smoke and he was left alone again. He propped himself against a column and looked around him, wondering where everyone had gone. Assorted panhandlers and tourists remained but they seemed pitiful as orphans in the sudden hush. As if no train were ever coming for them.

On the far side of the column a man was standing with his back to Lowboy, in exactly the relation the cars were designed to prevent. A show of power, Lowboy said to himself. A territorial display. The man's right hand held a black leather briefcase, the kind people handcuff themselves to in movies, and his left hand held a plain brown paper bag. The bag was rolled shut but Lowboy could tell what was in it. The smell was sweet and dank and unmistakable. The thing in the bag was a Jamaican beef patty.

Here we go, Lowboy thought. He felt himself gliding forward. He tried to keep his guts from making noises but there was no stopping them. His arms had gone slack and his bones cracked like pieces of kindling. The platform had begun to fill again, like a theater lobby at intermission, but he never took his eyes off the bag. I wonder if he'll eat it all, he thought. I wonder if he'll throw it away. The man was bald and thickheaded and his rumpled grease-smeared trenchcoat ended just above his shoes. The trenchcoat matched the briefcase perfectly. He ought to have sunglasses on, Lowboy said to himself. He looks like an unemployed spy.

The briefcase seemed heavy. What could there be inside it? The man set it down on the platform, less than a foot from the column, as if to offer him a better view. It never occurred to the man to look behind him. He's daydreaming, Lowboy said to himself. He's composing a poem. No wonder he got fired from Her Majesty's Secret Service.

The man unrolled the paper bag and started eating. The smell of it was everywhere by then. By the time the patty was two-thirds gone Lowboy could barely keep upright. At one point he thought the man had noticed him: he stopped in mid-swallow and his head ticked very slightly to the left. But then he was taking another bite, grunting softly as he chewed, glaring down at his fists as though they were somebody else's. His chin glistened like buttered rubber. Lowboy stepped back against the column and let his eyes rest flatly on the ground. His stomach was spasming and turning cartwheels but the man in the trenchcoat couldn't have cared less. His briefcase was less than an arm's length away, blacker and more official-looking than ever. It vibrated coldly against the concrete. There was some kind of machinery inside it.

Lowboy held his breath and reached toward the briefcase. The man with the patty gave a cough, cleared his throat petulantly, then coughed a second time. Down the wrong pipe, Lowboy decided. That's all it is. He closed his hand around the mottled snakeskin grip. It came to eager life under his touch.

"How was your weekend with Shakila, by the way?"

A second man had appeared beside the first. He was fine-boned and yellowish and he stared sleepily out at the tracks. The man with the patty had his mouth full. He held up a finger and nodded.

"Noisy," he said at last.

The second man laughed. "You should spend your time more constructively, my brother. Chess or model airplanes. Pay-per-view."

"It was all right, actually. Pretty nice."

"Shakila," the second man singsonged. "Shakila. Shakila. Shakila."

The first man took a slow, thoughtful bite of his patty. Two or three more and it would be gone forever. Lowboy bit his lip and pulled the briefcase closer. No one on the platform seemed to notice.

"I'll tell you something about that girl," the second man said. "Shakila isn't even her real name."

Lowboy craned his neck to get a better look. The conversation seemed to harbor another message inside it, a confidential message addressed to him and him alone. A great show was being made of not seeing him crouched there against the column with his right hand on the briefcase. The not-seeing had been worked out masterfully. The man with the patty had finally finished and was wiping his fingertips one at a time on a dirty bandanna. Lowboy could easily have bitten the man on the calf. A mechanism inside the briefcase was keeping him from picking it up and running: a gyroscope or an electromagnet. A magnet, he decided. He felt the same charge pass through him that he'd felt at MUSEUM OF NATURAL HISTORY when he'd let his fingers rest on Andrew Jackson. This is what power feels like, he thought, clenching his jaw to keep his teeth from rattling. Rich people feel this way every day. They plug themselves into it like toasters.

"Want me to tell you her real name?" the second man said, looking every possible place but down at Lowboy.

"You'd tell me either way," the first man answered, bringing the bandanna up to wipe his nose.

The second man smacked his lips. "It's Emily."

At the sound of that name Lowboy fell over backward and staggered to his feet and started running. The briefcase was rattling and throwing off sparks but its current was propelling him forward now, feeding into his legs and stomach, working his body by remote control. Emily, the man had said. The word seemed senseless to him, a random assortment of everyday noises, but he knew that it was connected to the briefcase and to the feeling of power that was carrying him up the escalator and out through the turnstiles and into the late morning light. Emily. From the platform to the sidewalk he had no other idea. By the time he reached the curb it had come quietly to rest, taking root against his memory like a virus, flooding his consciousness with copies of itself.

"Emily," he said in a reasonable voice, staring out into the traffic. Already it was the only name he knew.

Clouds hung low over midtown, pressing against the roofs and water towers and LED displays, but the sky above his head was high and blue. He looked up and saw that the cold couldn't last. That summer had been the hottest ever, the hottest in the last one hundred years, and the summer before had been the second hottest. Nobody denied that. Nobody could. He looked over his shoulder at the stainless steel globe that divided Broadway from Central Park West, glowing so brightly in the sun that he could see it even when he closed his eyes. The globe was less than thirty years old, younger even than Violet, but already it was almost obsolete. Antarctica doesn't look like that, he thought. Not anymore. Greenland doesn't either. The knowledge made him feel melancholy and privileged at once, predestined for glory, a noble and underestimated prophet. He could make the clocks run backward, after all. He could keep the world from ending with the help of just one person. Such a small and ordinary thing. But that person was nowhere to be found.

His head was clear again, obedient and still, and the machinery had quieted to a purr. He remembered where he was and turned and walked into the park. The briefcase was almost weightless now. Trying to cooperate, he decided. It wants me to get it open. But even as he had that thought his face flushed with embarrassment. It's a *briefcase*, he reminded himself. An item of luggage. It doesn't give a shit whose hand it's cuffed to.

A dozen steps into the park he came across a sheltered patch of lawn. He waited for a dogwalker to pass, keeping his face averted, then laid the briefcase flat against the ground. It gave the faintest shiver. He hesitated a moment longer, listening closely, but he heard nothing but the ambient panic of the city and his own hurried breathing. The briefcase was completely silent now. A screwdriver ought to do it, he thought, fingering the catches of the lock. But there was no need for a screwdriver. He pulled the briefcase toward him and the lock popped meekly open.

"What the hell," said Lowboy, making his Philip Marlowe face. "What the hell."

The briefcase was practically empty. It held one roll of duct tape, one small manila envelope, a stack of Xeroxed pages, and a fitness magazine. No machinery or ductwork to be seen. The hum must have been coming from some part of me, he thought. My right arm possibly. He'd just begun to consider this, opening and closing his right hand, when something about the magazine caught his eye. A talkshow host was taking his pants off on its cover and a caption next to his righthand nostril read

AB CUBING BLITZKRIEG . . . WHO STARTED THE FIRE???

The shape of the magazine looked wrong somehow. Lowboy picked it up with two fingers, listening closely, then held it cautiously up to the light. A second magazine slid out of the first and fell onto the grass. On its cover a middle-aged woman in a white paper smock was lying on an operating table.

Everything had seemed strange to him since leaving the school but the magazine was the strangest thing by far. On each page a woman was visiting the doctor. The skin of their faces was pulled back too tightly, like astronauts' faces at takeoff, and the rest of their bodies looked sunburned. They were sitting on upholstered vinyl tables or lying across them with their ankles in stirrups. They seemed to be upset. The hands of the doctor were just visible, too close to be in focus, holding a variety of expensive-looking instruments. The women's eyes were fixed on the instrument in the doctor's hands, or on the stirrups, or on some other object in the room. The text under the photographs was a jumble of medical terminology and profanity that made no sense to him at all. In the middle of the magazine, where the centerfold should have been, jars of honeycolored fluid were arranged in a tight black grid like pictures in a yearbook. At the lower left corner of the page, cut off along the bottom, the words ACTUAL SIZE were printed in fluorescent orange letters. Each jar contained a crumpled human figure.

Flipping slowly through the magazine, taking in each relevant detail, Lowboy wondered if the world deserved to end. When he reached the last page he took a deep breath and started over at the beginning. This can't be about sex, he thought. But the captions underneath the pictures told him that it was. Finally he laid the magazine facedown on the ground and wiped his hands back and forth in the grass. I'll save half the world, he decided. The other half can burn away to nothing.

The Xeroxes were even more confusing. Columns of tiny decimals, twelve or thirteen to a page, with minuses or pluses in between. The last number on the last page was 640.–, which seemed meaningless at first, but when he opened the manila envelope he found $640 in twenty-dollar bills. That changed everything. He felt like jumping up and down or letting out a Cherokee war whoop or kissing the next person he saw on the lips. But he contented himself with making his bankrobber's face.

"Got you now, Indian Killer," he said, grinning down at Andrew Jackson. The stack was almost thicker than his hand. Jackson said nothing but that was only to be expected.

Money has to do what you want, Lowboy said to himself. No matter how awful. And so do the people you pay.

. . . .

Ten minutes later he was back on the A. Crowley Academy was between two stops—Christopher Street on the 1/9 and West Fourth on the A, C, E—but he'd always liked West Fourth the best. West Fourth was where the college kids got out. He never grew tired of watching them, so grown up and self-sufficient in their expensive dirty clothes. There'll be more girls with that new haircut there, he thought. The one with the bangs. Emily might have it herself. But he knew even then that she'd look just the same, only taller and more serious, and that she'd be as patient with him as ever. That helped almost as much as finding the $640.

"Emily," he said under his breath. He'd been afraid of her until that moment, afraid of what she might do, but now he was the opposite of afraid. She'll be happy to see me, he thought. Happily surprised. He drummed with his fingers against his seat's hollow back and hummed a tune to keep from getting restless. "You Don't Learn That in School" by Nat King Cole. When he got out at West Fourth he walked past the college kids without looking at them once. He kept his eyes on the posters and the square-cut white tiles and the glossy gumspots on the cement floor. No time for sightseeing, William, he said to himself. It's already 11:45.

What happened when he got to Crowley was like a beautiful ballet. At 11:55 he sat down on a stoop across the street from the entrance and looked into the classrooms and waited. There were three of them all told, one to the left of the entrance and two to the right, each filled with identically inclined heads. Writing in their notebooks, Lowboy thought, and the idea relaxed him. All was well at Crowley. He sat and thought about Emily and watched the girls writing. After exactly three minutes an electric bell sounded and they got to their feet like ballerinas, revolving toward the hallway door in unison, falling willingly and easily into graceful double file.

At 11:58 the doors of the building swung open and the upperclass girls came outside: juniors first, still giddy at their lunchtime independence, seniors a world-weary minute later. He kept himself quiet and waited. At 12:03 she shouldered the lefthand door open, blinking skeptically in the midday light, swinging a black bookbag against her leg. The last of them all. Two redfaced blond sidekicks came out alongside her, talking in low courtly whispers, their awkwardness a tribute to her own. If she'd had on a dress they'd have been holding it up by the corners.

Halfway down the steps she stopped and dug out a pack of Salem Lights 100's without bothering to look behind her. The sidekicks formed a human screen to shelter her from Crowley's allseeing eye. She used to smoke Kools, Lowboy reminded himself. So did I. She was about to take another step when she stopped again, as though someone had called out her name or touched her, and brought her right hand up to shade her face. He himself had made no movement. The sidekicks were disoriented, unsure whether to break rank, but she said something under her breath and they laughed and went on down the steps without her. Neither of them looked across the street. Lowboy wondered what she could have told them.

She was studying him now, squinting slightly as she looked, as though a sunlit valley lay between them. He said nothing, did nothing, only waited for her to come across the street. He couldn't have gotten up to save his life. If he could have run away he would have done it. His calling and his belief in his calling had suddenly abandoned him completely.

He'd have run away if he could have because seeing Emily was more than he could stand. Violet had said that Emily would confuse him, that she would keep him from improving, but he'd never felt less confused in all his life. A memory came to him of their last day together, the day of the accident, when they'd met on the corner of Ninth Street and Broadway and she'd decided not to go to school. Let's run away, Heller, she'd said. Nobody will run away with me but you. Where should we go? he'd said, and she'd looked at him and said, You tell me where. Her hair had hung down into her eyes and she'd been crying. You're my best friend, Heller, she'd whispered. He'd laughed and said, Well, you're my only friend. I like that, she'd told him. That means you're all mine. She'd taken his hand and put it in her back pocket. He hadn't felt confused then either. It's all right, Emily, he'd said. I'll take you somewhere. I'm going to take you with me underground.

Slowly and cautiously he held up a hand. She shook her head and stubbed her cigarette out against the railing and coughed into her palm. The look on her face wasn't serious after all: it was wiped clean, opaque and transparent at once, like the windows of a midtown office building. The doors swung open behind her and two teachers skipped girlishly down the Crowley steps, passing her without a glance, laughing and chattering and fixing their hair. They seemed younger than her by a hundred years.

Suddenly she was in motion again, perfect in her deliberateness, crossing the wide spotless sidewalk in front of the school. It took her a long time to reach him. She stopped at the bottom of his stoop, whispered something to herself, then came up in a rush and sat above him. He looked sideways at the streetblackened cuffs of her jeans and saw that her feet were bare inside her sneakers. She never did like socks, he reminded himself. Not even in winter. He tried to catch her eye but she was staring back across the street at Crowley. I'm invisible, he said to himself, making his illusionist's face. I'm invisible until she looks at me. He brought a hand up in slow motion and let his fingers close around her ankle.

"I caught you smoking, Emily," he said.

Now she looked down at him. "Don't talk to me," she said. "Don't talk to me for a second." She slid her shoulder out from under the strap and pressed two of her knuckles to her lips. Her voice was uneven. That little lisp of hers, he thought. I'd forgotten that too. He let go of her ankle and waited for her to go on.

"Jesus Christ, Heller," she said finally. "Holy shit."

"I've thought about what you said to me," he said, smiling up at her. "At Union Square that last day. Remember? Right before we went into the station."

She didn't answer.

"I know you remember, Emily." He cleared his throat. "I want to do it now."

She blinked at him. "You came to my school, on my lunch break, to tell me that?"

"That's right." He was quiet a moment. "Also I wanted to say that I was sorry."

"Sorry for what?"

The answer was so obvious that he hesitated. She looked as though she wanted to say something else but she said nothing. She pressed her knuckles against her mouth and rocked backward and forward like someone on a swing. She turned away and he disappeared again.

"For pushing you onto the tracks," he said.

She laughed at that and sat up very straight. Did I say something funny? he wondered. He tried to remember. He tried to catch her eye but she ignored him. She was looking up again, directly ahead of her, possibly at her own desk. Something that she saw there seemed to bother her.

"You should be dead," she said.

He didn't know what that meant so he kept quiet. She said it a second time.

"I'm not dead, Emily." He shook his head. "I never died. I just came here to ask—"

"Shut the fuck up, Heller. I told you to shut up. Can't you do a single thing I tell you?"

He shut up then and let his head hang down.

"My dad told me a hundred times that this would happen. He said if it did I should speed-dial this number." She set a cellphone on the step beside him. "It's the police, Heller. Don't you care about that? Are you trying to get locked away again?"

He touched his forehead to his knees and considered her question and did what he could to keep calm. "I'm not trying to get locked away," he said.

"You're supposed to leave me alone. You're supposed to not *see* me."

"I know."

"There's a court order, Heller. Fifty feet at all times. There's no way you could have forgotten that." She picked the cell phone up. "Did you forget?"

"You're the one who crossed the street, Emily."

"Go fuck yourself."

He nodded at her and shrugged his shoulders and began to cry. His eyes were wide open but he couldn't see much. Two black sedans parked back-to-back across the street. An old man teetering in place at the edge of the curb, waiting for the next thing to happen. Crowley bright and bloodcolored behind him.

"What did they do to you?" Emily said.

"Where?"

"You know where. In that place you got sent."

A schoolbus went by.

"They put me in a bed."

"And then what?"

A second schoolbus passed. "Nothing. I just stayed there."

"For a year and a half?"

He didn't say anything.

"I thought they did things to you." She looked down at him sternly. "But I guess that's worse."

"They did things," he heard himself saying. "They did things." He said it three more times before she stopped him.

"Why did you come back, Heller? Don't you know how retarded that was? What makes you think that I won't call this number?"

She was staring at him now the way a nurse would stare at a sick baby and he knew that it was going to be all right. She might kick him or laugh at him or push him down the steps but she wasn't going to use her cellphone yet. She wasn't as angry as she was excited. He pressed his back against the sandstone steps and counted down from twenty. She wasn't going to send him back to school.

She asked him again what he wanted and he told her.

"Don't act like nothing's different, Heller. Everything's different. The whole world turned to shit while you were gone."

"I know that," Lowboy said. He smiled at her. "That's why I'm here."

She twisted away from him then and kept her mouth shut for what seemed like a week. With anyone else he'd have started to have his doubts. Some girls leaning against the Crowley fence waved at her and giggled and one of them blew her a kiss. An Utz Potato Chips truck rolled toward them at the slowest possible crawl. He started to tell her more but stopped himself. There was nothing to do but let her think it over. The Crowley girls waved again but she ignored them. Finally she coughed three times into her sleeve, a put-on smoker's cough, and waited until he was looking at her. Her face was as serious as he'd ever seen it.

"Apology accepted," she said, pursing her lips. "What do you want to do now?"

Ulysses S. Kopeck's practice was tucked discreetly away in a courtyard of The Phaeton, a West Seventy-second Street monstrosity that cut across its block like an Italianate aircraft carrier. "The largest residential building on the island, actually," the doctor had said after Will's first appointment. He'd said it modestly, in his trademark half-apologetic way, and Violet had nodded and smiled and said, "How interesting." Like all desperate mothers the desire to defer to some expert, to anyone at all, had become her greatest passion by that time: he could have fed her any variety of horseshit and she'd have taken it as gospel. And in fact that was exactly what he'd done.

Returning to The Phaeton now was like waiting for the show to start in an abandoned theater. It seemed unnatural to her, even obscene, but there was no denying that it also thrilled her. For two years the building had been no more than a stageset, a backdrop to her greatest disappointment: occasionally it had menaced her in dreams. But now she was following a man, a virtual stranger, demurely through its burnished Roman doors. She walked into the lobby as though she was expected, as though The Phaeton had been built just to receive her.

She noted her reflection in the antediluvian lobby mirrors, cow-eyed and compliant, no different than any other prospective patient. Her footsteps seemed to make no sound at all. Lateef kept half a step in front of her, the stiff-lipped official on confidential business, ignoring the doorman's dull suspicious greeting. He was less sure of himself than he'd been in his office, conflicted in some way she couldn't name, but his professional manner still came effortlessly. He was the parent on this visit, she the child. She found herself remembering Will's stricken face during his first appointment, his mounting confusion, his anxiety when they reached the doorman's desk. She'd gotten him past by putting her hands over his eyes and guiding him gently forward with her hips.

There were four identical lobbies in The Phaeton, each graced by an abstract expressionist poster from the permanent collection of the Met. The Rothko in Kopeck's lobby suited him perfectly: he was as warm and indistinct as a color field, a mildmannered and uninsistent spirit. His bell had been broken three years before and it was broken now. Lateef pressed it, waited, shifted from foot to foot for a moment, then pressed it again. A minute went by. God knows why I'm not telling him, she thought. She was already eager for things to speed up, for the meeting with Kopeck to be done with. But it was beyond her power to do anything but wait.

Lateef glanced at her a second time, pursing his lips, then knocked on the door with military correctness. When Kopeck's door swung open she found herself standing neatly at attention.

"Dr. Kopeck?" said Lateef.

"That's me, Detective." The same voice exactly. The same bookish awkwardness, the same studied calm. "Lateef, was it? Yes." He tilted his bald childish head to take her measure. "Hello, Yda."

"Hello, Doctor." She glanced involuntarily down the hall, measuring the distance to the lobby doors, picturing her escape just as Will had done three years before. Kopeck smiled at her as though there was some joke between them.

"I have to apologize about that bell of mine: it works about one time in sixty. Come in, both of you."

Lateef nodded and stepped aside for Violet. He doesn't want to go in either, she thought. Kopeck had already turned his back on them, shuffling past the threadworn sofas and stacks of *In Style* magazine to his antiquated, guidance-counselorish office. She knew from experience that he was muttering to himself, the potty old bachelor uncle. Not a thing had changed about him. There was no cause whatsoever for alarm.

Lateef cleared his throat behind her. "Thanks for making time for us on such short notice, Dr. Kopeck. We'll try to keep this brief."

"Not a problem, Detective. Though I must say I'm surprised to see you in the flesh."

"We're waiting on a call, Doctor—trying to make use of the time. There's really not much else that we can do."

"Of course. Sit down here, please." Kopeck perched on his desktop. "May I ask your first name?"

Lateef's discomfort was plain. "Ali," he said quietly.

"Good to meet you, Ali. I'd appreciate it if you'd call me Ulysses."

Lateef took the seat indicated, a hardbacked vinyl armchair that looked borrowed from some dated airport lounge. He glanced cautiously around him, then at Violet, as though unsure who was meant to do the talking. He's at a disadvantage in other people's offices, she decided. She resisted the urge to pat him on the shoulder.

"As I explained over the phone, Doctor, Miss Heller's son is currently in some part of the MTA network—"

"You gave me the details, Ali, and I remember them. Please call me Ulysses."

"Of course," Lateef muttered, more ill at ease than ever. "As I mentioned to you, Ulysses, the boy was last seen in the company of a forty-year-old homeless woman named Rafa Ramirez. Mrs. Ramirez has since been questioned, but she didn't give us much; one thing we've managed to establish is that the boy is not, at least at present, in a violent frame of mind." He coughed into his palm. "Just the opposite, apparently."

"You've managed to establish that, have you?" said Kopeck. He was no longer smiling. "You're certain that he won't act violently?"

"I didn't say that," Lateef said quickly. "I, for one, wouldn't be surprised—"

"What is it that I can help you with, Ali?"

"Anything." Lateef shrugged his shoulders. "Anything you could give us would be helpful."

"Can you explain the note?" Violet blurted out, regretting it at once. "We've got a copy of it with us. I can follow it fairly well until—"

Kopeck shook his head. "I haven't seen or treated Will in almost two years, Yda." He let his mournful pink eyes rest on her until she gave him the nod he required. "What I knew once—what I *believed* I knew—may no longer apply." He paused again. "I also feel the need to point out, for Detective Lateef's benefit, that you had little confidence in my relationship with Will. In point of fact, Yda, you had him removed from my care." He turned to Lateef. "This happened shortly before the boy's arrest."

She watched him breathlessly, still standing within easy reach of the door, waiting for him to go on. She had no doubt that more was coming, benign though he might look. He hadn't met her eyes once, hadn't asked her to call him Ulysses, and she was grateful for that, if for nothing else. But at the same time she was desperate for his answer.

"All right, Ali." A sigh. "You want to know whether the boy is likely to act aggressively. Is that it?"

Violet felt the floor pitch underneath her. "That's not it at all! We know he won't. We just thought you might—"

Kopeck's eyes remained fixed on Lateef. "Let Ali answer, Yda."

"Please, Dr. Kopeck—*Ulysses.*" She paused to catch her breath. "If you'd take a quick look at this note—"

"Miss Heller," Lateef said softly. He waited for her to sit down before continuing. "What I'd like to know first of all, Ulysses, is whether or not Mrs. Ramirez's version of events strikes you as plausible. Is she telling the truth?"

"That's impossible for me to determine, Detective. Mrs. Ramirez is not one of my patients."

"You won't be asked to sign any affidavits, Doctor. I'd simply like to hear your opinion."

Kopeck glanced at Violet and shrugged his shoulders. "Schizophrenics rarely tell lies, especially when in psychosis—which doesn't mean, of course, that one should take their statements at face value. In this case, however—assuming that Mrs. Ramirez has been correctly diagnosed—I see no particular reason to disbelieve her." He turned back to Lateef. "I'm saying this informally, you understand. Based on nothing but the small amount you've told me."

"You mean he actually tried to have sex with that woman?"

"For better or worse, Ali, Will's schizophrenia doesn't excuse him from being a sixteen-year-old boy."

"But what could possibly have been the reason—"

"To lose his virginity, of course. Isn't that what all teenagers want?"

Lateef looked hard at Kopeck. "Could it have been a straightforward assault that Mrs. Ramirez—" He stopped again. "Could she have misinterpreted it as sexual?"

"Some things are hard to misinterpret, Ali, even for the mentally ill." His face went grave. "Which brings me back to my original assumption."

"What would that be?"

"That you came here to find out whether Will may become violent."

No one spoke for a moment. Lateef inclined his head toward Violet but did not look at her. When he answered he spoke very mildly. "It's my responsibility, Doctor, to act under the assumption that he will."

"A sound assumption," Kopeck said, bringing his palms together.

Even Lateef seemed startled. "What are you saying, exactly, Doctor? Are you telling me the boy—"

"I'm telling you that Will has never responded well to stress, and that he's under enormous stress now. What's more, his current environment has acted as a trigger for him in the past. If it's true, as you tell me, that he's gone off his meds completely, then I'd advise you to alert the MTA at once—every transit post along the line—and instruct them to use extreme caution. Every train that goes by is a temptation to Will."

That was too much for Violet at last. "What the hell are you saying?" she murmured, feeling herself lurching to her feet. "A temptation to what? Don't you understand that this man is a—"

"This man is a policeman, Yda. His duty is to the public safety. The safety of everyone, not just your son. Kindly sit down."

"Sit down, Miss Heller," Lateef said absently.

She stared at them both without speaking. The confirmation of the thing that she'd most feared made her feel almost clairvoyant. Will was a public danger now and would be dealt with as such, just as she had foreseen. Hunted with the blessing of his doctor. She sat down tremblingly beside Lateef.

"The common perception of schizophrenics as violent is inaccurate, of course," Kopeck went on. "They're no more violent, as a group, than the rest of us are." He smiled at Lateef. "But most likely you knew that already."

"I didn't, actually," said Lateef. "In my job, I tend to get the raving—"

"That said, however, Will has always been exceptional." Kopeck nodded toward Violet. "Let's reason with the worst that may befall."

"Will put his trust in you," Violet said through her teeth. "Will thought of you as a friend." It made her stomach cramp to speak the words.

Kopeck leaned forward on his elbows, reasonable, regretful. "I don't doubt that Will thought of me as a friend, Yda. I was trying to help him, after all. But you certainly never thought of me that way."

Lateef coughed into his fist. "With all respect, Doctor, this hardly strikes me as the moment—"

"Permit me to finish. You never thought of me as Will's friend,

Yda, and you were perfectly right. I *wasn't* Will's friend, which is precisely the reason I could help him: I was able to talk to him plainly and unsentimentally about his life. And Will, in turn, was able to answer me plainly. Which is presumably the reason that you're here." Kopeck studied his hands, rubbing the fingertips together, as though he'd picked up something faintly greasy. "You're here because Will told me things he wouldn't have said to a friend, and most definitely wouldn't have told you. You're here to find out what Will said to me in confidence."

Lateef made as if to speak, then coughed once more and sat back in his chair. Violet couldn't have said whether he looked exasperated or content. She herself felt nothing whatsoever.

Finally Lateef took a breath. "I couldn't care less what the boy said to you in your sessions, Doctor. Nobody's trying to make you break your pledge." He passed a hand over his face. "But we need to find him quickly—you said as much yourself. You might not care for Miss Heller, but I hope that you can appreciate my problem, and the boy's. I'd like to know where you think he might go."

"Have you ever been in therapy, Detective?" Kopeck said amiably. "Something tells me that you have."

"Where do you think the boy might go, Doctor?" Lateef repeated. But Kopeck seemed not to be listening.

Violet brought a finger to her mouth and bit it. She was shaking severely now, shivering with fear and foresight, but she managed to keep her voice intelligible. "Answer the question, hypocrite," she stammered. As always when she was enraged or terrified she found herself having to translate her thoughts from the language she'd spoken as a girl, to struggle to keep her accent within bounds, but today it was almost more than she could do. The last of her composure fell away as she stared into Kopeck's damp, insipid face. She hated him more desperately now than when she'd first discovered his fraud, first realized that he'd been setting Will against her. She hated him with unabashed devotion. "Answer the question," she heard herself hissing. "Answer the question, cocksucker."

Lateef was on his feet before Kopeck could say a word. "I'm going to have to ask you to wait outside, Miss Heller," he said hoarsely. Whether he'd gone hoarse out of anger or amusement made no difference to her, although she would wonder about it later. Later she'd ask herself which side he'd been on, but not then. She got up obligingly and followed him out without a word of protest. Kopeck clucked but said nothing. She had no doubt that he'd gotten what he wanted.

For the briefest of instants, looking back from the door, the hope she'd felt three years before revisited her. The heavy armchairs and curtains hummed invitingly, like a bed at the close of a long day, and the diplomas and framed certificates on the walls glimmered like proof of promises upheld. I expected so much from this room, she thought.

"Move," said Lateef. His hand on her forearm was a creature of pure authority. A practiced grip, she thought, stumbling ahead of him like a hostage. He held her just tightly enough to call attention to the strength held in reserve. She'd been the child when they'd come into The Phaeton; now she was the difficult child. Before the door had shut behind them she was twisting and kicking and cursing at the top of her lungs, but even now he acted with economy and restraint. The doorman leaned out from his terracotta grotto, vanished for an instant, then rose up imposingly before them. To her astonishment he called her by name.

"You okay, Mrs. Heller?"

For some reason his civility shocked her. She remembered him now: he'd once given Will a toffee that he'd spit onto the floor.

"Yes, Stavros," she said. "Thank you. I'm all right."

"Who is this gentleman?"

"Police," said Lateef. She waited for him to flash his badge but he did nothing. He knows what I'll do if he lets go of me, she thought.

"It's fine, Stavros," she said finally. "I promise." But the doorman had already disappeared.

"There's a man who still has respect for the law," said Lateef. He grinned at her and let go of her arm.

For some reason she decided to behave. "You see what Kopeck's like," she whispered. "You saw for yourself what a son of a—"

"I don't see that at all, Miss Heller. I see a doctor who treated your son for more than a year, apparently with some success, and who's taken time out of his busy day to help us." He shook his head tiredly. "I don't know what happened between the two of you—"

"Nothing happened," she said. "That's what I'm trying to tell you. He promised to cure my son and nothing happened."

"I doubt he said any such thing." Lateef was standing between her and Kopeck's door, both his hands slightly raised, as if to keep her from storming back in. "Therapists don't make those kinds of promises."

"That's all they *ever* do," she said, bracing herself against the wall. Her anger had made her lightheaded. "That's all they ever do. Then nothing happens."

"What I can't figure out is why he's so angry at you," Lateef said thoughtfully. "What did you do to him, Miss Heller?"

"He was in love with Will," she heard herself answer. Her head was still spinning. "Everyone was. But I broke up their little love affair."

"You sound like a jealous husband."

"Fuck you, Detective."

He shook his head at her in plainfaced incredulity. "Miss Heller, you might just be the most foulmouthed complainant I've ever let into my Nissan. Does everybody talk like you in Denmark?"

She blinked at him. "In Austria, you mean."

"Get your story straight, Miss Heller."

By the time she could think of an appropriate reply he'd darted back into the office like a spider, pulling the door shut behind him with a wink. Make a note of that, Yda, she said to herself. One of his better tricks. She took a small step forward and rested her head against Kopeck's door, not at all embarrassed by what she'd done. At the moment she felt nothing but relief. She tested the doorhandle with her left hand, turning it to see if it was locked, but she made no attempt to open it. "I'm fine out here," she murmured, nodding to herself the way certain people do in public: the lonely and the aged and the mentally ill. The doorman was back in his prescribed position, running a comb carefully through his immaculate hair, looking everywhere in the lobby but at her. The Rothko glimmered sorrowfully in its warped Plexiglas frame. Kopeck will talk, she thought, bobbing her head. He'll have to. He'll talk just to prove me wrong.

The stillness of the lobby made her thoughts incline toward Will. Nothing about the place had changed: everything was rapt, expectant, suspended in the sepiacolored air. It seemed preposterous without Will's presence, stripped of its only context, an empty filmset with the cameras running. The relief she'd felt was already subsiding. She tried to steer her mind clear of Will but it refused. For a moment she stood at a remove from herself, saw the barrenness of a life lived to one end alone, the bitterness and futility of such a life; but the feeling soon passed. You don't live only for him, she thought. Not anymore. And he doesn't live for you at all.

A sentence from Will's letter came to her unbidden, in Will's dull deliberate voice: *Anything else you could help me with, Violet, but not with this.*

Then all at once she knew where he was going.

Kopeck's door opened in that same instant, while she was still in the first flush of her discovery, as though the force of her idea had thrown it open. Lateef stepped out and shut the door behind him. Apparently the conference was at an end.

"He'll go to her," she said. "He'll go to Emily."

Lateef walked right past her. "To be honest with you, Miss Heller, I'd been hoping not to get the girl involved."

"Why the hell not? If he's going—"

"It's policy." He said the word with a complacency that chilled her. "We try not to cause alarm if we don't have to."

She put out a hand and caught him by the sleeve. "Please listen to me, Detective. I'm trying to tell you that I'm absolutely sure—"

"We'll find the girl, Miss Heller," he said evenly. He was making a great show of patience. "You and our friend Ulysses happen to agree."

When they reached the lobby doors he held them open for her. "What else did Kopeck tell you?" she said as offhandedly as she could. "Plenty about me, I bet."

"I didn't ask him about you, Miss Heller. Should I have?"

"He thinks I'm bad for my son. That I should keep away from him."

Lateef shrugged his shoulders as if that were a given. He offered no more than that, and she lacked the courage or the recklessness to press him. "What happens next?" she said, if only to say something.

"What school does Emily go to?"

"Crowley Academy." She thought for a moment. "But she's a senior now."

"Junior, senior, what difference does it make? If he shows up there—"

"It makes a difference, Detective. The seniors get to leave the school for lunch."

They were outside The Phaeton now, back in the breathable air, strolling almost blithely to the curb. Lateef kept half a step ahead of her.

"You agree with me, don't you?" she said, drawing even with him. "You see why he'll go to Crowley?"

"I don't see anything, Miss Heller." He was patting down his pockets for the keys. "But since Kopeck seems to think—"

"Good old Kopeck." She could afford to be magnanimous again, knowing what she knew. "I figured you'd get him to spill."

Lateef raised his eyebrows at her. "Spill?" he said vaguely.

"I've got cable, Detective. I know how you people talk."

"Get in the car, Miss Heller."

Neither of them spoke until they'd crossed Fourteenth Street and were coming up on Crowley. Things were happening so quickly. She sat slumped in her seat with her eyes not quite closed, counting the streets as they passed, trying to brace herself for seeing Will. It was impossible to imagine him on some arbitrary corner: she couldn't conceive of what he might be doing. Emily might be with him, she reminded herself, and that somehow made it easier to picture. To her surprise it even reassured her. Emily was a clearheaded girl, able to look after herself, and she'd always had the upper hand with Will. She'd underestimated his illness, of course, but the accident and the trial had ended that. No more romanticizing. If Will did find her she'd most likely call the police, or at the very least report him to Crowley. She would handle it quite well unless she panicked. Will was off his meds now, which couldn't help but give her the advantage, knowing everything she knew. Why hadn't they gone to her at once?

Emily will mind him, Violet said to herself. She'll take his hand and talk to him and keep him calm.

Lateef glanced at her from time to time in that odd way he had, studying her as if to confirm some theory, but she had too much on her mind to pay attention. Part of her was still in The Phaeton's dark expectant lobby and the rest of her was on the street with Will. It was a good thing to know what was going to happen next. It made you feel that randomness was not the universal law: as if a thing you'd been taught to think of as hollow were suddenly shown to have substance. There was comfort in that belief, if you were willing to put reasonable doubt aside. She wondered whether Will took comfort there.

"Kopeck did tell me some things about you," Lateef said after a while.

The mention of Kopeck annoyed her, coming when it did, but she gave him a cordial smile. "What sort of things did the good doctor say? Am I needy, yet distant? Is my affect inconsistent? Did I keep my son from masturbating freely?"

"Nothing like that."

He was keeping his eyes on the road in a way that immediately made her think the worst. "It's true, Detective," she said brightly, keeping her expression fixed. "A joint now and then. But never when I was pregnant with him, I swear."

His awkward laugh put her further on her guard. When he spoke again his voice was oddly smooth. "Why did you take your son out of Kopeck's care?"

"I told you why. He's a fat, self-satisfied, condescending—"

"Violet."

The sound of that name from his mouth brought her up short, but it was the look on his face that disconcerted her: an expression of almost fatherly concern. It was not a look she'd have imagined him capable of.

"I took Will away from Kopeck because he wasn't getting better. Kopeck admitted that much himself." She stared down at her loose mannish jeans, running her eyes along the wrinkles and the seams. "What I hadn't considered, of course, was that he might get worse."

"Worse in what way?"

"Violent," she said. A motorcycle roared past as she said it.

"What's that?"

"That he'd become violent."

"I see."

"He'd never attacked anyone before Emily. Not once. It's true that he was scared by things, more frightened every day, and I don't need a psychiatrist to know what that can lead to. But Will hadn't been in a single fight in fourteen years. He'd never lost his temper, never raised his voice, never kicked or cursed or threw a punch. Not even—" A second motorcycle passed, closer and louder than the first, and she was glad of the reprieve.

"I'm sorry, Miss Heller. Could you say that again?"

"Not even when he had a reason to."

The motorcycles came together in front of the car and the riders leaned casually toward each other. Both of them were women but it took her a moment to see it. They had the bodies of middle-aged men, slump-shouldered and sagging at the middle, the shape all bikers' bodies tended toward. Like old avocados, she thought. By the time Lateef asked his next question she felt better.

"What kind of reason could your son have had?"

The same one that I had, she thought.

"Miss Heller?"

She shrugged her shoulders.

"Look at me for a second, Miss Heller."

She turned and met his look. That was easy enough.

"I asked you what reasons your son might have had—"

"Will was making no progress in Kopeck's care, so I stopped taking him. There's no mystery there. But it wasn't Kopeck's fault. Not really."

"Why not?"

"Because Kopeck was only with him for an hour a day."

Lateef hesitated. "And the rest of the day he was—"

"Most of the time he was with me. Some of the time he was with Emily." She brought her hands together in her lap. "Some of the time he was down in Richard's basement."

They were rolling slowly now, advancing at a creep along a line of cars whose bumpers weren't quite touching. On the far side of the cars laughing girls promenaded. Some dragged their bookbags on the ground behind them, some balanced them on their heads, some held them to their chests like nursing infants. Half a block west stood the blunt sandstone ramparts of Crowley.

"I'm going to pull over here—are you listening to me, Miss Heller?—and I want you to stop watching the goddamned street and pay attention. If there's anything significant about your son's personal history that you haven't told me, any detail at all, it is absolutely mandatory that you tell me now. You have no choice in this. Do you understand?"

"There he is," she said calmly, looking past Lateef's shoulder.

Even as Lateef spun in his seat Will was disappearing around the corner, moving in a way she didn't recognize, his pale hair sticking out behind his ears. She hadn't seen his face yet, but that didn't matter: she'd have known him by the back of his neck alone. He was wearing the navy blue corduroys she'd sent him at Christmas and a shirt that looked meant for a boy of ten. Where the hell did he get that thing? she thought. She felt pity for him then, as if he were a stranger, and at the same time a sharp spasm of jealousy at the idea of anyone else picking out his clothes. He's not dressed for this weather, she thought helplessly. He's dressed for July. She glanced toward Lateef, not sure what to do next, and watched him rifling through the glove compartment. He seems confused, she thought. Maybe he didn't hear me. But of course he wasn't confused at all.

"Will doesn't carry a pistol, Detective. I don't see why you need yours."

He looked at her kindly. "I'm getting my badge out, Miss Heller. Just to make this official." Then she saw that the pistol was already in his coat pocket.

By the time he spoke again they were out of the car and running, pushing past the schoolgirls the way police do on television, ignoring their cries with studied equanimity. She'd seen Will exactly the way she'd imagined seeing him: from the window of a moving car, a stone's throw from the Crowley steps, Lateef gruff and oblivious beside her. But the correspondence was somehow too complete. It would have calmed her a great deal, helped her to trust in what was happening, if there'd been no trace of Will around the corner: her faith in the world's indifference would have been reaffirmed. Instead he was less than a block away, holding hands with a girl she didn't recognize, tipping his head back to look at the sky.

"That's him?" Lateef said, reaching a hand out to stop her. "That's your son?"

What's he trying to hold me back from? Violet wondered.

"Of course it's my son. Don't you think that I—"

"Is the girl Emily Wallace?"

"She must be. But she looks different somehow. I'm not completely sure—"

"All right, Miss Heller." His grip on her forearm tightened. "I want you to stay right here and let me do the rest. If he recognizes you he might start running. Do you understand?"

"We're wasting time," she murmured.

"Sit down here on this stoop and wait for me. Can you do that?"

"Just go, Detective," she said, leaning away from him. "Please go now." For some reason his hand was still locked tightly around her wrist. They stood there like lovers for a measureless span of time, posed together absurdly, while the children drifted slowly up the street. It made no sense at all. She'd just asked herself whether Lateef might be punishing her when Will leaned slightly farther back and saw them.

In 1985 Jacques Cousteau, the famous deep-sea explorer, was testing a diving suit off the coast of France. The suit was made out of pressure-treated bauxite and industrial steel and Cousteau believed it would let a man go past sixty meters, the world depth record at the time. A clear day in June had been picked for the test, the time of year when currents are at their weakest. The dive was planned for 3:00 p.m.

Cousteau was an old man by then, but he insisted on wearing the diving suit himself. A doctor and an engineer stood by on the *Calypso* and Cousteau's son Émile manned the oxygen tanks. The only other witnesses were the *Calypso*'s crew, half a dozen merchant seamen from Marseille, and a reporter from the local Sunday paper. The sky was clear and blue. Some yachts were anchored close by, but nobody paid much attention. After the water temperature had been taken and the fittings on his helmet doublechecked, Cousteau had himself lowered into the water.

He was careful not to go too fast at first. Every three meters he'd stop and check each of his gauges, then make a note in chalk on a little slate tablet. But at nine and a half meters—the world record for unassisted diving—he had a huge shock. A man was suddenly next to him, treading water and waving, dressed in nothing but a pair of cotton briefs. Cousteau decided to ignore the man and continue his dive. To his amazement the man followed him, and after five more meters they were side by side again. Cousteau did his best to push on, but when, at thirty meters—sixteen and a half feet past the free-diving record—the man was still with him, he gave in and wrote him a message on his slate, asking how he was able to stay alive at such a depth. The man took the slate from Cousteau, wrote down an answer, and handed it back.

"Well?" said Emily. "What did it say?"

"You asshole! I'm drowning!"

She put a hand over her mouth. "I don't know about that one, Heller. It's not very funny."

"I know that," said Lowboy. "I couldn't even make jokes yesterday."

"Good on the details, though." She stubbed out her cigarette and pushed the hair out of her eyes. "What's bauxite?"

"They make diving suits out of it," said Lowboy. He pinched his nose and buckled at the knees.

"I've got one for you," she said, passing him the lighter and the pack. "Ready?"

"Ready."

They were at the corner of Christopher and Seventh and people and cars flew by like startled birds. She caught hold of his arm and stopped him, as though she could tell it only by standing still. A billboard behind her said METH = DEATH. She took a breath and stared at him until he was paying attention, then let the breath out. A three-wheeled police buggy puttered past.

"A bear and a bunny are taking a shit in the forest. The bear asks the bunny, 'Do you ever have a problem with shit getting stuck to your fur?' The bunny thinks about it for a while, then says, 'Not really, no.' So the bear—" She squinted at him. "Still with me, Heller?"

He nodded. "Not really, no."

"The bear wipes his ass with the bunny."

Lowboy looked up at her. She was still a bit taller. Half an inch, he decided. She was standing flatfooted with Christopher Street behind her and her hair snaking this way and that like the hair of a woman possessed. A woman, not a girl. Smiling as though she'd known him since the day that he was born.

"Funny," he said finally. "Poor rabbit."

"You should laugh, then, Heller. It's polite."

She did his laughing for him and led him west between the parked cars toward the river. Past storefronts selling Greek food and fetishes and videos and haircuts and rubber suits and tarot cards and tapas and tattoos.

"Where are we going?"

She frowned and pursed her lips. He'd forgotten that too. "Nowhere," she told him. "A place that I like."

"A good place?" he said, but only to make some kind of noise. He could just as well have barked. He'd pissed out the last of his meds at the corner of Grove and Bedford but he felt happy and attached to things and not at all confused. If this is sick, then I'll take a dozen, he said to himself. If this is sick, then meds are a sin. An evil worse than The Atomic Bomb.

Fat Man & Little Boy, he said to himself. Another perfect name for Skull & Bones. He thought of them now with a kind of affection. He wondered whether they'd given up yet and gone home. Maybe they're having lunch somewhere, he thought. He pictured them eating pancakes in a diner.

"A good enough place," said Emily. "I thought you said you didn't give a shit."

One second's gone by, he thought. Less than a second. How could I have had all of those thoughts? He held his hands out in front of him, palms upturned like a saint's, admiring their squareness and their weight. He could have run a marathon on those hands. He could have rearranged the cars like three-card monte cups. The city was newlooking, glistening in the daylight, an onion with its outer skin sloughed off. He saw dimes in the pavement and vinecovered housefronts and old useless flagpoles and shopping bags hanging like vampire bats from the trees. He saw awnings and bellpulls and limos and dogs dressed in parkas. There were so many things to see that he got dizzy. Babies see the world this way, he thought. Then they forget.

"People are after me," he said finally. "Two of them."

Emily didn't answer. He took a breath and decided to try again.

"From the school," he said, watching her. She was walking with her hands in her back pockets. "From the place that I got sent to. Skull and Bones."

"They sent you to a place called Skull and Bones?"

"I'm seeing the world the way a baby does," he said, covering his face and looking out between his fingers. "It's interesting."

"I used to think that you looked like a baby." She grinned bashfully down at the pavement. "I don't think so anymore."

He wanted to shut his eyes tight, to have her lead him through the city like a Seeing Eye dog, but he had to look to see where he was going. She was standing a few steps ahead of him, turned halfway around, looking back up the street for enemies. His father had once shown him some Red Chinese money and the way Emily was standing, with her chin held up high and her mouth slightly open, reminded him of the girl on the fifty-yuan note.

"You should have army pants on," he said. "You should have an Uzi."

She heaved a sigh and took his arm again. "I probably should," she said. When she said it herself it stopped being a joke. They were at the corner of Christopher and Hudson and the traffic was sliding by them without any sound at all, as though the city had been tipped and everything with wheels was rolling down to Chinatown. She looked ten years older now than when they'd sat together on the stoop. She looked committed to a great and hallowed cause. Suddenly he was afraid that he might still be too young.

"Emily," he said faintly.

"Don't worry, Heller. You're not a baby."

How did she know what I wanted, he thought. How did she know what I was going to say. "How warm is it right now, Emily, do you think?"

She smiled at him. He hadn't told her yet about his calling. "It's the middle of November, Heller. It isn't warm at all."

"It is," he said. "It's fifty-nine degrees."

"Fifty-nine doesn't count as warm, you retard. And it can't be more than forty-five right now." She shook her head and steered him out into the street without waiting for the light to change. People from the city could do that. When his mother crossed the street she kept her eyes fixed on the cars, looking straight at every driver, so that her face would haunt them if they ran her over. Sometimes she cursed or said a prayer in German. But Emily looked like a freedom fighter, like someone with a bomb hidden under her clothes. She didn't have to look at the cars to stop them. None of them even came close to her.

"They can't touch you," said Lowboy. "If they came close to you they'd melt."

She tugged at his elbow. "Watch out for the curb."

"They're made out of wax," he said, not because he believed they were made out of wax but because it was simpler. "I don't really believe that," he told her. But then he thought: That would explain about the quiet.

Emily looked up the street and shrugged. She seemed unexcited. "How many boys have you done this to before?"

She made a face. "Done it *with*, Heller. Not to. I'm not going to take your tonsils out."

He nodded slowly, touching a finger to his neck. No need for any operation, he thought. This is the opposite of what happens in hospitals. But the question still stuck to his lips like a piece of dead skin. At the corner he stopped short and planted his feet. Behind them the cars were still rolling downtown, veering and guttering like badly cast marbles. It took him a long time to reshape his question, to take it apart and put it back together, but Emily didn't seem to mind. She thinks I'm like everyone else, he thought. Maybe a little slower. Not sick. The idea bothered him somehow. For a moment he found himself missing his doctors.

"What I mean to say is, have you done this before?" He took a deep breath. "Have you done this with anyone else?"

"It's safe to say, dumb-ass, that I've never done this before. Never skipped school with an escaped mental patient. Never hid a fugitive from justice." She smiled at him. "And I've definitely never held *hands* with somebody I was going to put out for."

That satisfied him. He was different from the others, exalted, distinguished, if only because he was sick.

"Emily," he said, and laid his right hand flat against her belly. There was nothing sly about her anymore. He was old enough now and she knew it. Both of them did. It seemed incredible that she'd helped him cross the street.

"What is it," she mumbled. It wasn't a question. Her stomach was shivering under her clothes. She had on a red shirt and a purple thriftstore sweater. His little finger traced her bottom rib.

"I know you didn't mean to push me, Heller." She was leaning into his hand and her hair was in his eyes and he could feel her heavy breath against his face. "I know you didn't mean to. But I want to hear you say it."

"I told you I was sorry."

"I don't care about that. Sorry only matters if you *meant* to."

He forced his eyes shut but her outline persisted, the afterimage bright against his brain. A green girlshaped pillar rose through the veins of his retina like ivy twining through a chainlink fence. As soon as his eyes were closed her beautiful face began to disassemble. He'd suspected it would. Her features came apart like knitting.

"I drew pictures of you, Emily. I drew one every day. In the end there was just a house: a house with a hairy roof. I didn't know that you were still inside it."

"That's not an answer, Heller. Answer me."

Her stomach pulled itself back from his fingers. He was old

enough to know that her question was a sign of love or at least of passing interest and he struggled to find an answer that would please her. What he wanted most was to not answer at all, to bring his second hand against her ribs, to hold her there until the next thing happened. To not have to remember the flat time or anything like it. There was nothing there that he cared to recall.

"I wouldn't have done it if you hadn't touched me," he told her.

She nodded and let her shoulders slump toward his. Her hair hung dark against his face but her eyes shone on him like stagelights through an old motheaten curtain. That was why her stomach had pulled back: she was bending down to meet him, folding over. All at once her face was under his. "You were frightened of me," she whispered. "You thought that I'd become another person. You told me so."

"I didn't know what you wanted to touch me for."

"I was frightened too. That's why. To keep you quiet."

"It was hot in the station. Hot and wet, like in a greenhouse. A policeman was coming up the platform to catch us. A highpressure system. You'd gone flat, playing tricks, not like Emily at all. I wanted to cool down. I wanted to take my clothes off. Then you came and wrapped around me like a blanket."

"I touched you," she said. "You didn't recognize me. You thought I was some other person. Not Emily anymore."

He felt her cautious breath against his neck. Her breath smelled of licorice and cigarettes and fetid greenhouse air. Her ribs were suddenly back against his knuckles. Everything's happening suddenly lately, he thought. Emily bit her lower lip and started walking. Not taller than he was anymore. After three short steps she stopped and waited for him.

"You're Emily now," he said, taking her compliant hand in his.

Some time later they passed the window of a bakery and stopped in front of it and looked inside. She appraised the shelves of bright potbellied jars and he shifted and blinked and sidestepped his reflection. With his head behind hers they looked like a twoheaded baby. He liked the idea of that. "What's in there?" he said to Emily, but he'd already seen for himself. The wall behind the counter was graced by a menagerie of pastel forms. Green and pink clots cupped in pleated waxpaper. Green for her afterimage, pink for his skin. He could tell by her expression that she was inspecting them closely.

"This place only makes cupcakes," she murmured. "Sometimes there's a line around the block."

He leaned back on his heels. "Cupcakes?"

"Not worth waiting in line for," she said. "Too much frosting." But her forehead was pushed flush against the glass.

"You want one," he said.

She stuck out her tongue. "To be honest with you, Heller, I couldn't—"

"Wait here."

Before she could answer the powderblue shopdoor was closing behind him. People were standing alone and in clusters, sighing and whispering, running their fingertips along the glass. Across the top of the case sat the row that he'd seen from the street. That part of it was easy. A girl behind the counter smiled and asked him what he wanted.

The rest of them are thinking, he said to himself. Thinking it over. They're having a hard time making up their minds.

"What can I get you?" the girl said again. She was taller than he was by at least half a foot. There was some kind of construction underneath her: some sort of a platform. To lend stature or the illusion thereof. He decided to keep the conversation brief.

"Cupcakes," he said, pointing at the display.

The girl sighed and propped her elbows on the counter. "What can I get you?" she said a third time, as though he hadn't spoken. He felt like the stranger in the first scene of a Western. The encounter at the saloon. When he repeated his order her head rolled lackadaisically to one side.

"Cupcakes is the only thing we sell."

"Those," said Lowboy. He tapped the case with his knuckles. "The pink ones and the green."

Her head clicked woodenly into place. "Angelfood cake and red velvet."

Lowboy blinked at her and nodded.

"Which do you want?" said the girl. "What kind?" A second girl slid into view behind her. Not a girl at all but a woman with a wrinkled mouselike face.

"Give me the cupcakes," he said under his breath.

The girl's eyes dug into him. Her pink mouth hung open. "Red velvet's the favorite."

"Give me those. The red velvets."

"How many would you like, sir?" the woman cut in. The girl moved the least possible distance away from the glass. Gawking at him pigeon-eyed and leering.

"How many?" said the woman. "The red velvets are $2.75."

Lowboy considered her question. The sun through the window made the two of them look spotlit. "I don't know the answer to that," he said finally.

The girl started laughing. The woman turned toward her and she stopped, staring slyly at the other customers. Everybody held their breath at once. The woman licked her lips and frowned at him. "Why don't you tell me how much you want to spend," she said. Leaving off the "sir."

Lowboy put his hands into his pockets. He squinted at her and looked around the room. He was careful not to look over his shoulder. "I have $640," he said.

Someone behind him laughed next. A grown woman or a little girl. The laugh was muffled and lilting, not necessarily unkind. At first he thought of Emily but he knew her laugh too well. Maybe she has two laughs now, he thought. Maybe she has dozens. He was afraid to look behind him then: afraid that she was watching him, afraid that she was gone. But he was afraid of the woman's question even more. A man to his left took a few paces backward. Women and children whispered as they will. He touched each of his fingers to the glass.

"I'll take five."

"Five red velvets," the woman said. She seemed to approve. The girl hovered at her elbow with an open paper bag. Her face looked bloodless and surprised. Because I gave the right answer, Lowboy thought.

"$13.75," the woman said.

Lowboy bit his lip and counted out the money. The bills were moist and rumpled in his hands. The girl slipped the cupcakes into the bag with inexplicable delicacy and care. As though they were hazardous objects. He caught the girl's eye and she looked away at once.

"What's she doing with that bag," said Lowboy.

"What do you mean?" said the woman.

"What's she putting inside it."

The woman opened her mouth but the girl answered first. "Just your cupcakes," she said. "Your five velvets. That's all."

Lowboy looked at the girl more closely. He took his time about it. She was not as young as he had first supposed.

"How old are you?" said Lowboy. "Have you ever been hot?"

"Your change," the woman spat out, snatching the bag from the girl. That brought him some relief but not enough. The room had the same theaterlike calm that he remembered. The hush beforehand. The smells were being sucked back into the ovens. The woman cupped the bag tenderly, protectively, her mouselike face gone featureless and stiff. What's in the bag, Lowboy said to himself. What's in it. Her damp varicose palm cradling the bottom. A faint but unmistakable sound of ticking.

"Put the bag down," Lowboy said to her. "Step away."

They were wondering about him now: they couldn't help it. He was wondering himself.

"Put that fucking bag down. Take out the machinery."

He drew himself up straight and made his inquisitor's face. He stood righteous and clear-eyed and unafraid and he scared them to death.

"Out," the woman stammered. "Get out of my store." Holding the bag in one hand and his money in the other. Sword and scale, mirror and scepter. Suddenly he recalled that the rest of the world was behind him. He saw the shop as Emily was seeing it: the pastels, the clustered heads, the jars arrayed in cold bilateral symmetry. The order of the world is not my order. He left the bag where it was and retreated. He moved surefootedly and smoothly, letting himself be sucked backward, the last five minutes playing in reverse. Eyes on the floor like a minesweeper. Ears alive to the tiniest tick. Passing out through the door he felt a dryness, a sterility, a high desert wind. The pavement coated with dust as in the last scene of a Western. Emily long since swallowed by the sunset.

He found her at a payphone across the street. She was searching for something in the bottom of her bookbag. When she saw that he was coming she zipped it up and waved at him to hurry.

"You found me," she said brightly. "Any luck?"

"Uhhh," he said.

"What happened, Heller? Did something go wrong?"

"Sold out."

She picked the bookbag up and started walking. "I didn't want one anyway. They sweat."

He turned her answer over for a time, reviewing it from every side, trying to find some way inside it. "What does that mean?"

"The frosting." She was walking faster than he was, a full step ahead now, not looking back to see if he was following. "You have to eat them quick. On hot days you've got maybe a minute." She was talkative now, reciting meaningless phrases, chirruping little false notes. "We could have split one, I guess. That would probably have worked."

"You said it wasn't hot today," he mumbled. "You said that it was forty-five degrees."

"Huh?" she said. Not paying attention.

He took a deep breath. "You told me—"

"Here we are," she whispered, tugging at his sleeve. "Stop walking, Heller! This is the place."

He teetered to a halt and looked around him. A low and graceless brownstone with a skin of withered paint, its left side buttressed by a padlocked church. Hudson in front of them, Charles Street behind. Between the brownstone and the corner a bright purple storefront selling latex chaps.

"In there?" he said.

She rolled her eyes. "Sorry, gayboy. Over here."

He turned away unwillingly to a narrow staircase leading underground. A handpainted sign read SAINT JEB S BUY·N·BARTER. Dustcovered windowpanes lit by anemic fluorescents.

"What did we come here for?"

"For clothes, André Benjamin. You look like an usher at the Special Olympics."

"Oh," he said. He nodded reasonably.

"Come on, then."

"Who's André Benjamin?"

He let her pose him and twist him like a dressmaker's dummy. He let her muss and rearrange his hair. Her fingernails sharp and cool against his scalp. Her breath coming in flutters through her teeth. A corner of the store was curtained off for privacy but she followed him in and cursed and fussed and fretted. His corduroys were elastic at the waist and she laughed softly at that, sliding her thumbnail along his hip. "Sansabelt no good," she said, pulling them down with a jerk. "Sansabelt for men with bladder troubles."

"The school made me wear them, actually. Everybody's pants were like that there."

"What the hell for?"

"Safety reasons," he said, smiling down at her. "No belts. No laces. Nothing anyone could use."

She stopped what she was doing and frowned at him. "Okay," she said at last. "I get it." It didn't seem to bother her at all.

She came and went in businesslike rushes, draping things across his chest and disappearing. Giggling and unamused at once. The smooth-faced dandy at the register ignored them. She came and went faster than his dazed eyes could follow and smiled and hissed at him to stop his fidgeting. He thought about his mother painting eyes and lips on mannequins. Had she taken the day off, he wondered. Of course she had. Was she still out looking for him or had she quit. He pictured her having lunch with Skull & Bones.

"All set," Emily said. He took a step toward her but she held up her hands. "Stop right there." She squinted at him. "Okay, Heller. That's a billion times better." She tipped an imaginary hat. "Allow me to welcome you to New York City."

What do I look like, he asked her. What person place or thing do I resemble.

She steered him toward the mirror but he pulled free of her grip. "Tell me," he said, stepping back and standing at attention. "I want you to tell me." A lock of her hair still connected them. She made a face at him in a proprietary way. A grocer's face.

"All right," she said severely. "Here we go." She was willing to do it because it was part of the game.

"You've got on sixties-style jeans with a little pair of dice on the back pocket. It looks like somebody stitched them on themselves. Straightcut jeans, not the tapered fairypants the college boys are wearing. These sit low on your ass. They'd look even better if you had a skateboard."

"I used to have one." He wrinkled his nose. "I never really knew what it was for."

"Shut up. A blue gingham shirt with a buttondown collar, tucked in in front but not in the back. A black crewneck sweater with moth holes in the sleeves. I didn't want that but you've got to have a sweater. Because it's cold outside, Heller. Koko says it's forty-eight degrees."

"Koko?" Lowboy said, looking around him. The dandy raised a liverspotted hand.

"I kept the shoes because they're so totally hideous that it looks as though you're wearing them on purpose." She nodded to herself. "Also they look sort of comfortable."

"They *are* comfortable. I like these shoes."

"Come back in here," she said. "I want you to try one more little thing."

She guided him into the corner and pulled the sheet closed after them. She had a belt in her hand, green with black enameled rivets, but she didn't give it to him. She seemed to have forgotten it existed. Her small round face was flushed and close to his. Her lips were chapped and parted. Tomboy's lips. The teeth behind them sharp and closely set.

"Should I put on that belt?"

She pressed two fingers to his bottom lip. Her dark hair clambering up the wall behind her. The ancient tubelights muttering. The damp discolored wallpaper alive now and a witness to their secret. His mouth filled with breath. He saw what was behind her so clearly, saw all of it at once, as though she were a detail in a painting. Blackhaired Girl with Curtain. Like everyone else she was part of the visible world. Girl with Mouth Open in Yellow.

Behind his own head everything was white.

"You almost killed me," she said sweetly. "Did you know that?"

He said nothing. The wallpaper rustled and hung from the ceiling in coils.

"I could have been cut in half, Heller. You did that to me."

What could he say to that but I'm so sorry. She took his hand in both of hers and brought it to her stomach. She made a place for it under her shirt. His hand felt a current: a mustering there. Her ribs shifted upward with three precise clicks, like the bones in the back of a snake. His hand found her hip, no thicker than a doorhandle, and she gave the least imaginable shiver. His weight carried him toward her. Her thumbnail caught the hollow of his neck. His lips came apart and a small defenseless thing was lost forever.

"Open your mouth wider," she told him. "Let your tongue out."

He fell back against the wall and did exactly what she told him. He was falling in slow motion. His body didn't know that it was falling but there was no doubt whatsoever that it was. She took a half step forward, a self-conscious shuffle, and let her knuckles catch under his jaw. A stricken feeling and a voluptuousness. To put your tongue where another tongue was kept. There was no way of telling was it the best thing or the worst thing that could happen.

"You see now," she said to him once it was done. Her voice was strange and dull and out of focus. "You see now. Don't you, Heller?"

He smiled and nodded and kept his lips shut tight. Now that it was over it had been a good thing without question. A ticklishness inhabiting the teeth. A prickling against his gums like soda water or like Perrier. That was the reason it was called French kissing.

When Lowboy's eyes came open he was alone behind the sheet. He looked down at himself: the loose jeans, the black sweater, the green belt curled around him like Ouroboros. To his surprise the world appeared unchanged. He heard her laugh, then curse, then laugh a second time. He breathed but it was hard to fill his lungs. She was at the counter talking business with the dandy. Their voices carried softly through the rows of pleated pants and ruffled blouses and by the time they reached him they were barely whispers. He passed the belt through his beltloops. It fit perfectly. He'd just gotten it buckled when her arm came around the sheet, casting for him blindly, fingers flapping like a hand without a puppet.

"$37.20," she said. "The $.20 is optional." Laughing from some as-yet-unfinished joke.

He laid his cleanest bill across her fingers and they shut and withdrew with hydraulic precision. He remembered that she used to do the Robot when she was happy, to commemorate certain pivotal events. Watching her slight body rotate and tilt had thrilled him in a way he'd had no words for. A sense of some momentous thing impending. The answer to a question. He wondered whether he could name it now.

When he got to the counter with his clothes under his arm she was doing the Robot gravely for the dandy. He stood beside the register holding the clothes out in front of him but he couldn't seem to catch the dandy's eye. Emily was lost to the world, shooting down flying saucers, and the dandy was watching her do it. Lowboy wondered what his real name was. To the left of the register stood a crepe-lined case cracked and yellow with neglect and inside it paste jewels and Bakelite clasps were laid out like exhibits from forgotten murder trials. He set the clothes down as discreetly as he could. His giddiness had passed and he felt small and insignificant and content.

"Koko says you look tasty," Emily said. "Koko says there ought to be a law. I told him as a matter of fact there is."

The dandy looked at him steadily, letting the statement hang exactly where she'd left it. Emily didn't look at him at all. Lowboy ducked his head to study his reflection in the glass. "What's your real name?" he said. "I bet it's not Koko."

Emily stopped in mid-pivot but the dandy only shrugged. "Ernest," he said. "Ernest Copeley Johnson."

"Nice to meet you, Mr. Johnson. My name's William Heller."

"But people call you Lowboy," said the dandy. "Why is that?"

Lowboy bit his lip and looked at Emily. He had no memory of having told her.

"I've been away at school," he said. "I had a hard time there."

The dandy heaved a sigh. "Didn't we all."

"A lowboy is an item of furniture," Lowboy said. He hesitated. "Also a dog."

"Very interesting, Mr. Heller. Which are you?"

"He's a man on a mission," Emily said, taking him by the hand. "Can we leave his old crap with you, Koko?"

"That's what I'm for," said the dandy. "Run along." He hummed a tune at them as they went up the stairs, jaded and magnanimous and wise, the smile lingering bittersweetly on his lips. He said something just as the shopdoor swung shut but the noise of the traffic eclipsed it. "What was that?" said Lowboy.

Emily took his ear and pinched it. "Something about liking your new look."

They crossed the street like other people, like people with nothing between them, and she steered him gently back the way they'd come. He had to ask her twice where they were going.

"I'm a lame-ass, Heller. I forgot something at Crowley. Can we go back for just a second?"

"What did you forget?" he said, slowing. Crowley was finished, a completed episode. "Was it something important?"

"Take my word for it, Heller."

He didn't want to take her word for it. "What is it?"

She mumbled something that he couldn't hear.

"Emily?"

"Rubbers. It's *rubbers*, Heller. Okay?"

"Okay," he said. "I guess that's all right, then."

They walked half a block without saying anything else. He was thinking about rubbers, about what rubbers were for, and about the look on her face when she'd finally answered his question. An impatient look, almost resentful, as if the word was somehow too specific. And it was too specific. It turned a cold blue light on what was going to happen.

"It's not like I keep rubbers in my locker all the time," she said, keeping half a step ahead of him. "I don't want you to think that I'm a slut." When he said nothing to that she gave a laugh and took out her pack of Salem Lights. "Or maybe I *do* want you to think that. I don't know."

She slowed down to let him catch her, knocking a cigarette out of the pack, waiting for him to say something.

"Can I bum a smoke?"

She sighed and dropped the pack into his palm. There were only three left and that made him uneasy. Sometime soon they'd have to stop at a bodega.

"You never used to smoke, Heller. You used to be afraid of it. You even used to be afraid of matches."

"Everyone smokes at the school." He found a cigarette he liked and shook it out. "There's nothing else to do."

She lit a match for him. "Didn't you have board games or anything? Wasn't there any TV?"

"The TV was just a bunch of moving pictures."

She frowned at him. "Was the volume broken?"

"There wasn't anything—" He stood still for a moment, thinking of a way to make it clear. "No story. There was nothing behind it."

"Sounds like regular old TV to me."

"No," he said. "Sometimes there's a story. Like today."

"You're right about that," she said, smiling at him. "A little something for the *Daily News*."

"Or the *Post*," he said. "They wrote about us once. Do you remember?"

She shook her head. "Just you. I wasn't in it."

"You'll be in it this time," he said. "You're going to be famous, Emily."

"You don't have to make me famous," she said. "You only have to make me someone else." She pulled him closer. "I want to be a different kind of person."

"I'll make you someone else," he said softly. "I promise I will, Emily. I'll make you a slut."

She let out a cough and pulled her body backward. At first he thought she was laughing but she only rocked back stiffly on her heels. Her tongue made a hollow sound against her teeth and she put her cigarettes away and started walking. Lowboy didn't move.

"I don't want to go backwards, Emily."

"Why not?"

He shook his head. "That part of it is over. No more Crowley."

She shrugged and started walking even faster.

He understood then that there were two ways of making her look back at him: the sick way and the well. The way that would keep her and the way that would lose her forever. What would Violet say, he thought, then closed his eyes and shook his head to clear it. Violet wasn't well. Neither was Kopeck. Neither was the world. The best thing to do was to kneel down and cry. The best thing to do was to run screaming out into the street.

"Emily," he called out. "Hold on, Emily. I'm sorry."

When she turned to look at him her face was wet. "You don't look sorry," she said. "You don't look sorry at all."

"That's what they told me in court." He smiled at her. "Before I got sent away. That's what your father said."

That brought her up short. "My father," she murmured, opening her eyes wide.

He waited for her to laugh or spit at him or slap his face.

"Do you know what my father did when I told him I didn't want to testify? Do you want me to tell you what he did to me, Heller?"

A picture came to him then of Emily's father, pale and hulking on the sofa, staring pigfaced at the seven o'clock news. He remembered her cringing mother. "I don't want you to tell me," he said.

"He couldn't make me, though." She crossed her arms. "Things have changed with him and me since then."

"Changed how?"

"They've gotten worse."

"But I'm not your father."

She laughed. "That's true. You're fucked up in a totally different way."

"I love you, Emily."

She nodded absentmindedly. "I know."

He took a deep breath, as much as he could fit into his chest, and held on to the air until it hurt him. He thought of what he could do to prove he wasn't lying.

"How are you feeling, Emily?"

"I'm okay, Heller. Don't worry about me. I don't feel bad anymore."

"All right, then," he said. "Let's go to Crowley."

Hello Violet how are you?

They gave me or deposited me in a new room which the Headmaster says is a Real Sign of Promise. Not a room necessarily more like a corner with a shitcolored tarp around it but a bed & nobody else can sleep there. & a light that I can turn on when I want & obviously this pen or else how would I be writing. How are you?

Today Dr Prekopp said How awesome Willy that you asked for your own room & a pen etcetera now that's what we like to call Progress. Only please don't tell our dirty secrets thank you in advance. Hugs & Kisses. So I laughed because how could I do it? Secrets are secrets because nobody says them out loud. If nobody can't then I can't Violet. I'm a 24 hour student now but nobody here has taught me how to tell. I won't do it I said no worries Dr Prekopp. I don't tell secrets. Also I said to him don't call me Willy.

There was a Flat Time Violet as you know but things happened without me & yesterday the Headmaster said William you've been here for

6 months. I didn't take that as a fact but Dr Prekopp said it was or he corroborated it & showed me my chart so I could count the days & doses for myself. When the cat's away he said Help yourself Willy no skin off my pimply behind. Dr Prekopp! I said. You'll make a bighearted woman a bigbellied husband one day & he laughed & asked me what song I was quoting. (Potbellied Blues) I told him something about you Violet but I haven't told him yet that you are blond. Are you still blond actually? Or has there been a wig?

I've seen terrible things Violet. Somebody had to see them. Somebody low. If you meet anyone who knows me at PAYLESS SHOE SOURCE or DAFFY'S CLOTHING BARGAINS FOR MILLIONAIRES you can tell them I've seen terrible things. But don't tell anyone at BERGDORF GOODMAN.

I was sitting in the Smoking Room reading the Wall Street Journal when I saw the Schoolmaster aka Dr Fleisig sliding sideways down the hall. Fleisig is a friendly Mediterranean man he looks a little bit like Jacques Cousteau. But this time I jumped up & dropped my cigarette & ran to the door. Because I knew by then it wasn't exactly Fleisig. He was changing his haircut every 6 or 7 steps & playing temperature games inside his body. & at night he used my hands and mouth to eat with.

Truth Be Told Violet! we used to watch Underwater Movies. My father would make seafood soup & beer & you cooked me a beautiful Jell-O. Why Underwater, Violet. Why Movies. You had Pam Anderson hair but I didn't know it then. You kissed him on the shoulder. You said "Stop it, Alex." You were younger then at least than I am now. Also 63 years old. Also CRAB CAKES. My father making fun of Jacques Cousteau or was it me. Which one was it. Don't tell Will what's in the soup he said to you one time. He might possibly lose his shit.

The room turned green and blue when we had dinner. What did he say to you Violet I can't remember. But you laughed & kissed him on the shoulder & that was all there could be in the world.

A man goes into a bar Violet he asks for any kind of beer but please not Schlitz. Why not Schlitz says the bartender Schlitz is a quality beer. Yes says the man but last night I drank Schlitz and blew chunks. Happens to the best of us says the bartender. You don't understand the man says Chunks is my dog!

Skull & Bones told me that one Violet is it funny.

There was a time or an occasion when Fleisig appeared at my bedside wearing your stepfather's head. Playing temperature games was a favorite of his at that time. Fleisig the schoolmaster making the whole schoolhouse hot. He used crude oil to do it actually & electronics. Fossil fuels Violet. At times he put degrees into my body. Me thinking all the time How can I lower the temperature? How can I keep it low? Since the day I was born 12 September 1992 the MGT (Mean Global Temperature) has gone up by 7 and one half degrees.

There's a language of numbers Violet if you can follow it: 2773664748 565758933 5758489 757. 47458959 3263647478548585858 2632. 37 4855959 967009858483783. 72726 7474. 7474. 7474. 7474.

There's still time Violet. Things get brighter suddenly as in a theater. People get better. Things have been known to laugh at me for example Clouds In The Sky or my own mouth. Tom Brokaw said this: Scientists believe the warming will continue, not on a straight line but on a curve. Which is my idea Violet as you know very well. How did Brokaw find out did you tell?

Fleisig is a German name which means hardworker or industrious in that language. Be Fleisig, people say to their children. Make sure to always be Fleisig. Of course you know that Violet since you come from Austria, not Germany at all but a country most of us have never heard of. Or we've heard of it Okay but we don't care. Do you know about Fleisig Violet? He knows all about you. Fleisig is the Superintendent of the School. Always be Fleisig. Approximately 6 times he inserted into my body an electronic device or molecule no bigger than a little piece of skin. This molecule was I later found out "bioengineered" & soft like a piece of old jelly. Some times he put it in my right arm some times he put it in my neck. Always professionally done & no discomfort. As a result the school was able to get intimate with me & generally to speak its Proper Mind. But could I speak my mind Violet I could not. Most of the time I couldn't say a word.

The lights get brighter suddenly as in a theater & I'm in the audience & not even in a good seat. People things & colors look "projected." How can I believe in things Violet. How can I believe in "people." There's talk in the theater about William Heller. Will he be able to perform the miracle? Will he lower the temperature? Is it the voices of real people or is it my own voice or is it just another joke of Fleisig's. Machinery and wires under the stage giant turbines just to keep the flashbulbs going. That's why it's always so hot. Stars are there & also paparazzis. You're there too Violet smiling & holding hands with your Projection. The movie is dubbed but dubbed badly. The School is a movie like that. How funny that Fleisig looks like Jacques Cousteau.

I found an article yesterday in The New York Times. It's called

IN CHILDBEARING, A BATTLE ON MANY FRONTS.

Dr David Haig plays a scientist who makes some discoveries about mothers & their embryos. People find his discoveries Upsetting. "Natural Selection favors offspring that get enough nutrients from their mothers to grow up healthy," the scientist says. However Violet. "Natural Selection favors mothers who retain enough nutrients to have larger families." The scientist tells people that This leads to conflict. The Mothers and the embryos fight for Nutrients in the mothers' blood. The New York Times calls this THE SILENT STRUGGLE. "Dr David Haig suspects that this conflict may add to the risk for mental disorders, from depression to autism" etc. This may explain your mental illness Violet.

I got low during the flat time Violet As You May Know. Too low actually you would have laughed. There were even Pampers Violet please don't tell. They thought I was asleep because my eyes looked shut but I was seeing Every Little Thing That Happened. Somebody had to see it. Everything was quiet Violet you know what that means Everything Was Dubbed. Badly dubbed in fact and out of Sync. Sometimes worth paying attention to sometimes not. Occasionally sexy. There was interest in my penis Violet. It was difficult!

The question of my penis is an ongoing question. My penis seems to be a kind of Answer. I took it out during TV hour & Prekopp & Fleisig & everyone else stared & hummed at it & let it happen. Another sign that things might be improving. My unzipped pants like Direct Cable Service. I'm not dead Violet. I'm not even tired. I'm making myself an airconditioned body.

Why was I born Violet? Can you tell me why?

I'm writing to inform you that I remember who you are & not to worry. I'm writing because I've gotten so much better. Men are going to visit you with questions. Men are going to make you Propositions. Please don't answer. Please don't worry about The last bad thing that happened. Or in the old man's house or in the basement. Those things should not be cited Violet & you didn't cite them so you should be proud. I AM PROUD OF YOU VIOLET. I am proud of you Violet. Please don't forget. Your son William.

The first thing Violet did when her son turned his head was to retch as though she'd swallowed something sharp. Lateef watched her go down with the calm of a man watching a rogue wave rushing toward a crowded beach, able to witness the event and guess at its meaning but helpless to keep the event from happening. The children broke into a run, but there was nothing to be done about that yet. He had time to catch her by the arm and plant his feet before she fell, time to ease her down onto the pavement and arrange her with her head between her knees. If he felt disappointment or frustration he was not aware of it. She was costing him time but there was plenty of that. The children were still less than a block away when he got back to his feet and started running.

Almost at once he became aware of a change in the way they moved. Half a minute earlier they'd been holding hands slackly, almost bashfully, shuffling past the storefronts as mildly as retirees: now they were sprinting in unison, not a glance or gesture wasted, with the single-mindedness of lifelong fugitives. More surprisingly still, the girl was out in front. He wondered what in God's name she was thinking. She shot across Seventh Avenue during a lull in traffic and the boy followed her without the least sign of concern. Stockholm syndrome suggested itself, certain celebrated cases, abductees taking the names of their captors. The comparison was a romantic one and he flushed it irritably from his mind. She's seventeen years old, he thought. That's a syndrome in itself. He worked his arms and kept his breathing even. The main thing now was not to lose his footing.

The children were more than a block away already, almost to Hudson, but Lateef chose to believe the gap was closing. The girl held the boy by his left hand or possibly his shoulder. "Thank God for small favors," Lateef said out loud. The handholding would slow them down a little. He drew his arms farther in and stared down at the pavement and set himself to lengthening his stride. Someone shouted as he passed them and the cramp that he'd been nursing since Seventh Avenue bloomed in that instant, as though the pain had its source outside his body, in the parked cars or the pavement or the daylight. The children were closer now, standing perfectly still, penned in by the traffic at the corner. The girl had her thumb hooked into the back of the boy's collar. They didn't seem to want to turn uptown.

How much can I do, Lateef thought. How much farther. He was not in embarrassing shape for his age, he was strict with himself, but his last foot pursuit had taken place in the previous century. Runaways rarely bolted when you found them: most of them were relieved to be brought in. He let out a laugh, a senseless discharge of breath, and the cramp crept cheerfully up into his stomach. He was a few hundred feet from them now, keeping as close to the curb as he could manage. A groan of pain slipped out of him with every step he took. Through the tinted windshield of a Lexus he saw the girl's hand hovering at the base of the boy's neck.

They've done it already, he said to himself. Look at them. For some reason the thought of it made him feel faint.

For the briefest of instants he was able to admire them both, the picturesque pair they made, each of them the other's complement. The boy was a sight to behold: even Lateef could see that much. Pale and finefeatured but in no way girlish. He had none of the awkwardness one would expect, none of the hesitancy, none of the fear. He was more beautiful even than his mother, perhaps because he seemed so self-assured. More than self-assured: exalted. The girl seemed proud to have him by the collar. You never would have guessed he'd tried to kill her.

Just then the girl turned on her heels and looked Lateef straight in the eye. The boy didn't bother.

"Stay right there," Lateef shouted. A vain and senseless gesture. By the time he'd stepped around the Lexus they were lost in a clot of pedestrians outside a café and he was standing up straight again, blinking and groaning, stumbling after them like a lovesick drunk.

Motherfuckers, Lateef thought, struggling to keep his balance. Neither of you even looks athletic.

The sidewalk cleared quickly once he'd passed the café and he saw that he was closer than he'd thought, maybe two dozen steps back, close enough to talk to them if he wanted. A question might do it, he thought. Ask them a question. Name, age, destination, antipsychotic of choice. Break their rhythm, distract them, make them consider what might happen next. What *will* happen next, he corrected himself. He felt grotesque and hamfisted, a cop on a sitcom, a show that never made it past the pilot. Not like those kids, he thought. Not like them at all. They run as if somebody's filming them.

And yet in spite of it all he seemed to be gaining ground. The children were moving differently than before, less automatically, less sure of their purpose. The girl glanced back at him more often: with each foot he gained her self-assuredness weakened. She was careful to keep the boy from noticing, keeping herself just behind him, but her doubt and her fatigue were obvious. Slowly Lateef came to understand her, to categorize her, to arrive at an adequate profile. She's not in too deep yet, he said to himself. She's starting to think. She'll feel nothing but relief when this is done.

But in the excitement of this new intelligence he'd forgotten to consider the boy. The boy saw her looking back and pivoted in mid-stride and pulled her toward him. That was all he did, but it was enough. They were moving in concert again, better and more easily than before, and the girl was smiling at him gratefully. They crossed Greenwich without the slightest effort. As Lateef's foot left the curb the girl glanced back one last time, as if to commit him to memory, and he called out her name but by then it was already finished.

Consciousness returned to him delicately, measured and mild, as though there were no need to hurry. His eyes were shut tight and he took his time getting them open. A man in a turquoise helmet was addressing him from a great height.

"—for a nigger," the man in the helmet was saying. He reached down and took hold of Lateef's blazer. He seemed to be trying to read the label.

"Helmut Lang," Lateef said, sitting up. "The collection."

"The which?" gasped the man, scuttling back like a crab. A mountain bike lay on the tarmac behind him. He wore scuffed spandex shorts and his arms were tattooed to the elbows. He looked to be well over sixty.

"Nothing," Lateef said, getting to his feet. He still felt at a slight remove from things. He held up his badge and asked how long he'd been lying in the street.

"Don't know how long," the man said thickly.

"Take a guess."

"Maybe a minute." If the man was pleased to see Lateef alive and in working order he kept his pleasure to himself. "Next time you cross the street, Officer, you might want to pull your head out of—"

But by that time Lateef was up and running. The pain was back in all its glory but it was somehow less insistent than before. He judged that he'd lost two blocks, possibly three, and that the children were still heading west on Tenth Street. He had no evidence for either theory, but there was no sense in questioning them now. If he did that he might as well lie back down in the street.

Soon enough his lightheadedness returned and with it came a dull surge of indifference. The accident knocked something sideways, he said to himself. Something got tipped. As he had this thought he felt his body coming to a stop, slowing like a watchspring at half-coil, and his eyes struggling to close against the light. What he wanted most at that moment was to let the children go. It occurred to him to look at his reflection to find out whether he was bleeding and it turned out, not surprisingly, that he was. He reached into a pocket of his JCPenney blazer and pulled out a lintcovered napkin and pressed it to the back of his skull.

I'm Rufus White, he thought suddenly. The thought came to him in an odd voice, faraway but insistent, like the thoughts that sometimes visited him as he fell asleep, or the voices reportedly heard by schizophrenics. Rufus White, the voice repeated, not unkindly. For Rufus White, it seemed to be saying, you've done better than anyone expected.

He sat down on the stoop of a bodega and waited to hear what else the voice might tell him. That morning he'd felt well suited to his work, but at some point unknown to him that feeling had been abolished and the old uselessness had claimed him absolutely. It's the boy, he thought as the first wave of nausea hit him. The boy and Violet together. He knew that the accident was behind it and he recognized the symptoms of concussion, but the true cause seemed to be the case itself. It should have felt familiar to him but it did not feel familiar. The boy was different from all previous SCMs, somehow out of proportion, and everyone who knew him seemed to have been sent out of plumb. His girlfriend, his doctor, his mother. His mother especially. Lateef knew that he wasn't thinking clearly but the idea calmed his nausea regardless. He'll change me too if I allow it, he thought. Maybe he already has.

Sit up, Rufus, the voice told him. Don't fall asleep. He recognized it as his own voice now. His other name hadn't left him, only been temporarily obscured. The roof of his mouth had a flat metallic taste that put him in mind of childhood accidents. He drew his knees in to his chest and let his head hang slack the way Violet had done some time before. How long before he had no idea. I need something to drink, he thought. Seltzer water. A Coke. A Glenfiddich with water. Rufus Lamarck White, Detective Second Grade, he thought. Forty-six and one-half years of age. Sitting on a bodega stoop and bleeding in an unassuming way. His right elbow was propped against a stack of day-old copies of the *Post*, and he tossed one to the ground and tried to read it. A polyp had been removed from the vice president. A warm front was approaching. The corpse of a woman pulled out of the Central Park Reservoir had been identified by tracing the serial numbers on the implants in her breasts.

With time he began to feel better. The bodega clerk was still nowhere in sight. He passed a hand over his face and pushed his head slowly backward, taking sharp, shallow breaths, compelling himself to revisit the last quarter hour. Like a multiple exposure his every thought was colored by the image of the boy. He'd been so docile as he followed the girl's example: so comfortable, so self-possessed. It was impossible to conceive of him as violent. Even while sprinting into traffic a part of him seemed to be standing apart and still. His mother's that same way, Lateef thought. That same stillness. There's a wrongness to it, even though she's beautiful. Everything she does is done in spite of herself.

He remembered how the boy had looked running. From the back the resemblance to his mother had been absolute. He'd moved differently, of course—in a loose, disjointed way that called attention to his sickness—but that had only emphasized their sameness. His sickness somehow made him more like her. There was a mystery there that Lateef could not enter. Yda and William Heller. Violet and Will. In some way they were interchangeable.

She wanted to keep him locked away, he thought. She told me so herself. She petitioned for an extension of his sentence.

Why was that?

Just then a blond head was spotlit by the sun on the opposite corner, closecropped and boyish, flickering in and out of sight along the storefronts. No sign of the girl but of course that meant nothing. He got up as best he could, supporting himself on the newspaper rack and the doorframe: the door gave a squeal and swung angrily inward, forcing him to jerk upright. The head was plain to see above the cars, the lone golden object in a monochrome field. He fell in step with it as though joining a religious procession. Another ridiculous comparison, he said to himself. He put one foot in front of the other with fanatical precision, gritting his teeth from the effort of keeping upright. Even once he was sure that it was Violet and not the boy he made no attempt to call her name out or to catch her. The avenue seemed wider than before, a river at full head, something any sensible man would be afraid of. At the corner of Tenth Street and Washington he finally mustered his courage and eased himself gingerly out into the traffic. He was halfway across before he realized that the bloodspattered napkin was still dangling absurdly from his neck.

She'd seen him by then and she stopped and watched him tottering toward her. At no point since they'd met had he felt more at the mercy of her judgment. She was studying him closely, shading her eyes with her sleeve, as though trying to recall where they'd last met. Her lack of urgency would come to perplex him in time, to add to his misgivings, but in that moment he was grateful for her patience. His head was misaligned somehow, out of step with his body, and the ground under his feet was vague and fluid: he had no choice but to take things at face value. All he asked of the world was that it keep reasonably still.

He'd thought she might show some trace of chagrin herself—frustration at the very least, possibly even anger—but she seemed carefree and serene. She smiled at him as he came alongside her and took him amicably by the arm. "You're bleeding," she said, wrinkling her nose. She might have been pointing out an inkstain on his shirt.

"I was knocked down by a bike."

"Yes," she said placidly. She stopped him and lifted the napkin away from his neck. "You ought to see a doctor."

"How are you feeling?"

"I'm fine, Detective. Why shouldn't I be?'

"Because—" he said, then stopped himself. He felt oddly cautious. "You had that spell. I thought you might be sick."

"Let's worry about you first. Are you having trouble walking?"

He wasn't used to solicitude from complainants and he found it particularly hard to bear from her. He slid his arm out of her grip as goodnaturedly as he could. "Miss Heller, if you have any medical condition, such as asthma, for example, or are prone to lightheadedness—"

She shook her head sweetly. "No asthma, no lightheadedness, no scarlet fever. How long ago did you lose track of my son?"

Here it comes, Lateef thought. He stared down at his feet like a schoolboy, feeling his toes curling inside his loafers, casting anxiously about for a reply. "Five minutes," he said finally. "Maybe ten."

"That's all right, Detective." She took out a cigarette and lit it. "I know where they are."

It took him another long moment to answer her. "How?"

She smiled at him and shrugged. "They've gone to the river."

"The river," Lateef said.

"That's right."

He waited for an explanation but none was offered. "Which river, Miss Heller? The East River? The Hudson?" He squinted at her. "Not the Harlem, I hope?"

"The Hudson is closest," she said soberly.

"Why didn't you tell me this earlier, if you don't mind my asking? I could have arranged—"

"I couldn't tell you earlier." She took his arm again. "It just came to me."

He nodded morosely and loosened the knot of his tie. He ought to have been relieved that she'd taken his failure so well. They'd already begun walking west, toward the parking garage and the pier at the end of Houston Street. Judging by the way she moved there wasn't any hurry.

"Can I ask you why?" he said finally.

"Why what?"

"*Why* would they be going to the river?"

The question seemed to gratify her. "Will's grandfather used to tell him stories to help him fall asleep. His favorite was about an underground city, the exact size of Manhattan but backwards—"

"Backwards?"

She pursed her lips. "'Backwards' is the wrong word—upside down. Deepest where Manhattan is tallest." She paused until she was sure that he was following. "The city had its own river, called the Musaquontas. Even Will knew that it was a fairy tale, but Richard always swore that it was true." She took Lateef's arm again, either to urge him onward or to keep him from falling over, and made a face that he couldn't decipher. "The Musaquontas comes out under the West Side Highway."

Lateef took a breath. "But what would the, ah, Missaquorum—"

"The *Musaquontas*," she said patiently.

"Why would your son go there now?"

"Isn't it obvious? He's got Emily again but he doesn't feel safe. He'll want to take her with him underground."

The image came to Lateef of a rat darting into its burrow and he turned away to hide his face from her. Her theory seemed far-fetched at best but he supposed that it was as good as any other. Don't forget that she's his mother, he thought. They're bound to think alike up to a point. He said nothing further, letting her usher him forward, marveling at her self-possession. Look at this woman, he said to himself. She's completely convinced that we'll find her son around the next corner. It would never occur to her that I might disagree.

He did not disagree. He stopped very briefly to let his head clear, bracing himself against her, then let her steer him up the street like a wheelbarrow. Even given her confidence there was something incongruous about her lack of hesitation, about her measured, unhurried, entirely deliberate walk. She's obsessed with her own son, he thought. She told me so herself. But I didn't appreciate it at the time.

When they reached the West Side Highway the light turned green as if on cue and she crossed the uptown lanes in six smooth steps. She was moving even more purposefully now, all but carrying him forward: she seemed to have forgotten his injury. Her eyes were focused on the middle distance, ticking from side to side, noting every relevant detail. She crossed the downtown lanes almost casually and turned up her collar and stood graceful and composed on the near curb. A wind was blowing off the river and she raised a hand to keep it from her eyes. She seemed less to be scanning the crowd flowing past them than waiting to keep some prearranged appointment. She expects him to come to her, Lateef thought incredulously. The pain and the nausea were largely gone and in their place was a kind of listlessness, a heaviness in the bones, a reluctance to act that he could not account for. It was tempting to blame the accident for his helplessness—head trauma, blood loss, a possible concussion—but the feeling had begun before the accident. He'd known from the beginning that he would fail to catch the children: he hadn't been able to make up his mind to catch them. He still couldn't make up his mind.

"There they are," said Violet.

He followed her gaze to what looked to be a Catholic school outing: girls of assorted shapes and ages, wrapped in identical tartans, staring mournfully across the water at New Jersey. A matron in a quilted coat, much too warm for the weather, gesticulated at them like a mime. What the hell could she be telling them, he thought. There's nothing behind her but an air vent for the tunnel. It took him a moment to make out the children: only their heads were visible, one jet black and one blond, both of them facing due south.

Violet was sprinting already, her thin coat furling out behind her, her head set low as if to brace for a collision. The children were on the far side of the group, ignoring the matron, their heads inclining dreamily toward each other. They seemed to be lost in contemplation of some Lower Manhattan landmark: the Woolworth Building, possibly, or the construction at Ground Zero. I thought he wanted to take her underground, Lateef thought, struggling to catch up to Violet. But by then he'd realized that they weren't the same children at all.

He called her name out as she reached them but of course it did no good. He couldn't see her face but he could guess from the girls' reactions how it looked. The woman in the quilted coat made a sound like a popping cork and reached for Violet's sleeve too late to stop her. The girls themselves shrieked or swore at her or simply froze in place and watched it happen. Violet had the nearer of the pair of them by the collar and was looking back and forth from her tartan skirt to her cropped blond hair with an expression of simple animal disbelief.

"Police," Lateef shouted, searching in vain for his badge. Violet was saying something in a dull voice that he took to be gibberish before he realized that it was German. She was bobbing her head now, her eyes flat and blank, and the girl she was holding seemed to be mimicking her. Lateef found his badge at last and held it above his head like a semaphore, reciting the word "police" with as much believability as he could muster. The only one who noticed was the matron. She spun around sharply, as though she'd been propositioned, and slapped him expertly across the face.

"Violet," Lateef said, pushing the matron aside. "Let her go, Violet. Violet, for Christ's sake."

She lowered her head stiffly, her boyish blond head so much like the girl's own, and he made out a few strands of gray. For the first time it struck him as unnatural that she looked so childlike. Her head was still lowered when she let the girl loose, bowed as if in submission, and her lower lip looked to be bleeding. The schoolgirls fell back when she got to her feet as though the ground were coming open underneath her. Lateef took her arm in his and guided her awkwardly past them. At that moment he was afraid of her himself.

"I'd like to go home, Detective," she said under her breath. "Would you take me home in your electric car?"

"T"ell me what happened to you," Emily said. The A and C# interrupted her and the car doors met behind her like a kiss. "Tell me about your time in that asylum."

Lowboy looked at her sideways. "My time at school, you mean."

"It wasn't a school really, Heller. Was it?" She opened her eyes wide to tease him.

"I'd rather not talk about it."

"I bet it wasn't boring." She watched him for a while with her mouth hanging open. "It wasn't boring, was it?"

"It wasn't anything."

"You might as well tell me, Heller. I'll just keep on being a bitch until you do."

They were on the downtown 6. Before that they'd been on the Shuttle and the C and the Brooklyn-bound F. Lowboy looked out through the cracked pane behind her, watching the nothingness draw itself sorrowfully past. The gap between the train and the tunnel wall was the deadest place on earth. Nothing could happen there. School had been another place like that, at least during the flat time. A hundred well-lit rooms enclosing nothing.

"Are you still going out with Skippy Fadman?"

Her mouth clicked shut and her eyes pulled back into her head. "Who told you I was?"

He smiled at her and shrugged his shoulders.

She gave him the finger. "Skippy Fadman is a bounder and a cheat."

"Say that again with an English accent."

"That *was* my English accent, dumb-ass."

He reached over and tucked the tail of her shirt back into her jeans and she let him do it. Her features were apparent to him and particular and real. The nails of her left hand were bitten down to little purple lozenges. The nails of her right hand were painted the color of blood.

"What was the name of Skippy's band again?" He tried his best to think. "Was it Mangina?"

She laughed and turned blue at the temples. Most people blushed red but not her. "Don't try to dis him, Heller. You can never dis Skippy. He's seen a dozen faces and he's rocked them all."

He studied his new clothes in the glass. It looked as though somebody else was wearing them. "What's the name of his band really?"

"Priapussy."

When he said nothing to that her face turned even bluer and she looked restlessly up and down the car. "They're a punk band, you know. They've all got names like that." She let out a slow breath and shut her eyes. "It's sort of a joke, anyway. It's basically a joke. Even Skippy knows it sounds retarded."

He took her square tomboyish hand in his. "It's a beautiful name, Emily. It means something." He nodded solemnly at his reflection. "It means that he has more than just a penis."

Her eyes went sharp again. "It means what?"

"He can have sex with himself, that's all. Like a sea cucumber."

"Lucky him."

"If I could do that I could save the world."

Instead of asking why she started laughing. He turned back from the window and watched the laugh run through her, shaking her ribs and her vertebrae, making her teeth buzz and click like transistors. She seemed to be laughing at a conversation that he had no part of, something at the far end of the car, or even in another car completely. It confused him. He waited patiently for her to finish, watching the laugh spill out of her, feeling the air between them shudder as she breathed. Her breath had no smell whatsoever.

"Why are you laughing?"

She stopped right away. "I'm sorry, Heller. Wasn't I supposed to?"

"Things are going to end, Emily. Things are going to stop happening."

She bit her lip and watched him for a while. Then she crossed her arms and nodded. "When?"

He'd meant to tell her the hour and the minute exactly but something held him back. "Soon," he said. He made his voice kinder. "Very soon. Today."

"Okay," she said. She put her hands in her back pockets. "Okay, Heller. Today it is."

For the next three stations neither of them spoke. Lowboy kept his face set and solemn but in his secret heart he was gratified beyond words that she believed him. She had always believed him, never made him feel sick, but this time it made all the difference. He slid closer to her and let the screeching of the train enclose them in a shimmering tent of noise. Inside the tent it was luminous and still. Her eyes had gone shallow, reflecting no light, and her forehead twitched as though she were asleep. She neither inclined toward him nor away. The last time we stood like this she was taller than I was, he thought.

"Look," she said sometime later. "Look at those funny tags." He turned his head to see what she was seeing: turquoise letters oozing by like toothpaste from a tube.

"I can't read it," he said. "I don't know what those letters mean."

"It's somebody's name, that's all. Like a signature. It doesn't mean anything."

"It means something," he said. He watched the letters coil and kink and slither. "It has to mean something."

They watched until the last of them was gone. "Is that why you want to have sex with me, Heller?" she said under her breath. "Am I supposed to help you save the world?"

The way she said it put him on his guard. Also someone might hear. He glanced over his shoulder at the half-empty car, taking an unhurried census, squinting through the busy silver air. Seven women and six men and one undecided. A pageant of storebought faces signifying nothing. No one listening. He smiled down at Emily and drew her contentedly toward him. They couldn't have been safer at the bottom of a well.

The train bucked and switched to a parallel track. Emily let her head rest on his shoulder. He kept his eyes wide open. In the middle of the aisle something fleshcolored glistened, a quivering wetlooking heap, and he tried to figure out what it could be. None of the other riders seemed to see it. He leaned forward to examine the thing more closely, narrowing his eyes so he could see it better. It cringed subtly under his sight.

What is it, Lowboy asked himself. What could it be. The thing wasn't fleshcolored at all: he saw that now. It was hot pink but encrusted in a layer of filth, like the skin around the ass of a baboon. It trembled with the tremblings of the train. It could have been pudding or housepaint or latex or something that a cat would bring indoors. It could even have come from a human body. Pencaps and paperclips were lodged in its surface like daggers in the backside of a bull.

"What are you going to do, Heller?" Emily murmured. Her face was hidden in the sweater that she'd bought him. "When they find you, I mean."

"I'll run."

"You won't get far."

"I've got $640."

She pushed him away from her. "Where the hell from?"

He grinned and put a finger to his lips.

"Jesus, Heller." She dug a fist into her forehead. "It's going wrong already, isn't it? It's already turning to shit."

"I thought it was," he said. "Now I don't know."

As he said that they arrived at Union Square. Here of all places, he thought. All 469 stations in the tunnel. A sign within a sign, a harbinger, a reminder of his half-forgotten calling. They were in the head car and the whole station rolled by and Emily had her back turned to the window. Her eyes might have been sewn shut for all she saw. He kept his own eyes open and saw everything for them both. The mezzanine, the sootstreaked tiles, the platform like a fat beckoning finger. As always he asked himself why they'd built the station at a sudden turning. The city fathers were cautious men and fearful, every detail planned so carefully, but not this. The platform came to meet the train on grooved robotic feet, sliding out to cover the mistake, squaring the circle. That was why they called it Union Square.

"I'll tell you something funny," Emily said. "I never thought of what happened here as something that you did. I always thought it would have happened anyway." She looked at him. "Even though you pushed me off the platform."

"I didn't push you off the platform," he said kindly.

"What?"

"I didn't push you off the platform, Emily."

Her face turned a color he couldn't have named. "Don't say that, Heller," she murmured. "Don't say that to me."

He tipped his head to one side, his every movement easy and efficient, and kissed her on her chapped unparted lips. Her body was unyielding but her mouth was still the mouth that he remembered. They were pulling out of the station now, pulling out as easily as they'd arrived, gliding silently past the spot where it had happened. Where she'd put her arms around him a woman now stood, picking her nose with her thumb and middle finger. He looked down at Emily to see if she'd noticed but Emily had her hands over her face.

"We're pulling out again, Emily. Back into the tunnel. The crushload of this car is one hundred and eighty passengers but there aren't even half as many now. There's plenty of room. We're under Lafayette and Ninth. We're exactly fifteen feet under the sidewalk. The cars on this line used to be called Redbirds, Emily, do you remember? They were painted red to keep from getting tagged. They used to run on all the old IRT lines—the 2, 4, 5, 6, and 7. Do you know what happened to them, Emily? They went into the ocean. They got dumped off of barges into forty feet of water and turned into reefs. *Underwater* reefs, Emily. Like in Jacques Cousteau. Fish swimming where we used to sit together. Sharks in the conductor's booth, squid in the cab. Isn't that funny, Emily? Isn't that a good joke?"

He held her against him and she let herself be held. His chin rested lightly on the crown of her head and he studied the things that moved outside the glass. He saw the doorjamb and the concrete wall beyond it and he saw himself between the concrete and the doors. He saw himself in that dead space holding Emily. Astor Place rolled by with its seablue tiles and terracotta beavers and Bleecker Street with its bright green bricks and Canal Street with its squat mosaic glyphs. If the C# and A rang out he didn't hear them. With each station the train got emptier and lighter until finally its wheels hovered over the rails. The temperature in the car was seventy-two and seven-tenths degrees.

Not long after that they were alone. No one else in the car. The intercom made noise but he ignored it. He knew without listening that it was the end of the line.

"Where are we now?" said Emily, rubbing her eyes as though she'd been asleep.

"City Hall."

She blinked nearsightedly at the empty car. "We ought to get out, then. This is the last stop."

"We're not going to get out, Emily. We're going to stay."

"What for? We'll just—"

"Shhh," he said. He took her arm and led her to the corner. "Sit here next to me. Keep your head down."

"Are you trying to get us caught, Heller? The conductor—"

The C# and A cut her off. It was louder and more final than before. Another omen. "We're going somewhere else," he said. "You'll like it there."

She stared at him then but before his doubts could come she'd looked away. He felt tenderly toward her and his doubts could find no purchase in his thoughts. His thoughts were as cool and smooth as porcelain.

"I'm not ready to get caught," she said. "Can you hear me, Heller?" She took him by the shirtsleeve. "Hello? Will?"

Hearing her say his name was a delight. The train was in motion again, clumsy and vacant, dependent on the two of them for its purpose. Without them it would not have been a train. He pictured it late at night, following its ghost through its melancholy circuit, empty as the shell of a cicada. The thought of it made him lightheaded. He imagined the world that way, carbonized and disemboweled by fire, brittle and egglike, cycling through its orbit like an automated car. No more arclights, no more sidings, no more stations. No more passengers. His eyes tipped backward in their sockets and he stared into the dead starcluttered future. He was part of the future but only as a wisp of stellar gas. No life anywhere to speak of. No tunnel any longer and no hurry, no calling, no need for any kind of sacrifice. Only space and knowledge without end.

"Look at this, Heller! Look out the window!"

Slowly and reluctantly his eyes recollected the world. The left-hand windows were dark and unassuming but the windows on his right side gave out onto a glittering skylit tomb. Vaults of red and green and coppercolored tile arched gravely over desolated stairwells. Vents rose toward a city no one knew. The lights of the train did nothing to dim that prehistoric vision. Its walls shed water like the belly of a ship.

"What is it, Heller?"

"The old City Hall Station," he heard himself answer. "The place that I wanted to take you. They shut it down in 1945."

"Yes," she said hoarsely. "Yes. Take me there." Her hands left dappled palmprints on the glass.

He stood and led her from one car to the next as the train canted through its long turning. She was playful again, almost coquettish, darting ahead through each set of steel doors and pretending to be surprised each time he followed. She thinks this is a gift, he thought. A token of affection. Suddenly he understood how much there was to tell her. It was clear to him now that she knew next to nothing. He remembered the sound she'd made when he'd hinted at his calling, the harsh nervous laugh, almost cruel, and the look on her face when he'd cut her laugh short. A doubtful look. All at once he wanted to be left alone.

But he was not alone. The train was full of light and heat and noise. And behind the noise and under it were the voices.

They began as a rustling. They carried up from the floor, from behind the linoleum and woodgrain, bypassing the intercom and the doors. They made no announcements. Quiet as always at the beginning, a conversation overheard in a neighboring room, a meeting of the minds. They began as a rustling but soon he heard three of them clearly. The hum of the turbines was in them and the draw of his breathing and the clatter of the undulating train. His name was not spoken. Each time was different of course, like turning on a radio, but there was no trace of the old familiarity. Instead there was sadness and also a kind of impatience. The end of the world was not discussed, never once made mention of. And yet the voices had no other subject.

Now therefore was the time to make things happen. "Get Up and Get Courtin'" by Jelly Roll Morton. He pulled open the door at the end of the car and stepped out into the hot rush of the tunnel. The shocked air beat against his face and ears. Not long now, Lowboy thought, and the thought helped to calm him. Not much longer now until it happens. Get on up. Get on up. Get on up and get courtin'.

When he pulled the next door open he found Emily waiting there
with the conductor.

"*There* you are," said Emily. She looked happy to see him. "I guess
we're not supposed to be on this train."

"I guess you're right," said Lowboy.

The conductor was a mediumsized man with two tiny Band-Aids
above his right eye. His skin was a deathly shade of grayish pink and
the Band-Aids were the same color exactly. Did he do that on purpose, Lowboy wondered. Could he possibly have had them custom-
made.

The voices expressed no opinion.

"Why are you on my train?" said the conductor. He was looking
at Lowboy with his left eye only. His right eye was looking at Emily.

Lowboy shrugged and hummed the Oscar Mayer theme.

"What's that?"

"Nobody told me that this was your train."

The conductor grinned. "You thought it was your own damn train,
I guess."

Lowboy didn't answer.

"Sit down a minute, son. Not next to your girlfriend. Over here."
He patted the seat next to him the way the Sikh had done a hundred
years before. He wasn't the police or a transit guard either but his
uniform was a beautiful midnight blue. It had folds and creases like
any other garment but none of its folds or creases cast a shadow.
Why was that.

Lowboy nodded and sat down. Next to no time was left. The conductor was sitting spread out on the bench and their elbows and
their knees were almost touching.

"You're not supposed to be on this train," said the conductor. "But
you knew that already."

Lowboy frowned and made himself as thin as possible.

"City Hall was the last stop," said the conductor, breathing wetly through his open mouth. He blinked and wheezed and clicked his teeth together.

"Where are we going now?" said Emily.

"You're not going no place," said the conductor.

"I mean, like, what's the next stop?"

"City Hall."

"But you said City Hall was the *last* stop. Didn't you?"

The conductor looked at her with both eyes now. "That's what I said."

Emily sat back and sighed. "I guess we really *aren't* going no place."

Lowboy laughed and the conductor let out a kind of groan and grabbed him by the collar of his shirt. There was a song by Bootsie White called "Mashed Tapatoes" and for some reason it came into his mind.

"I'm going to hit you," Lowboy shouted. "I'm going to mash your face like a tapato."

"Try it," said the conductor. Emily had been laughing too but now she stopped and stared at both of them. Then she laughed again. The conductor let Lowboy loose and wiped his hands with great dignity on his midnight blue pants and sat looking straight ahead of him at nothing. The train bucked hard to the left and then righted itself and eased into the station with a sound like a dog going to sleep. The same station of course but in reverse. Emily winked at him behind the conductor's back. "Through the looking glass," she said under her breath.

The conductor got up and pressed his knees together. "You kids get off of this damn train," he said. The doors shivered open and they got to their feet and stepped contritely out onto the platform. The conductor stayed where he was with the knuckles of his fist against his forehead. The doormusic sounded and the doors came together and still he made no movement whatsoever.

"I guess we hurt his feelings," Emily said.

"He's a ghost," Lowboy whispered. "He's made out of fiberoptics. I reached into his mouth and shut him off."

She took him by the shoulders then and spun him around to face her. She twirled him in her hands like a baton. "Listen to me, Heller. You're beautiful and you make me laugh and I want you to take me to that place that we just saw, but you need to stop saying things like that. They creep me out, okay? And you're not creepy." She nodded at him until he nodded back. "That's right," she said. "You're sweet. You're sweet and you're a genius and you look really good with no clothes on. So shut up about ghosts and fiberoptics." She smiled at him. "I mean it, Heller. You should never be allowed to put on pants."

"At school sometimes I wasn't," he said. "At school sometimes they put me in a smock."

"A smock? What for?"

"I don't think you want to know that, Emily."

He thought she'd laugh at that but she kept quiet. "It might make you feel good to tell me," she said. "It might make a little room inside your head."

He brought a hand up wonderingly to his skull.

"That's right, Heller. You've got it. Right in there."

"How do you know what I look like with no clothes on?"

"Come on, loony. Let's get going." She took five quick steps and turned back like a duelist. "Come on already! I thought you said we didn't have much time."

I never said that, thought Lowboy. Not out loud. But he caught up with her and followed her to the end of the platform. A monitor hung there above an overflowing Dumpster and Emily looked up at it and waved her arms. Its screen was chipped and dust-covered and sheeplike figures moved across it dumbly.

"What are those things?" said Lowboy.

"People." She waved her arms again but nothing happened. "People behind us."

They stood under the monitor and waited. Two of the sheeplike figures drifted closer.

. . .

"You're right," said Emily. "They really do."

"Do what?"

"They look as though they're sharing the same face."

Again he had no memory of having spoken. Between the tunnel and the platform was a waist-high aluminum gate, the kind that parents put at the tops of stairs for safety. The mouth of the tunnel smelled sweetly of piss. Abandon All Hope Ye. He nodded to Emily and pulled the gate open. Ye Who Enter Here, he said to himself. The voices agreed. The hinges were black with grease and made no sound.

Once they'd passed the gate the voices got ambitious. Still a room away but closer now, more plaintive, tapping on the brittle wall between. If he whistled or hummed they dimmed but only slightly. Talking was better. What is there to talk about, he asked himself. There's got to be something. Emily was barely moving now, both hands against the wall, cursing herself in steady mouselike hisses. What was there to say that wouldn't scare her. The seam was wide enough to walk along, not too rough or too slippery, with mancatches every six to seven steps. He couldn't help but think of the last time, of Heather Covington moving effortlessly through the dark, shuffling ahead of him in her Saranwrapped feet. Reaching back to pull him stumbling after. Little baby, she'd said to him. Little dollar bill. Emily had stopped moving altogether and the next 6 train was coming. He tried to step past her but she put out a hand and caught him by the shirt. Fucking Jesus, Heller, don't you rush me. Tell me something. Tell me a story. He looked at her and touched her face and wondered. All right, Emily, he said finally. Here it is. They went forward together, tottering like some half-assembled thing, and he told her what had happened at the school. He couldn't believe that he was telling her and neither could she. Even the voices held their breath and listened.

They put me in a kind of bedroom Emily. Someone else was in it. They took my clothes and my Benson & Hedges 100's and my box of colored pencils and my wallet with the picture of you inside it and they put me in a room with rubber beds. Somebody was wrapped up in a blanket. Who is that I said. They told me to shut up. Big beautiful brownskinned nurses who blew kisses at you while they kicked your ass. What kind of school is this I said. What kind of study. It's summerschool William they said. Take a look outside! I went to the window and saw high cottony clouds and yellow leaves and my own face and sailboats on the river. I saw everything I was supposed to see. I see everything I said to them. That's right sweetheart they said. We can see for miles up here we way up high. The name of this establishment means Pretty View in Spanish. Lucky boy. They blew a kiss at me and shut the door. I don't want to be up high I whispered. I don't want to see everything. I can't. But they were already gone off down the hall.

The person in the blanket never saw me. He stayed wrapped up wheezing and chewing on his lips and shouting to the nurses to let him out of bed to eat their pussies. Once a day they came into the room in twos and threes and rolled him into the next bed and wiped the rubber sheet down with a sponge. As soon as they touched him he went quiet and sat there showing off his dripping lips and sighing. He had a soft woman's body and he slept bare assed in his blanket and they dressed him in a smock and called him Baby. When they gave him a fresh blanket he'd smile and laugh at them and piss himself. And they'd smile back and take off the smock and bunch it up and wipe his body with it and go outside and shut the door behind them. Someone told me he used to be a policeman.

I tried drawing pictures of you when they let me have a pencil but by then I had forgotten how you looked. Don't laugh Emily. Reading was a problem the meds made it hard and also certain words were not as they appeared. Light for example was Girl and Kick was House but Kick was also Bed. Up was Down and Hot was Cold et cetera. The clocks were in degrees instead of hours. I told time from the ice on the East River. I wrote you a letter when they let me have paper in fact I wrote you seven in a row. Do you remember? But they told me you'd already moved away. Also they told me you were thirty eight years old.

Around that time the Temperature Games got started. I was watching the Summer Olympics. A doctor I'd never seen before took me out on a date they told me his last name was Fleisig and his first name was called End Of Days. He took me into a room Emily and taught me a lesson. The room was exactly like the TV lounge without the TV. No boardgames either. There was a table in the middle with a sort of couch built into it and he asked me respectfully to sit or lie down across it and then he put degrees into my body. I know he did Emily I could feel it and also I could see it on the clocks. First just a few but then dozens and then sixty whole degrees in Celsius. Why in Celsius Emily? It was interesting.

How have you been feeling Will? he asked me. I'm fine Doctor but right now I feel just a little hot. Well what do we have you taking now he said. Let's see. Itching powder Doctor I mean Geodon.

I see he said. And would you say that's working for you buddy? I suppose so Doctor but right now I feel very hot actually I can't breathe. Well all right then Will I'll tell you what we'll do. Hot flashes are a known side effect of Geodon but I could prescribe some Risperidone for you in addition if you'd like. Risperidone has been known to help matters though it brings with it the slight possibility of obesity which would be a shame as you are such a handsome fellow. What do you say amigo?

Who? I said. You of course said Fleisig. You are the amigo. William Henry Heller Esq. Would you like me to modify your regimen? Is that something you might like? I shut my eyes and mouth I didn't answer. Beyond that there's not much I can do he said. The whole world's getting hotter so they say. I opened my eyes and looked at him. The whole world's getting what? Nothing he said he cleared his throat he took the degrees back out he wrote me a Risperidone scrip on a creamcolored ticket. Let's see how this feels amigo mio. Then he called the nurses to come and take me but it was too late by then the miracle had already happened.

The world was in my body and my body was hidden deep inside the world. In its guts Emily. It was the most interesting thing. I could feel it getting hotter even on the coldest days the windows fogging up from the degrees. The miracle was that I could do something actually. The miracle was that I had got this calling. Baby sat up and watched it all happen he couldn't shit himself without directions but I could still get up and go down to the TV lounge. I wasn't like Baby that is to say I wasn't like him yet. Now listen up Emily I'll tell you a classified secret. The window above the toilet wasn't locked. It was too small to crawl through but there was a ledge outside and sometimes in the winter there was snow. When the feeling came on of Too Many Degrees I'd put snowballs in my hands to make it colder. Like the little steel balls they sell in Chinatown do you remember? And it did get colder Emily. This past January was The Coldest In Recent Memory I'm quoting from the New York *Daily News*.

In October someone started to call me Lowboy. A very sick man with a soft way of talking he used to make believe that he was healthy. You know what a lowboy is? he said. He never looked at me he talked in a sad fancy voice. You ever heard of one? I told him I hadn't and he nodded and made a sad face. A lowboy is a kind of a low chest of drawers he said. Often though not always with cabriole legs. A lowboy is similar to the bottom of a highboy. It is squatter and flatter however. I didn't say anything and after a while he forgot I was there and he started to spit at the nurses. When I saw him the next day I asked him why he called me Lowboy. He stopped and thought it over for a while. A lowboy is a useless thing he said. Not so a highboy.

Then one day the nurses all came in together and the bright lights came on. I pressed my face into the rubber sheets. Baby sat up and held his hands out for the smock but they walked right past him. No one smiled no one whistled. Tsk they said when they got to my bed. Tsk tsk tsk.

Where are you going! Baby said. Look at me. Look at Baby. Pus was running down his cheeks onto the blanket. No one looked. They slid me out of bed like the drawer out of a dresser and put me in my buttondown shirt and corduroys. They brushed my hair and cleaned my face for me. They tied my shoes and pinched my cheeks to make them look warmblooded. They tucked in my shirt. Goodbye Baby I said. Take care of my honeys for me. They all laughed. You not leaving us yet Will. They someone to see you. Who is it? I said. They shook their heads all together. Ask me no questions, Robert P. Redford. But me no buts.

She was sitting in the visitors' lounge with the TV on behind her. She was smoking a Newport with three yellow fingers. Alive With Pleasure. Her hair was longer than it should have been. I wondered was she visiting or staying. You need a haircut I told her. She laughed. I knew you'd say that. Sit down Will. I stared at her. Aren't you happy I came? she said. Aren't you glad to see me?

You told me this was going to be a school I said. A school Violet.

She shook her head then. You were very sick Will. Terribly sick.

You know that yourself. She smiled. But we can talk now if you want. Dr. Fleisig says you're very nearly better. I looked around the room for cameras. Dr. Fleisig says. That's right she said. I smiled back at her I gave her my best face. What do you think Violet. Do you think I'm better. I'm not a doctor Will she said. You look. Well. You look like. She stopped talking. What's that? I said. What do I look like Violet? She took her eyes away from me and turned her head. She looked down at the table. Dr. Fleisig puts degrees in me I told her. In my body. She said nothing. Why did you come here I said. She moved her hand to where the ashtray was. Half a cigarette was in it and she picked it up and smoothed it out and looked around for matches. She couldn't find a matchbook anywhere.

Can't you please sit down Will? Just for a minute? *Du hast mir so gefehlt—* Don't talk to me in that language I informed her. That language doesn't exist. Take me out of here Miss Heller you know what it's like yourself sign the papers please and write them out a check. I haven't told on you yet. I haven't. She closed her eyes then. The alternative to this is prison Will. Prison. Is that what you want? I nodded my head Yes. I was in prison once she said. Did you know that? Of course you did. I told you all about it. Do you remember any of the things I told you?

The TV changed colors behind her. I know you can hear me she said. Kindly give me an answer. I remember what you were in prison for I said. I remember that Mom. Do you want me to tell them? She was watching me now. She pushed her lips together. I don't think you want to do that Will she said. If you do that they might not let you come home.

I'll tell you something Violet I shouted. Go get fucked. You put me in here. You signed all the papers. Skull & Bones told me that and I saw it in a movie in the lounge. Go to hell Violet. No don't cry. Your face is falling off did you know that? Your face is falling off Miss Heller. My father is coming to see me tomorrow not some rotten-faced bitch and we're going to watch the Underwater Movies. Not you Miss Heller you aren't invited. You're drying up. I never came out of you your face is coming off your bones your body and your spirit are diseased. You disgust me Miss Heller. You're a dried out crust of a something you're a museum exhibit you're a dead Egyptian mummy of a cat. Your guts are buried somewhere in a jar. I can't have you here I can't look at you kindly get out of this room. Don't say that to me Will she said. Don't say that. Thanks for coming Violet I shouted. Don't worry about me I have got ideas. Good luck to you Miss Heller. I pray to God every day that you'll get well.

Not long after that the flat time started. It got hotter and hotter I couldn't sit up I couldn't get my body out of bed. Every day the world got flatter like a pancake or a candle on the dashboard of a car. Everything in the world was made of paper. I woke up one night with paper in my mouth and paper stretched across the room and light blue paper on me like a dress. The nurses came in I looked at them I pointed with my finger at my mouth. That's not paper sweetheart they said to me that's medicine. You eat it. I pointed at Baby's bed they said That's not paper Will that's a divider for reasons of privacy. Don't you like privacy? Baby was dying but they didn't tell me that. I pointed at my dress they said That's paper all right sucker that's a bright blue disposable paper smock.

That's how I found out what was going to happen next. I was going to be the new Baby. I liked the old Baby all right but that morning I got elected because the incumbent was deceased and I lay down comfortably in his bed. I knew how to be Baby I'd had most of the year to practice. Are you listening Emily?

Are you there?

Say something Emily. Say the next thing I say. You had to be the new Baby Will that's just terrible. That's terrible Will I love you very much.

After that the school spread out flatter and wider it was probably the widest thing on earth. The ceiling came and brushed against my face it wasn't painful but it was difficult to watch. Things kept on moving. The nurses for example. But how did they keep from sliding into each other Emily how did they keep from tearing themselves up. I had creases in my body I was afraid to touch water my stomach was full of confetti. People TVs gurneys sliding around like microbes in a dish. The big white microscope with the big blue eye behind it. Are you still listening Emily I saw one doctor Dr. Dickworth they called him or was that a joke he was ripped across the middle like a postcard. Dr. Cocksnot I said to him if you're looking for your bottom half it went under the bed. No I prefer not to accept my meds at this time there's no room in my neck and my stomach is full of confetti. I mean to say Yes thank you very much for these delicious caplets. Indebted you Dr. Franks & Beans may I please have another. Paper pills paper medledgers paper scrips. My bed like an envelope with a letter inside it a love letter sprinkled lightly with perfume. Eau de Bedpan someone called it. I could have mailed myself to you Emily but you'd have returned me to sender. No? If no then another question did you read the letter carefully did you give it your complete attention Emily did you understand it. Have you noticed about the tunnel it's a funny thing it's the one and the only The Tunnel Of Love. Did you understand my letter Emily are you listening at all. I hear you listening I hear you breathing I don't have to ask are you flat or dried up or alive. I'm in love Emily! Could you help me a little. Could you help me by taking your clothes off and spreading your legs.

'm sorry I did that," said Violet. They'd been riding in silence for a half-dozen blocks and she couldn't have stood it for an instant longer. If he'd been angry at her she'd have minded it less: he'd been angry before. But there was nothing resentful or sullen about his reluctance to look at her or to speak. He's frightened of me, she thought with a kind of sick wonder. He's asking himself what I might do next. She put her hand on his shoulder and apologized again.

"I'm sorry, Detective. I really thought those two girls—"

"No need to say anything, Miss Heller." The gentleness in his voice surprised her. "I wish you'd stood back when you spotted them and let me do my job, but you were excited. I can understand that."

She watched him for a time before she spoke. "I wasn't sure you'd catch them. You seemed hurt."

"You're right. I wasn't steady on my feet." A car pulled out in front of them and he tapped the brake. "Not to mention that I'd lost them once already."

She didn't know what to say to that so she kept quiet. The sick feeling was gradually receding. He hadn't looked at her yet but that would come.

"How are you feeling now, Detective? Any better?"

"Much better, Miss Heller. Thanks for asking."

"You're sure about that? You won't pass out and drive us off a pier?"

He smiled. "Not on your life. I love this car too much."

"And you're not angry with me?"

"I'm driving you to your apartment, aren't I?"

She blushed at that but he was looking past her. "Maybe you shouldn't, Detective. Maybe you should keep on—"

"I've got people in the stations, I've put the traffic police on notice, I've got a bulletin out with both of the children's descriptions. There's not much else I can do, to be honest, until the next sighting comes in." He smiled again, this time seemingly to himself. "Believe it or not, driving around aimlessly takes up a lot of my day."

"Driving hysterical mothers around aimlessly, you mean."

"You're not hysterical, Miss Heller." He squinted calmly at the car in front of them. "Not anymore, at least. And we're not driving around aimlessly. I'm taking you home."

The rush of gratitude she felt was so strong that she was tempted to take his hand from the wheel and kiss it. I have to do something, she thought, breathing in stutters like a twelve-year-old girl. I have to do something with this feeling.

"There's something else," she said before she could stop herself. "It's about Will."

He looked at her now. "What is it?"

She fussed with her seatbelt to buy herself time. "I didn't tell you earlier because I didn't think—" She hesitated. "I didn't think you'd try to understand me."

She felt the car lose momentum as he watched her. "I'm trying to understand you now, Miss Heller."

It took her most of the next block to decide where to start. "Now

that Will's with Emily—now that she's run off with him, I mean—
I want to tell you about his ideas on the subject."

The car slowed even further. "What subject is that?"

Already she found that she could barely answer. "The subject of
girls."

"Of sex, you mean."

"I'm not so sure that you could call it that." She cleared her
throat. "Will never cared about girls—not the way most boys do. Not
as far as I could tell. He didn't seem to think of them as different."
Why am I so inarticulate, she thought. Why am I so prudish.

"Different how?" said Lateef.

"He could see the differences between people, like any other
child—he could see that you and I aren't alike, for example—" She
hesitated again, afraid to give offense, but Lateef only nodded. "He
could see that much, but he didn't seem to be able to put people into
groups. He just saw the people themselves, I mean. The individual
people. Does that make any sense?"

"I suppose so," Lateef said. He sounded uncertain.

"Alex and I didn't give it much thought when Will was small, of
course, but by the time he'd turned eleven or twelve we'd started to
worry. I've always known that I kept Will too close, that I was too
greedy, and I've been told that does things to a boy." She gave a sharp
laugh. "Richard said so, for one. 'You're turning that boy into a fag-
got, Yda.' He loved to say that. So when Will brought Emily home—an
actual girl, and pretty in a tomboyish sort of way—all I felt was relief."

"It must have surprised you a little," said Lateef. "That the girl
took an interest, I mean."

"It didn't surprise me at all. Girls have always liked Will." She
stopped herself then, knowing how she must sound, and waited for
her defensiveness to ebb. "It was his indifference," she said finally.
"Girls never made him nervous, because there was nothing that
he wanted from them yet. They mistook that for confidence." She
shrugged. "Maybe it was, of a kind. Will always did exactly what he
wanted."

"What sort of things did he do?"

You wanted to tell it, thought Violet. So tell it. But she found her-self talking in euphemisms and half-truths, filtering and dissem-bling, if for no other reason than from force of habit.

"I went through a bad time after Alex died, and Will had to stay somewhere else for a few months. Richard's was the obvious place, but the two of them had just had one of their fights: Richard could be difficult, as I've said. I asked Will if he'd be okay at Richard's house, if they'd get along, and he nodded in a bored sort of way and told me they'd get along fine. He was going to pretend he was a cat."

Lateef frowned at her. "What does that mean, exactly?"

"I asked him the same thing. He just rolled his eyes at me and said 'Meow.'" She shrugged. "A few months later, the next time I saw Richard, he told me Will had kept it up for three whole weeks."

Lateef took in a breath but didn't speak. For a brief moment she thought he might start laughing. "Is that what you wanted to tell me?"

You know it isn't, Violet thought. But his disingenuousness no longer bothered her. It was a marker for her, a sure sign of his inter-est, and as long as she held his interest she was safe.

"A few months before Will brought Emily home, I'd had quite a shock: for the first and only time, I found a girlie magazine—one of the more harmless ones, I think it might have been a *Playboy*—lying open on the floor next to his bed. I laughed out loud when I saw it. This ought to shut Richard's mouth, I thought. I picked it up—a lit-tle guiltily, I remember—and flipped it open more or less at random. That's when I had my second shock. Parts of the girls had been cut out, very carefully and neatly. Not the parts you'd expect: it was the arms and legs mostly, sometimes the head. I found out later that Will was gluing them onto the comics he was making, onto the super-heroes' bodies, because as he got sicker he was losing his ability to draw."

She glanced at Lateef, trying to read his expression, but he was staring fixedly out at the street. It doesn't matter what he's thinking, she said to herself. It's too late for me not to tell the rest.

"When Will came home I asked about the pictures. We were sitting on his bed, I remember, and the magazine was lying open between us. He didn't seem the slightest bit embarrassed. He started to tell me about his day at school—what he'd eaten for lunch, the train ride home, that sort of thing—and turning the pages of the magazine while he talked, as though it was one of my *National Geographic*s. I just sat there on the bed and listened to him. I'd felt more and more helpless since that night in Richard's living room: sometimes Will would be fine, the same as he'd always been, and the rest of the time he'd be impossible. It never seemed to matter what I did. Will's illness had made me obsolete." Lateef was shaking his head at her but she ignored him. "I found myself wishing that Alex was there, something I never wished for anymore. Alex would know what to ask him, I said to myself. I sat there looking at the side of Will's face, still so delicate and babyish, trying to make sense of it somehow—to interpret it, I suppose." She rolled down the window and let the wind hit her. "But really there was nothing to interpret. Just my thirteen-year-old son, chattering on about his day, flipping casually through a cut-up *Playboy*. I'd already made up my mind that it had no special meaning for him—that it was a magazine like any other—when he turned to a page that was different from the rest. He'd ripped it out and done things to it and slid it back into place very precisely. He stopped talking about his day and stared down at it with a—" She thought for a moment. "With a sly sort of smile on his face, the way any teenager would look at a dirty photograph. 'What's that a picture of, Will?' I asked, feeling ridiculous as I said it. Then he laughed and held it up for me to see."

When she kept quiet for a time Lateef shifted in his seat and fiddled discreetly with the rearview mirror. How patient he's gotten, she found herself thinking. Just like I was with Will. He must not know how to act around me either.

"The picture took up a full page—it was the centerfold, I guess, or something like it—but the things Will had done made it hard to decipher. A woman was coming out of the water, I think. She might have been at the beach. Will had taken a Magic Marker and blackened the water, if that's what it was, and filled in the sky with what looked like hundreds of tiny rings or bubbles, though I found out later that they were degrees."

"Degrees?" said Lateef.

"The symbol for a degree. The temperature symbol."

He pursed his lips but said nothing.

"It was the only photograph in the magazine that Will hadn't taken things from—hadn't used for his comics, I mean—but he'd cut into it everywhere. He must have gotten hold of a razor, though I was careful not to have one in the house: I even kept the breadknife locked away. The face was just a ball of cuts—deep, heavy gouges— spreading out from the middle like an asterisk." She closed her eyes. "He'd made it into a kind of opening. At least that's how it looked to me. There wasn't any face left."

Again Lateef made as if to ask a question but kept quiet.

"He gave the picture to me so that I could see it better. Wavy lines were coming out of the opening like spokes, or like the light behind a saint's head in a painting. It reminded me of portraits of the pope I'd seen when I was a girl." She paused again, trying to remember exactly. "Her chest and her stomach were covered in a kind of black mesh."

Lateef coughed into his hand. "What about the girl's genitals, Miss Heller? Had he cut those away?"

"He hadn't cut anything away. He'd taken a cutout from some other page—a hand with bright blue fingernails—and pasted it over that part of her. That was the most horrible thing about the picture, at least to me. The hand wasn't covering her sex so much as growing out of it. When I asked him what it was his face went blank. 'That's the problem, Violet,' he said. I asked what he meant but he just shook his head. I began to feel dizzy. I was frantic to say something else, I remember, something to keep him from seeing my disgust. 'What's that, then?' I said, pointing at the cut-apart face. That made him laugh. He rocked back and forth on the bed and hummed and nodded to himself, the way he'd done on that first terrible night at Richard's. 'Oh, *that*, Violet,' he said, and laughed again. 'I can tell you that. That's the solution.'"

When she stopped for a moment to compose herself she could see that he thought she was finished. There was more to tell of course but it could wait.

"Why didn't you mention this to me before, Miss Heller?"

"I'm mentioning it now," she said. "Because of Emily."

While she'd been telling the story they'd arrived at her building and now they sat idling in front of it. The sight of its blandly lit foyer depressed her beyond words. When Lateef finally spoke she received it like a stay of execution.

"There's something I don't understand," he said after a long spell of quiet. "Why would Emily have run away with your son a second time? What could she possibly want from him?"

She considered the question, still staring into the foyer, and decided that she didn't want to answer it. "She's in love with him, Detective. Isn't that enough?"

His smile was so regretful that it shamed her. "You know it's not, Miss Heller."

She nodded at that and closed her eyes and shivered. She dreaded being asked to leave the car. The thought of climbing the stairs to her lightless apartment and waiting there meekly for news brought a sob out of her that she had no way of suppressing. It rang out in the cramped car like a gunshot. Lateef sat up at once and took her arm.

"What is it, Miss Heller? Should we get you upstairs?"

"I have something else to tell you," she managed to answer. "Something else about Will."

He sat back wordlessly and waited. Give him what he wants, she told herself. Don't test his patience.

"A week or so before what happened at Union Square, I came home from work and sat down at the kitchen table, trying to get interested in making dinner. I heard Will and Emily in the other room, but that didn't surprise me: she was eating most of her dinners at our house by then. It got quiet for a while—quiet enough that I noticed—and then Emily came out alone. 'I'd like to ask you a question, Yda,' she said. There was something different about her, something formal. I smiled at her and asked her to sit down. I already knew it would be about Will—what else did we have to talk about?—but I couldn't have predicted what came next. I was about to say something else, maybe ask what she wanted for dinner, when she made a sort of face and said, 'Why won't he touch me?' She said it louder than she'd meant to, I think, because afterwards she pressed her lips together. When I didn't answer she said it again, more quietly this time, still standing in the middle of the kitchen. I had no idea what to say to her, as usual: I must have mumbled some cliché or other. 'He thinks I'm beautiful,' she said. She said it as though she was daring me to doubt it. 'He *told* me that.'"

Lateef tapped his fingers restlessly against the wheel. "Go on," he said, not looking at her. He thinks he knows what's coming, Violet thought.

"I looked at Emily for a while, trying to see her the way Will saw her, and for once it actually seemed as if I could. I felt sympathy for her then, genuine sympathy and fondness, for the first time since the day Will brought her home. 'Emily,' I said. 'You understand that Will is special, don't you?' I actually used that word—that stupid, hateful, patronizing word. 'I know he's in pain,' she said quietly. 'That's what I mean,' I told her. 'That's what I mean exactly.' We sat there looking at each other for I don't know how long, neither of us saying a word. What a remarkable girl, I thought. So articulate and thoughtful. She could easily pass for someone twice her age."

She stopped very briefly, watching as a taxi rattled past. But she began again before Lateef could prompt her.

"I was wrong about that, of course. Emily was a teenager in spite of everything, a fifteen-year-old girl, as self-obsessed as anyone at that age. 'I know how hard it is for him,' she said. 'How hard it is to even talk.' I nodded at her, still happy just to look at her and listen. But the next thing she told me undid everything."

"What was it?"

"She said that Will had told her that he loved her. She said that it had to be true because of who he was. 'I read a book about schizophrenia,' she said, as if letting me in on a secret. 'Schizophrenics never lie, you know, Yda. They *can't.*'"

She turned her head to gauge Lateef's reaction. She was afraid that he'd have no response at all, that he'd fail to understand, that her solitude would become absolute. She wondered what would happen if it did.

"That's not been my experience," he said finally. "Everybody lies."

She nearly laughed with relief. "I hope you're not including me, Detective."

"Let's get you upstairs," he murmured, opening his door. His face looked small and blank.

She stayed where she was. "Emily said one more thing that day but I ignored it. I was too upset by then to think it through."

"What was it?" said Lateef. His left foot was already on the curb.

She took in a breath. There was nothing else now. "Will called her his favorite problem."

When he'd told Emily everything she looked at him and laughed. "Why are you looking at me like that?" she said. "Was I supposed to recognize the tune?"

"Tune?" he said, forcing the word out of his mouth. His voice sounded wet.

She nodded and laughed again and squeezed his hand. He'd told her everything and she hadn't heard a word. He took a breath and tried to start from the beginning but he didn't know where the beginning was. He couldn't think of it. Violet was at the beginning but Violet didn't matter to him now. Neither did Dr. Fleisig. Neither did the school. He tried his best to have a single thought. He closed his mouth and pushed his teeth together. The beginning had actually happened just that morning. Nothing else had any consequence or weight. On November 11 he had run to catch a train.

He was just starting to think as they stepped out of the tunnel, starting to get his thoughts together, but he stopped thinking right away and so did she. They had no choice but to stop. They stood side by side on the platform like petitioners, both their mouths hanging open, staring up at the glittering vaultwork. No earthly sound impinged on them. The air in their throats was the air of a forgotten age. They were deep beneath the city, almost too deep to breathe, yet by chance or fate a bloodless light still reached them. Her right shoulder dug into his left.

"Have you been here before, Heller?"

"Not ever."

She swore under her breath. "How come they closed it off? Do you know why?"

"Too beautiful." His voice was steady again. "Too secret." He watched the words curl up into the dark.

She took a few steps forward and stretched her arm out toward the terracotta. "I can't touch anything," she said. "I don't belong here."

"You belong here, Emily. I brought you here."

The fact of it didn't seem to reassure her. She shrugged and took another few steps along the wall, not quite touching it with her fingers, keeping as far from the tracks as the platform allowed. Lowboy stayed where he was. He would move toward her soon but not yet. He had to know if they had an understanding. It was important that she understood the reason for what was going to happen next.

"I was talking to you in the tunnel, Emily. I was trying to tell you something."

"What was it?" she said. She was running her left hand along the tiles.

"Slow down a minute. Are you listening? I was—"

"I don't want to talk anymore. Look around you, Heller! Look at this place!"

She leaned as far back as she could without falling and laughed up at the ceiling and shook her head in unabashed delight. She was different now, less beholden to him, less sincere. He barely knew her. Something had gotten misplaced in the tunnel. Some small necessary thing had been removed.

"We should stay down here forever, Heller. We should build ourselves a house." She caught her breath. "I feel like I'm seven years old."

"You're seventeen, Emily." He studied her closely. "You're half a year older than me."

"I know that," she said, rolling her eyes. "But with you I can be seven if I want."

"Why is that?"

She spun back to him and kissed him on the cheek. "Because you're William Heller," she said. "Because *you* know why."

"Why?" he said. But he already knew. "Because I'm sick?"

She squeezed his hand and spun away again. A small doubt flared up briefly and expired. No doubt could have endured in that sepulchral air. In place of his doubts was one solitary truth, no more and no less. But lesser truths than that had saved men's lives.

"We could make a fire out of these old benches, couldn't we? We'd just always keep it going." She giggled. "What did you say subway rats are called?"

"Track rabbits."

She chewed on her thumb. "I wonder if they taste like pork or chicken."

A song came to him as he watched her, a ballad his father had sung on half-remembered evenings. His beautiful pitiful ghost of a father. He began to hum it quietly and the melody beat back at him from the tooled and lacquered tilework as though his father himself were singing it in a bedroom on the far side of the world. I asked my love to take a walk. Just a little ways with me.

"I recognize that one," said Emily. "What's it called?"

Seven arches led to a Moorish staircase, seven led away. The glazed florets as pale as palmprints. The platform as symmetrical as the moon. Three times three skylights set with amethyst glass. Tiles green as tidewater, yellow as teeth. The number of steps and arches reckoned solemnly by mystics. Seven for Christ Jesus, three for the Trinity. Sixteen for the newest child martyr. Lowboy opened his eyes wide and stretched his arms up to the ceiling in hosanna. The platform had been expecting him since October of 1904.

"What are you laughing about?" said Emily. "What are you thinking?"

"You'll find out," said Lowboy.

She shut her mouth then. She stopped what she was doing and sucked in a breath.

"It's funny to be here, that's all." He lowered his arms and sighed. "It's been a very long time."

"You said you'd never been here before." She was at the staircase now, fidgeting with her collar, looking down at him as if from a great height. "Were you lying?" The look on her face was one he'd seen before.

"Come over here Emily. Don't go away."

"You're scaring me, Heller. Stop smiling like that."

"I can't stop." His smiled widened. "Come on down here and give me a kiss."

A sound came out of her then as she clutched at the railing. It reminded him of the mewling of a cat. "I don't like this," she said.

"That doesn't matter," said Lowboy. He was moving again. "It's not for me Emily. It's for everyone else."

"Heller—" she said, then covered her eyes with her hand. She was watching him through the cracks between her fingers. "Stay where you are for one second. Could you do that, please, Heller? I don't think I can—"

"Emily," he said. He was at the steps now. "It's getting hotter Emily. You can't deny that." His left hand closed playfully around the railing. "If you tried to deny it something bad would happen."

The mewling came again but nothing else. He said her name softly to see if she answered but she gave no sign at all. Had it happened again had his voice been disabled. What about her, he thought. What about Emily. Could she have done it.

He looked up and showed her his Will Heller face.

"I'm sorry to do this," somebody was saying. He was saying it himself. "I don't want to upset you. I'm upsetting you Emily. I can see it. I'm sorry to do this." He took a deep breath. "The truth is that I feel a little sick."

Nothing happened then. The Musaquontas whispered underneath them. Finally she nodded and coughed into her hand. "I know that, Heller. I got freaked out, that's all. Just please try not to—"

"I want to tell you something Emily. A human interest story. I read it or I saw it on the news."

She was on the third step by the time he'd finished. The third step already. He blinked his eyes and she was on the fourth. "Stop staring at me like that, Heller. You look like somebody else. You look like you want to—"

"Do you know the Great Lakes Emily? In the Great Lakes there's a problem with the fish." He looked at her. "The fish are extincting, all right? No more babies."

"Heller," she whined. "If you don't stop right now—"

"Shut your mouth Emily. Scientists came and found one kind of fish it might have been a perch. Do you know what a perch is?" He blinked at her. "A small fish and greenish. Not pretty."

She nodded at him from the fifth step. How many steps in all was it eleven. Was she trembling now. Was she crying. Black hair flat across her face like tinted glass.

"There was a problem with the perches Emily. There were less and less new perches every day." He caught his breath and tried to talk more slowly. "Were they dying out, though? Science said not exactly." He took two steps to her one. "No fucking Emily. That was the problem. Something wrong with the water." He clapped his hands and made his courtroom face. "I'm going to ask you to guess what that thing was. Are you listening to me? What do you think it was?"

She brought her left hand up beside her right. He kept as still as a dead perch and waited. He could hardly bear to keep still but he did.

"Was it too warm?" she said finally. "Too warm in the water?" The words came out badly. She sounded like someone from Austria.

"That's what the *scientists* thought!" He reached for her hand and caught it. "But something else was in it. Something funny."

She moaned and pulled her hand out of his grip.

"*Meds* Emily. There were meds in the water. Everyone pissing them into the toilets. The toilets go into the water Emily. The water goes into the fishes. There was one med called Traminex it made everyone happy. But it has a side effect Emily can you hear me?"

She nodded and pressed herself against the brickwork.

"Same as Zyprexa Emily. Same as Depakote." He winked at her slyly. "No fucking."

He pulled her shirt up and bent over to kiss her belly and she kicked away from him and up the steps. His hand was on the step behind her and it tore under her heel like toilet paper. Have I gone flat again he wondered. Is it the flat time now. She'd stopped three steps above him and he lunged to catch her ankle but when he tried to lift his head he could not do it.

"You tore my fingers Emily. You fucked them."

Take me back Heller please take me back there I want to go out.

"Out," he said blankly. "What kind of word is that." He folded his hand like a letter and tried to get up. His head spun and dipped and his arm vanished up to the elbow. See Emily, he told himself. He saw her. She came and sat down on the step above him. He said something to her and she answered him but there was nothing in it. There's nothing in it Emily he said. She shook her head and told him something else.

"You should still be where they sent you, Heller. I wish you were still there. I wish they'd never let you out."

He nodded at that and coughed and got up carefully. She slid away from him and pulled herself up and shivered uselessly against the railing. The blackness pulsed behind her like a searchlight. She seemed to want to keep going upstairs.

"Lift your hair up Emily," he said. "Come down here and sit. Take off your shirt."

Her body gave a jerk but nothing happened. She was talking to

herself now or to him or to some hidden other. "Stop crying Emily."
His father's song was playing somewhere sweetly. "Banks of the Ohio"
it was called. She was climbing or staggering up the last steps. There
was nothing behind her but gray sweating tilework and light. He
pointed his good arm at her like a rifle or some other deadly thing.

"Pull your hair back Emily I can't see you."

She turned and ran into the bellshaped stillness. Past a lightbox
and tripod burnt out since 1987. A light at each corner and a switch
in the middle it looked like a badly drawn robot. Emily did the Robot,
he reminded himself. She did it and she kissed me on the mouth.
How is that possible. Past the robot and up to a room like a chapel.
A dome toward which the keening darkness tended. A wooden
booth to one side like a Victorian commode. She was crouching in
the corner with her arms around her knees.

"You're frightened Emily." He slid his arms out of his sleeves.

"Don't come closer to me. Please Heller don't come closer."

"Sit on this," he told her. "Put this under your legs."

He threw his shirt down to her but she shrank back from it as
though it meant her harm. Something was different now he wondered what it was. Had he made some transgression. Had he made
some minor error or had she. When he closed his eyes he was alone
in the station but when he opened them he was less alone than ever.
She was rocking forward and backward on her heels and hissing
empty words at him and sobbing. Had there been a kiss behind the
yellow curtain? Had she given him clothes and food and cigarettes?
He looked at her. The halflight sent her features out of plumb. He
took a small step toward her and undid the top flybutton of his jeans.

"Lie down Emily," he said. "Put your feet apart."

She stared past him and did as she was told. The shirt still lay un-
touched at her right heel. Her eyes had gone soft. He looked down at
her and remembered the magazine he'd found in the briefcase and
compared what he saw with the pictures he remembered. She was
nothing like those women with their sunburned skin and makeup
but something in her face was just the same.

"What's the matter?" he asked her. "Do you need a doctor?" He frowned and slid his jeans down to his knees.

She sat up at once without saying a word and raked a copper key across his chest. She held the key sideways between her clenched fingers and clawed downward with it like a panicked kitten. He laughed at the thought and began falling backward but at the same time he knew that he was cut across the middle and that she was on her feet and running for the platform. Emily he called out but he couldn't even hear the words himself. His clothes were heaped against the concrete and his pants were bunched up like a shitting baby's. Blood was dripping onto them like water from a tap. He got up and called her name again and dropped back to his knees. The air and tiles and cracked rosettes exulted in his pain. She was running in frantic circles at the bottom of the stairs. Her footfalls resounded off the chandeliers and the vaultwork and the bowed walls of that glittering pitiless temple. She was searching for a piece of glass to push into his eyes.

I n no way was the apartment what Lateef had expected. It was long and pitched and nearly lightless, as hushed and airless as an attic, and its walls were painted a dusty Christmas red. No sound carried in from the street or the other apartments. She asked him in a cautious voice to take off his shoes, as if someone inside were asleep, and he obeyed at once. The separateness of the place was overwhelming. An opium den came to mind, and also a bordello, but no bordello was ever so intimate or so still. The redness and the airlessness and the glow of the black lacquered furniture combined to relieve him of his last sense of purpose. The walls were hung with pictures torn from magazines and books: a greenhouse, an obelisk, a naked arm, a railway tunnel somewhere in the tropics. Yellowed newsprint photographs in cheap unbeveled frames. He drifted from room to room in his unmatched socks, hands clasped behind him like an art collector or a suitor or anyone else out of his depth, waiting to have his role explained to him. The sadness of the rooms was unmistakable, as tangible as the pillows and the scraps of paper littering the floor. It was impossible to imagine them ever containing a child.

"How long have you been here?" Lateef said at last. She was making Turkish coffee in the kitchen. "Did you live here with Will?"

"I've been here for seventeen years, if you can believe it." Her voice lilted slightly, as though she were teasing him. "I could never afford this place now. Do you want milk?"

"Please. And sugar."

He heard what might have been a laugh. "I thought New York's Proudest always drank it black."

"New York's Finest, Miss Heller. We're not necessarily that proud."

She laughed again. "I don't believe that for a minute."

He stood by himself in the living room and listened to the clatter of saucers and cups, everyday domestic noises, exotic as birdsong in that halflight. She hummed to herself contentedly, disregarding him the way a woman can who has you at her mercy. But how can she know that, Lateef asked himself. How can she be contented. The memory of the schoolgirls in their tartan uniforms returned to him, and of Violet in the middle of them, stoop-shouldered and bleeding, whispering to him to take her home. An answer came to him a moment later: She can feel contented now because I've failed. The burden of uncertainty is lifted. She no longer expects a single thing from me.

It was obvious enough, listening to her in the kitchen, that she'd driven the past half hour from her mind. Never had he been more aware of the disadvantage her foreignness put him at than at that moment, waiting in her cave of an apartment for a cup of coffee he felt no desire for. If not for her foreignness he might have gotten her talking, have complimented the coffee or her self-control or her taste in furniture, confident that he was circling her secret. He'd have been certain, at least, that there remained a secret to find. But if the past three hours had educated him on any point it was that her character refused to hold still, refused to fall into a pattern, not out of resentment or contrariness but for some reason as yet unknown to him. There was nothing disingenuous about her, nothing studied, and that in and of itself was baffling. There might be nothing more to her than what he'd seen.

"Here you are, Detective. Strong and sweet. If you're not used to Turkish coffee it might knock you for a spin."

"For a loop, you mean," he managed to reply. She was standing in the doorway with a tiny cup on an enamel tray, smiling at him in a way that he was completely unprepared for. He took the cup from her hurriedly and drank.

"Watch out," she said, balancing the tray on the tips of her fingers like a waitress. "It's hot."

"It's delicious." He took another sip, then another. "Jesus Christ."

"It is good, isn't it. The Turks laid siege to Vienna for almost a year; we learned how to make coffee from them." She set the tray down and ran a finger absentmindedly through her hair. "I'm not so sure what they got out of it."

"You should try to get some sleep," Lateef said sometime later. They were sitting together on a shapeless rattan couch, cradling their cups with both hands like children at a birthday party. "This might end up being a long night."

"Who needs sleep, Detective? We've got Turkish coffee. Let's talk instead. Ask me a question."

"All right, Miss Heller." He considered her for a moment. "Why did you leave Vienna?"

Her smile tightened slightly. "Why do you think, Detective? I fell in love."

"With Will's father?"

She'd been sitting up attentively, a lady-in-waiting, but now she let herself sink back into the cushions. In the light from the Chinese lamp she could have passed for seventeen. "Will's father was a musician, Detective. A vibraphone player. I'm not sure if I told you that."

"You didn't." He sat with his cup balanced on his right knee, looking at her over his shoulder. For some reason he couldn't manage to recline.

"Well, he was. Jazz might be second to polka as the deadest music in America—"

"Jazz isn't dead music."

She brought a hand up to her mouth. "I think you've just revealed your age to me, Detective."

"Please go on."

She sighed. "Alive or dead, in Vienna in the eighties it was an exciting thing to us." He felt the couch move under him as she shifted her weight. "To some of us, at least. Compared to Johann Strauss, Miles Davis still seemed relatively young."

He laughed at that. "How did you meet Will's father?"

"I met Alex while I was still at the university. I was working three nights a week at a jazz club called Porgy and Bess. My English was good, and I knew a few things about jazz, so I usually made lots of money. And I had a soft point for American players."

He cleared his throat primly. "*Spot*, I think you mean. A soft spot."

"You like to correct me, don't you."

He avoided her look. "Heller was your husband's name?"

"We weren't married, Detective. I thought you knew that."

"You'd be amazed by all the things I don't know, Miss Heller. Especially today. I apologize if—"

"No need for that, Detective. We were unmarried by choice." She shrugged. "His name was Alexander Whitham."

Lateef couldn't help but give a start. "I know Alex Whitham," he said.

She seemed unsurprised. "Is that right?"

"Of course. He played with Ornette Coleman for a while."

"Now you've definitely shown your age."

He set the cup down carefully, turning its handle toward him, giving himself time to find a place for this new fact in his conception of her. Everyone knew Alex Whitham. One of the greats without question. He might have doubted the story if not for her beauty and for the small indifferent voice she used to tell it.

"You met Mr. Whitham at the club where you worked?"

She took in a slow breath and nodded. "I'll never forget the first time I saw Alex. He was the only white player on a bill full of legends—Ornette, Anthony Braxton, Ed Blackwell, Don Cherry—and he dressed to the nines to make up for it. The boys used to call him Vanilla the Pimp." She smiled to herself. "He walked into the club wearing a three-piece madras suit and silver sneakers. I thought he was the bestdressed man I'd ever seen." She slid her hand between the cushions and brought out a flattened pack of cigarettes. "A year and a half later I moved into this apartment."

He hesitated. "You moved in alone?"

"Sometimes Alex lived here." She found a lighter, tested it, lit a cigarette with it, and set it aside. "Sometimes not."

"Why the wait? Did you need time to finish your studies?"

The cigarette hissed. "I never finished my studies, Detective."

"I'm sorry to hear that."

She nodded. "I was studying to be a neurochemist."

The irony was too self-evident to acknowledge. "Couldn't you have gone to school here?" he said finally. "Transferred your credits, done your exams over, that sort of thing?"

"I did that, actually. My parents had some money put aside—retirement money, not very much—and they sent it over as a kind of punishment. I was in the graduate program at Rockefeller for almost seven months."

"What happened then?"

"What you see is what you get, Detective. I paint eyes and lips on mannequins for stores that I could never afford to shop in. Apparently I've got a talent for it."

"I hope you don't mind my saying—"

"Drink your coffee, please. It's no good cold."

He took an obedient sip. "I'm sorry for prying, Miss Heller. It's a habit with me when I'm working." He replaced the cup on its chipped and mismatched saucer. "Even when I'm not, to tell the truth. I'm not so good at regular conversation."

"Why the formality, Detective? A few minutes ago you were calling me Violet. Do we have to start again from the beginning?"

He finished the coffee and passed her his cup and through a great effort of will managed to meet her gaze and hold it. She regarded him steadily, without the least trace of amusement, bracing both her hands against the cushions. He tried and failed to guess at her intention. The directness of her stare was a thing he'd seen only in men about to assault him or in women who expected to be kissed. How laughable, he thought. How pathetic. I can't seem to think of any other reason.

"I thought I might have been presuming," he said finally, mortified by the thickness in his voice.

"You remind me of Elvin Jones," she said, refilling his cup. "Both of you seem too gentle for the kind of work you do. You ought to have been professors of something." She smiled and let her left arm brush his side. "Philosophy, maybe, or ethnomusicology. Something gentlemanly."

He returned her smile weakly. "It's not every day I get compared to a jazz virtuoso."

She said nothing to that.

"Why did you invite me here, Miss Heller?"

"I didn't invite you here, Detective. I asked you to drive me home in your little soybean-eating car." She seemed less fond of him suddenly. "I wanted to take a pill to calm me down, since you ask. That and maybe fix myself a drink."

That accounts for the change in her, he thought. That explains all of this. "I didn't notice you taking anything," he said, keeping his voice as dispassionate as he could. "Did you do it under cover of making me coffee?"

"I made *coffee* under cover of making you coffee, Detective." She closed her eyes. "I haven't taken my pick-me-up. Not yet."

"What were you thinking of taking?"

She fell back with a sigh and held out her crossed wrists. "Goofballs, Detective. Ya-ya pills. Lock me up and throw away the key."

He laughed in spite of himself. "You've spent too much time in jazz clubs, Miss Heller. What the hell are ya-ya pills?"

"Want to split one with me and find out?"

He watched her a moment. "Mind if I take a look at the bottle?"

"I'd have to see a warrant first, Detective."

"I'm not going to arrest you, Miss Heller. If you'd rather—"

"I'd rather show you this." She rose from the couch and glided with perfect economy of movement across the narrow room and out of sight. A moment later she was back beside him, hands tucked girlishly beneath her, watching him leaf through a battered photo album. Her breath drew past his right ear, unnaturally cool and even, as though he'd put his head to a screen door. She smelled of unwashed hair and cigarettes.

"I don't know what kind of picture of Will you have in that folder of yours, but if it came from the *Post*—"

"Is this your son here?"

"Of course."

An overexposed snapshot of a garden. A boy with his feet planted squarely in the center of the frame, his hair almost colorless, his arms held out like someone caught without a handhold on a train. Four or five at the most. Some quality or detail of the picture was remarkable but it took Lateef a moment to discover what it was, perhaps because it was the last thing he expected. The look on the boy's face was intelligent, of course—even confident—but it was more than that. It was knowing.

"You see it too," she said quietly. "Don't you see it?"

Lateef nodded.

"We were frightened even then, I think. It wasn't just the way he looked. He moved differently from the other kids, talked differently. It was Alex who decided we should take it as some kind of mark of genius." She sat back lightly on the couch. "Now I feel as though we both knew what was coming."

"It always seems that way, thinking back on things."

"Does it?"

"I don't see what either of you could have done differently."

"You see what I mean, Detective? You're much too generous for your line of work."

He was still staring down at the picture, still trying to see it as no more than a snapshot, trying to bring it into clearer focus. It took him another few seconds to notice the girl in the background. She was older than the boy, already into her teens, but aside from that she might have been his twin. The boy was too young to be beautiful yet but the girl was no less than a vision. She hovered in the upper lefthand corner of the picture, blurred along her left side, as if caught in the act of escaping from the frame. He found himself hesitating to ask about her for fear of the change in his voice.

"Who's that in the corner?"

"Who do you think, Detective?"

Of course it was her. Of course it was. Now at last she'd disarmed him completely. He turned and looked at her but she was too close to focus on, blurred about the edges, exactly like the face in the photograph. "How old were you when you came to this country?"

He'd expected a smile from her but she withheld it. "Too young to know better, apparently. Twenty-one."

"The girl in this picture looks about fourteen."

She nodded. "I used to hate how young I looked: it made no sense to me. As if I'd been put in someone else's body."

"You could have done worse, Miss Heller."

She frowned. "Alex used to catch me making faces at myself in the mirror—the ugliest faces I could think of. Will picked that up from me. Will makes faces all the time."

Unwillingly he turned back to the album. "When was it that Will's father passed away?"

"Two years ago this March."

"I see." Now he recalled a cursory obituary in the *Times*: a heart attack in some obscure airport motel, alone and in bed, with all the sordidness that kind of death implied. "Right at the time your son's condition worsened."

"Alex had stopped coming around by then. He had troubles enough of his own." She might have been talking about the sad fate of a man she'd once met on a train.

"No love lost between the two of you, I take it."

"Not by the end." She began to say something else but stopped herself. "That's a ridiculous expression, isn't it? 'No love lost.' When Alex was alive I might still have taken it literally." She sat up and took back the album. "More important things than that were lost, of course. Our son was lost."

As he watched her he became aware, dimly at first but then ever more clearly, how far from reason and prudence he was straying. Soon the fact of it was inescapable. His awareness, however, was a passive thing as he sat there and let her relieve him of his last defenses. In time it seemed to disappear entirely.

"I want to show you one more picture. Do you mind?"

"I don't mind at all."

She balanced the album on her knees and turned its pages measuredly, bashfully, playing the role of the doting parent. No. She's not playing any kind of role, he told himself. Don't belittle her because you want her. You put your head down freely on the block.

"Here," she said, smoothing the cellophane down. "Here he is at the library. A few months after his fourteenth birthday."

He leaned toward her and looked. The same delicate head, more beautiful now than seemed necessary in a boy, backlit before a flight of granite steps. The same wide-legged stance, the same carefully combed hair, the same downward tilt of the shoulders. The face was also the same but its expression had changed to one of simple panic. A grin was fixed to the front of it like a screen around an operating table.

She shifted away from him and coughed into her fist. "When I explained to Will that he was getting sick, a few days after we'd been to visit Kopeck, he read every book on schizophrenia that he could find. He learned that he didn't have much time—or maybe he could feel it, I don't know—and he asked if he could be excused from school. When I got him a note from Kopeck he seemed almost proud of it." She coughed again. "There was no need for a doctor's note, of course. He could never have gone back to school. He was hearing voices already, talking to himself, giggling for no reason, all of the usual symptoms. But he kept himself under control at the library, at least at the beginning, and by the end of that month he was practically an expert. I asked him one day—a particularly good day, I remember—what he thought we should do. He smiled at me in an indulgent sort of way and took my hand. 'We'll have to wait for the end of the world, Violet,' he said. He was treating me as though *I* was the patient, as though I was the one who needed looking after, and I suppose in a way he was right. 'What do you mean, Will?' I asked. 'What world is going to end?' He reached over and patted me on the shoulder. 'My world, obviously,' he said. Then he kissed me on the cheek and went upstairs."

Lateef sat on the edge of the couch and waited. Violet's eyes were closed again but she held herself stiffly upright. Say something to her, he ordered himself. But of course he said nothing. The lamp had started to flicker, like the beam from an old film projector, but that might have come from watching her so closely. He knew that his desire was obscene in light of everything she'd told him but the knowledge had no effect on him at all.

"You deserve better than this," he said dully. The air seemed to have been sucked out of the room. "A better kind of life."

She opened her eyes. "Are you proposing to me, Detective?"

"Miss Heller," he said. He took her tentatively by the shoulder. Her body twitched under his fingers, then relaxed. "Violet—"

Her eyes went flat. "No one but Will calls me by that name."

The telephone rang as he took his hand back from her shoulder. An actual bell, a bright and childish alarm, antique as everything else in that place. For the first three rings she sat motionless, staring helplessly at her hands, as though the sound incriminated her. Then she darted past him out into the kitchen.

When the ringing stopped short he assumed that she'd answered:

he waited for her to speak but she said nothing. Only then did it occur to him that she might not have picked up in time. The phone rang again as he got to the kitchen and this time she answered at once.

"All right," she said calmly. "It's all right now."

It was clear to him then that she'd been expecting the call from the beginning.

V iolet? Hello? Please say something Violet. Please be answering and saying *It's all right*.

All right. It's all right now.

I fucked up Violet. There's blood coming out of my clothes.

Are you hurt, Will? Is there any pain?

Will?

I don't know about that. Pain? There's no pain.

Good. That's good. Now take a breath, if you can, and tell me—

What's funny is she tipped me over backwards. She got up all of a sudden and that was a surprise and when she made the cut I fell and laughed out loud. She'd obviously been waiting with the key. It was a simple thing. She ran back down the stairs like a fucking track rabbit. I didn't want to do it anymore. I watched her go Violet. She just hopped right away. You don't know what I'm talking about. You don't even know what a track rabbit is.

That's right, Will. I don't know. Would you explain it to me?

Was I supposed to do it Violet? I thought I was supposed to. If I wasn't I'd never have pulled down my pants.

First tell me where you are. If you tell me that, then I can come and find you. I can listen to you then. I'd like so much to hear—

Hear what Violet? I don't want to hear anything. I want not to be hearing. I want everyone to shut their mouth already. Uhhh—

Who's there, Will? Who's everyone? Can you tell me that?

Uhhh. You know who.

I don't know, Will. I want you to tell me.

You know who. You know who. I stopped taking my meds.

Your meds are the only way to shut them up, though, aren't they? I talked to you about that. You made me a promise. Remember the promise you made to me, Will? Remember what Dr. Fleisig—

They shut up too much with the meds. It gets quiet. It all gets so flat.

You sound quiet too. There's a funny kind of buzzing on the line. Are you maybe calling from a payphone?

From a payphone in a station in a tunnel. That's all right. A payphone is a coin-operated machine.

Why are you being so quiet? Why are you whispering? Are there people around?

Close enough Violet. In the doorway. Three of them together. For a long time they were in the other room.

Can you tell me the name of the station? Which station is it?

A good station actually. One of the best. Ladies in raincoats are talking about us. Trains going by. It's one of the finest stations on the line.

They have raincoats, the ladies? Is it raining there?

Uhhh—

What kind of line is it, Will? Is it a letter or a number?

No Violet. Uhhh. No no no no.

That's just fine. It doesn't matter. Can you tell me what color it is? Can you tell me that?

I've been cut up actually. Emily did it. She sat straight up and chopped me in two pieces. She cut me right between the tits.

Where's Emily now, Will? Is she all right?

• • •

Will? Hello? Is Emily with you right now? Is she there?
Uhhh.
Will, please answer me. I'm begging you.

Yes and no Violet. Yes and no.
Oh God, Will. Oh God. Please don't say that.
I told her everything Violet. I didn't mind. I told her about the weather and my calling and about the Musaquontas. I told her a joke and I followed her and I put on someone else's clothes. A whole new look for me and sexy. I gave her money. Dark blue jeans with dice on the back pocket. An oxford shirt. A sweater. She gave me a green belt too behind the curtain. She did the Robot Violet. She gave me kisses.

Emily would never want to hurt you, Will. Emily's your best friend. Are you listening to me? Emily wouldn't—

Oh yes she would Violet. Close your mouth now. How could you know anything? Were you there? That fucker. I told her about my time at school but she tried not to hear it. She was stupid and she was scared shitless in the tunnel. She did too much talking. We got to the platform and she giggled at me and rolled her eyes like someone from the school. She couldn't hear a single word I said. She told me everything was *beautiful*. She liked the arches best. There were chandeliers and skylights. Are you ready? I asked her. She liked that too. She went up the stairs. I thought I was supposed to do it then. There was this calling Violet. It gave me directions. It called me up and said to do that thing.

What sort of things did it—

Have I told you about my calling yet?

Not yet. Maybe you could—

Who's that with you there? Who's talking?

Nobody's talking. No one's here but me. Tell me what your calling said.

Well listen carefully everybody! Attention please! Because there's not much time.

What are you talking about, Will? There's plenty of time. Just take a breath and close your eyes and try—

There is a hurry Violet. Time is actually very tight. First of all I've only got two quarters.

Can you tell me the number of the payphone there, maybe, in case you run out of money? It's all right to tell me. It's better.

I love you Violet.

I love you, too, Will. You know that I love you. I would never—

Why was I born Violet? Tell me why.

Goddamn it, Will, give me a straight answer. Slow down and catch your breath and tell me—

7186738197. It could be anybody's.

Hold on. 718. 673. 819—

Why are you saying the number out loud? Hello Violet? Who are you talking to?

You're in Brooklyn, is that right? Are you on the F line?

Payphones only ring in the movies. No one gets a payphone call. I've never gotten one ever.

That's not true. I used to call you at the hospital, don't you remember?

Will? Hello?

What hospital Violet? What hospital do you mean?

I'm sorry, Will. I'm sorry. I didn't mean to call it that. What I meant was when I called you at the—

You must think I'm stupid Violet. You must think I wear my underpants on the outside of my clothes.

Hold on a second, hold on—can you please wa.. ......nd—don't stop—

What's that? Violet? VIOLET?

It's nothing, Will. I'm sorry about that. I just dropped the—

Who's with you Violet? Who the fuck is that?

It's nobody, Will. No one's here. I told you already—

Will, can you hear me?

Will?

The sun was declining and the firepits were glowing and oil-colored nightbirds were warbling down from the trees. The birds and the fires and the voices made a chorus. His own voice was in it. Dead air whistled through the tenements and bottles cooed and sparkled in the weeds. Sunlight cut into his body like a blessing.

He walked down the street with his left eye shut against the sun and his fingers hooked together at his neck. Smoke rose straight up from the ground in silver lines. Two boys with socks on their hands were kicking something in a rolled-up paper bag. He walked with one foot on the curb and one foot off. There were cars on the street but most of them sat flatwheeled on the ground. Pelts of carbon swaddled them. He found one that he liked and climbed inside.

The windows were broken but the front seat was warm. A smell of sunbaked Naugahyde and shit. A sticker on the dash said STRICTLY FOR MY NINJAZ. He sat up and pressed the heels of his palms against the wheel. He revved and coughed and sputtered, shifting gears. His shirtfront snapped and crackled as he breathed. He tapped it with his finger and watched the bloodflakes settle in his lap. Snap crackle pop, he mumbled. He sat back in the seat and shut his eyes. Nothing left now but patience. Snap crackle pop. Nothing left to do but wait until the fire.

Under the street at that moment a train shot through a station unstopping. The rails sighed and protested as they will. Emily lay stretched between them. She looked up at Lowboy as the train hit the junction and gave him a thin Christian smile.

A noise woke him suddenly and he jerked himself upright with both hands still braced against the wheel. The two boys he'd seen before were squatting on the hood with the toes of their bare feet curled against the dash. Crumbs of windshield squeaked under their heels. They were lightskinned and somber and they seemed to know him well. The smaller boy pointed at something on the seat behind him.

"Happy birthday," said the boy.

"Girlfriend's first name," the other boy said. His voice was high-pitched and polite.

Lowboy looked cautiously over his shoulder and saw the bag that they'd been kicking up the street. Dark with tar or grease along the bottom. A bag for a Jamaican beef patty or a chicken cutlet sandwich or a beer. He reached behind him and brought the bag over the seat and held it toward the boys but neither of them took it. He opened the bag himself and looked inside and saw the carcass of a stillborn dog.

"Get up," said the small boy. "No sleeping." He worked the words out thickly through his teeth. The other boy yawned. The sun behind them made them look like cutouts. They frowned at him but he felt safe and careless. He felt sleepy and untouchable and still.

.   .   .

When he kept quiet the taller boy sucked in a breath and let it out and eased his body down onto the pavement. He squinted at his feet and shuffled slowly clockwise and let his knuckles drag along the hood. He stopped at the passenger-side door and opened it. The smaller boy's eyes never blinked. He ran his tongue along his teeth and nodded sadly. Lowboy stared back at the boy and listened to the glass chittering and wondered how he'd gotten to that place.

He was starting to remember when the taller boy's hand closed over his mouth. The hand smelled like rust and old treebark and crumbling bricks. It touched his face lazily, heavily, the way that it had moved across the hood. Aged fingers testing and exploring. When he sat up the hand covered his eyes.

A wheezing. A rustling. The crackling of paper.

The hand withdrew soon after but his eyes refused to open. He felt the seat sag and buckle as someone got in. Cursewords were uttered. It was not the small boy's voice or the other boy's either and it was like no voice that he had ever heard. He had never heard it but he recognized it. He had heard it since the day that he was born. Careful now, said the voice, and immediately everything went shrill.

"Okay, Alex," Lowboy said, covering his ears. "Okay, Dad." He had no idea what business his father had in that godforsaken place but he knew that it was no business of his. A hand slipped into his shirt pocket and he let out a frightened breath and slumped forward until the seatbelt caught and held him. He couldn't remember having put it on. He was about to cry out when the boys cleared their throats and the voices came to life and started shouting.

When he opened his eyes he was alone in the car. The sun was the same but the sky had changed colors and the seat was dark and cool against his back. The brown bag was empty. The glass had been arranged into small bright piles along the dash but he couldn't make sense of the pattern. He sat up and looked at the street. A group of women stood clustered at the far end of the block but other than that he saw no one. If he listened closely he could still make out the voices, at times even understand them, but the wind through the car was a thousand times louder and so were the sounds of his body.

He sat for a time watching the women on the corner, feeling the sun on his face and his forehead, adjusting to the faintness of the voices. Their laughable faintness. He wondered how on earth it could have happened. The piles of glass possibly, or the little dog's body, or some other trick he had no knowledge of. He decided that the two boys were behind it. They're the opposite of Skull & Bones, he thought. Two personal angels. So straightfaced and quiet. He pictured them to himself, the smaller boy talking and the taller one moving, as if picturing them would get them to come back. He decided that their names were Quick & Painless.

Now that it was quiet again he could think about Violet. He'd have liked to have her with him in the car. She'd have fussed about the bloodstains but that would have been all right. Now that it was over, now that he'd done everything he could, there was no reason for them not to be together. He turned his head and imagined her sitting in the passenger seat, smoothing down the creases in her jeans, picking bits of broken glass out of her hair. It's no good Violet, he'd have told her. I tried my best to do it. I tried twice. There's nothing to do now Violet and I'm sorry. She'd have taken his hand in hers and he'd have let her. He might even have laid down in her lap. He imagined her jeans against his cheek, the beautiful mannish jeans she always wore, warm and rough against his forehead like the canvas of a sail. He'd asked her once to take him sailing, he remembered. Come on Violet, he'd said. One of your boyfriends has to have a yacht. She'd laughed at that and called him Little Jacques Cousteau.

He covered his eyes with his shirtsleeves now and pictured her. Violet, he said in a whisper. Listen to me. Are you there. There were two little boys here Violet did you send them. Two little angels. If you sent them Violet could you please send them back.

. . .

He was still waiting for an answer when someone broke off from the group on the streetcorner. A blackhaired woman of no particular age, hesitating as if she expected to be called back, fussing with the catches of her latticed limegreen pumps. No one called her back. She took off her glasses, thick owlish lenses in tortoiseshell frames, and polished them with the hem of her miniskirt. The others ignored her. When she'd finished with the glasses she put them back on and started resolutely up the street. The pumps were high but she moved smoothly and easily once she started walking. The skin on her knees turned blue and gray and green as she came closer. She's cold, Lowboy thought. How is that possible.

She was even with the hood before she saw him. She cocked her head and arched her back and shivered. She was close to the window, close enough to touch, and though her body was set for walking she stayed still. She let her eyes roll past him up the street.

"That ain't going to ride you," she lisped. "Do you know why?"

He sat back in the seat and shook his head.

"Out of gas."

He looked at the gas gauge and saw she was right. "Is this your car?"

"Not from the South Side, are you, son." She squinted at him. "You look just like that actor. Bradley Pitt."

"Downtown," said Lowboy. "Not actually from the Bronx."

She curled her middle finger around the lock. "What you come to the Point for, Bradley? For a date?"

"I'm looking for some boys," he said. "Two small boys. Quick and Painless."

She laughed and coughed and laughed a second time. She kept her lower lip over her teeth. "You on the wrong street for that, Bradley. Try up on Edgewater."

"Not the wrong street," he said. "There were two little boys. They threw a paper bag into the car. A dead dog's body. They came around the car and touched my face." He hummed to himself and sighed and tapped the wheel.

She considered him awhile. "Best not stay out here, Bradley. You want to go someplace and call your mother."

"No mother," he said. He shook his head. "No calling."

"Your papi, then. Whatever." She pursed her lips. "Stay out in this ride you getting fucked."

"I want to get fucked," said Lowboy.

"You what?"

He frowned and slid away from her and pressed his hands together in his lap. "I've got money," he said. "I've got $600."

She slid her glasses down her nose like a professor. "$600?" she said. "On you right now?"

He bobbed his head and blew a kiss at her.

The door rattled open and the car's engine started and they were driving or else she was pushing him by the elbow down the street. The tenements the firepits the oilcolored birds. The song of Quick & Painless playing backward. He saw the two of them watching from under a stoop and he waved at them and they pulled back into nothing. They couldn't follow him where he was going.

She took him to a place where the street humped and narrowed and turned back on itself like Ouroboros. They stood side by side and stared up at a building. The steps were limegreen. A poodle looked down from the fire escape with its head stuck in a plastic cone-shaped bonnet. Does that make it bark louder, thought Lowboy. Does that keep its head out of the rain. He thought of the dog on his father's old records: HIS MASTER'S VOICE. What master, he wondered. What voice. They passed into a foyer with gray scalloped walls and then up a cracked waterstained staircase. Then down a low hallway. Then into a fivecornered room.

"What's your name?" said the woman. She was making the bed.

"Lowboy."

"That's not a name. What kind of name is that?"

"Like a dog," Lowboy said. He watched her bend over. "Like furniture."

"A dog, huh?" She laughed at him. "A pussy retriever? You look more like a little squirrel to me." She pulled off her sweatshirt. "Nobody tell me they church name, doggy. That's all right."

Lowboy said nothing.

"I got a name like that," she said. "Everybody call me Secretary, account of my glasses." She let the sweatshirt drop onto the floor. "I hate that shit."

"Who calls you that?"

She sat down on the bed and shrugged. "All of them dried-out bitches."

"Secretary," he said cautiously. Getting the sound of it. He reached over and took hold of her hair.

"Don't come up on me yet, doggy." She coughed again and pushed his hand away. "Sit down here next to me." She pulled her right foot up and unbuckled the pump. Her leg was as glossy and softlooking as a baby's. A line of stubble above the ankle with the shiny skin behind. She let her right foot go and lifted up the other. Why is she taking her shoes off, thought Lowboy. How do the shoes come into it. It occurred to him then that he might have the wrong idea about how it was done. But as he looked at her sitting squatly in her underthings, massaging her heels, he knew one thing beyond the slightest doubt. It would happen now no matter what else happened.

While he waited for her he looked around the room. Silhouettes bobbed and flitted past the curtains. Doubts visited him but he dismissed them. The room took up the whole of his attention. A door in the far wall hid behind a dresser. A tearshaped lightbulb jittering like a candle. A snapshot of a man in uniform. Her father, he decided. The wall above the mattress was festooned with curlicues of yellow paper. They twitched and rasped in concert with his breathing, working free of their staples, a sound like roaches trapped inside a box. In time he saw the slips for what they were.

"Receipts," he said. He pointed at them. Secretary was hanging up her clothes.

"That's my diary, doggy. That's evidence."

"Evidence?"

"Damn right."

He didn't know what to say to that. She was folding her sweatshirt. She did it very quickly and precisely.

"What's your church name?" he said.

She stopped and looked him over. The room seemed smaller than before. He turned his head and tried to count the staples.

"Maria Villallegas," she said. She said it as though he'd asked her something secret. "You can read it on those slips if you can read."

"Maria Villallegas," he repeated. The name felt brittle in his mouth. "Villallegas," he said carefully. "Is that right?"

She smoothed the sheet down under him and sat him up and pulled his zipper open. "How about you just call me Secretary."

"Secretary," he said loudly. *"Secretary."* She was between his legs now. Her lips came graciously apart. She was keeping him quiet by putting her head in his lap.

"You ready, doggy?" she said. "You look it."

How can she ask me that, thought Lowboy. He bit down on his tongue. How is it that she can say a word.

"Don't stop, Secretary," he said. She didn't stop. "I want to—"

Something tapped against the window and she stopped. A bottle or a watchface or a cane. Something ungiving. She stopped and cursed quietly and pushed herself up off the floor. She got up because a man was at the window.

"The fuck away, Ty. Somebody dating me." She cleared her throat. "A man. A little boy."

A little boy, Lowboy said to himself. He put a hand over his face and hid behind his fingers. A man.

The man at the window spoke measuredly and without any cursing. Secretary held the curtain closed. To hide the man from me, Lowboy decided. Or possibly to hide me from the man. Secretary cursed and spat and rolled her eyes but she never spoke until the man was finished. Their voices never touched. Lowboy wondered what would happen if they did.

Then the talking was over and Secretary came back to bed. The look on her face was hard to make sense of. Lowboy opened his mouth but she held up two fingers. "That's just Ty," she said. "Ty like to grieve me." She let herself sink back onto the bed. "He said we ought to done this on the street."

"I heard him," said Lowboy.

She looked at him now. "You heard all of that?"

"You never talk until he's finished talking."

She made a sharp sound with her tongue against her teeth. Then she made what sounded like a laugh.

"Why is that, Secretary?"

"Get them clothes off you, Bradley. Why you pull your pants up?"

"I was cold."

She pulled them down and shook her head at him. "Damn if you ain't good to go," she said. "I guess Ty didn't spook you much."

"Who's Ty?"

She was back on her knees with a towel under her and the front of his pants in her fist like a ball of old paper. What she was doing to him was terrible but he wasn't afraid of it yet. "That's my little Bradley. Look at that doggy dick." Her voice was high and toneless and impatient. A child actress, he thought, but that wasn't right. A fullgrown actress playing the part of a child. Talking straight at his stomach and keeping her child's eyes wide open. The top of her head was kinked and wiglike and his stomach itched where her hair brushed against it.

"You ready," she said suddenly. "You good." She pulled a coffeecan down from a shelf above the bed and brought out something

wrapped in silver foil. He knew what it was for and smiled and nodded. She bit open the wrapper and stared at him until he closed his
eyes. She held him down with one hand and put it on with the other
and brought her knees up level with his hips. He was afraid of her
now. He heard her squat and stop and shift and take a breath. She
was smaller than seemed possible and her body had no smell or
weight at all. "All right now," she singsonged. "All right." Her hand
held him pinned like a butterfly in a glass case. He thought of
MUSEUM OF NATURAL HISTORY and the skeletons set like jewels into
the tiles. When he opened his eyes she was smiling and looking him
over.

"You a sweet boy," she said.

He opened his mouth and closed it.

"You couldn't find a little girl to date?"

"I've got $600," he told her. "I've got—"

She moved her hand up to his mouth. "Quiet now."

Why was I born, thought Lowboy. Is this why.

She let out a thick breath and put him inside her. He tried to keep
quiet. He was underwater now and so was she. She was moving
above him like someone on camera, making small sounds so as not
to wake the neighbors. He forgot her and remembered her again.
She was moving the way he'd imagined her moving and the sight of
it flooded his body and brain with relief. It was happening now there
was no way to stop it. He was laughing apparently. The room had
gone silent and the light had gone dim and he opened his mouth and
the whole world went silent. Somewhere voices were screaming in
amazement and victory but the screaming was too far off for him to
hear. There was no need to hear. She was moving above him. He
could see out of the holes in her eyes and taste with her mouth and
feel every single thing that she was feeling. He felt the skin around
him breaking and the silence breaking with it. He seeped out of his
body like the yolk out of an egg. The world was outside his body
now, which meant he was alone. His body was on the outside of the
world.

. . .

"That's right, doggy," she said. Her eyelids fluttered like the receipts on the wall and her mouth hung wide open and he saw black spaces where her teeth had been. "That's right, doggy," she said. "Give it up."

Afterward she leaned forward and they came softly apart and that was all. But the world was so different. He was seeing out of his own eyes again. For the first time he noticed a poster behind the dresser of a deserted sunny beach and one above it of the singer Ricky Martin with two holes punched into his neck. The mark of the vampire, Lowboy thought sleepily. He felt easy and harmless. He raised a corner of the bedsheet and ran it slowly back and forth across his stomach. Now it's happened, he thought. Now the world can stop ending. He let his head fall back and looked at Secretary. She was turning out the pockets of his jeans.

"Where's the money?" she said. She dropped the jeans to the floor. "Where the fuck is my $600?"

She almost seemed to be saying it to herself.

They arrived at the precinct and found the right room just in time to hear Emily's statement. It was well after midnight but the building seemed crowded. Such a different place from the Department of Missing Persons, Violet thought. Everything so close together. No one asked them who they were or what they wanted. They found Emily sitting up straight in a room full of desks, a proud and solitary figure, watching the desk sergeant curse at his computer. If she noticed them she gave no sign of it. She seemed too old somehow, not the same girl at all, a stand-in for Emily Wallace. An understudy, Violet thought. Only when the sergeant had asked if there was anything else and she'd shaken her head no did she turn and look at them over her shoulder. Her forehead and her neck were smeared with soot and her jacket was ripped along the collar but her face was a careless mask of self-sufficiency. If anything she seemed very slightly bored.

She learned that from Will, Violet found herself thinking. That's Will's look on her face. Her own expression was not much better and when she realized that she forced herself to smile. The sergeant nodded to Lateef and withdrew discreetly behind the photocopier. Not a word passed between them. He stepped around Violet blankly, squinting down at his files, as though she'd been put in his way by accident.

No one spoke for a moment. Emily seemed to be looking at Violet but in fact she was looking at nothing. I'm going to make a mess of this, Violet thought. Emily's dislike of her expanded to fill the empty space between them. Violet opened her mouth, took in enough breath to speak, then bit down on the knuckle of her thumb. She felt her body tipping backward. Finally Lateef cleared his throat and sat down heavily behind the desk. He looked uncomfortable there. The sergeant's ergonomic chair gave a slow disdainful hiss under his weight.

"Hi there, Miss Wallace. I'm Ali Lateef, the detective in charge of Will's case. I think you know Miss—"

"I know her," said Emily. Her voice was clear and composed, the same voice she'd been using with the sergeant. "Hello, Yda."

"Hello, Emily. I'm so happy to see that you're okay." The fact of Emily sitting composedly before her, a little disheveled but otherwise in perfect health, was too much for her suddenly, too extravagant a gift. How could such a thing have happened, she thought. How could it have happened twice. But this second miracle was not like the first: Emily's empty face was proof of that. There was no love for Will to be found there.

"Something's happened, Yda. To Will, I mean." She smiled crookedly. "I know that sounds stupid."

"It doesn't sound stupid, Emily." Violet gritted her teeth and took a small step toward her. "Will's gone off his meds. He stopped almost two weeks—"

"It's not the meds. It's something else." Emily turned to Lateef. "He's a different kind of sick now than he was."

"Different how?" said Lateef.

"Something happened to him while he was gone. He tried to tell me what it was but I freaked out. I didn't want to do it anymore."

She made a face. "He wasn't ever rough with me before. I know he got sent away for assaulting me or whatever but I never agreed with that. He used to be afraid to let me kiss him. That's part of why he pushed me that first time." She hesitated. "I guess you know why he took me to the tunnel. What he wanted to do with me, I mean."

Violet let herself down on the edge of the desk. "I think so. Will seems to have confused—"

"He wanted to fuck me."

She was looking back and forth between them now, eyes wide and unblinking, challenging either of them to contradict her. There was nothing blank about her expression any longer. She sat on the backs of her hands, letting her full weight rest on them, as though to keep from doing something she'd regret. She seemed to have no idea that she was crying.

"Do you know what he wanted me for?"

Violet nodded mutely. I'm afraid of this girl, she told herself, framing the thought very clearly. I'm afraid of her because she's been with Will. Because of what he's told her and because of what she's guessed. The sooner this is over with the better.

Lateef shook his head. "Miss Heller and I understand, Emily. There's no shame in that." He cleared his throat like an embarrassed father. "You know that there's no shame in that, don't you?"

Emily rolled her eyes at Violet, as if they both knew that Lateef was being childish. "If he'd still been the same I'd have done it," she said. "It's not my first time, you know. Not like Will." She shrugged her shoulders. "I might even have done it anyway."

Lateef said nothing to that. Violet saw her chance and took it.

"You're right about Will, Emily: he's always been afraid of things, and he's still afraid. You agree with that, don't you? So maybe he hasn't really changed so much." She was smiling and nodding at Emily but she was talking to Lateef. "Look at me for a second. Would you do that, Emily? Let's think this through together. I've always tried to shield you from Will's bad spells, always kept him at home, so you've probably never seen him at his worst. I'm sure you remember, on certain days, how I wouldn't let him come to the door—" But by then it was clear that she'd made a mistake.

"That's bullshit, Yda. You're lying." Emily was on her feet now, no longer holding herself back, pointing at Violet like a detective on the last page of a thriller. "The reason you didn't let Will out had nothing to do with that. Who the fuck could *you* protect from anything?"

"Miss Wallace—" Lateef was half out of his chair, looking from one of them to the other, huffing and swaying like a man twice his age. "Miss Wallace, I'm going to have to ask you—"

"You're right, Emily," Violet said softly, reaching out to take her by the arm. "You're right about everything." But Emily had already started screaming.

"You're the reason Will's the way he is, Yda. What other way could he fucking be? You're his *mother*." She stood for a moment with her feet wide apart, bracing herself as if for punishment, taken aback by her own fearlessness. Then she said the thing that Violet had been dreading.

"What he did to me proves you're his mother, Yda. You know it does."

Violet said nothing, did nothing, made no reply or sound of any kind. Lateef was next to her but he did nothing either. He'll ask me now, she thought, and that was enough to keep her mute and still. She waited until she couldn't stand it, until she felt actual pain; then she turned around to face him. And still he didn't ask.

"Miss Wallace," Lateef said, as decorous as ever. "I'm going to have to ask you to sit down." Violet watched him as if through a telescope. She no longer felt the slightest trace of fear. He's not in on the joke, she thought. How could he be?

"She's lying," Emily said through her teeth. "She's lying, Detective Lateef. Just look at her."

Lateef kept his eyes fixed on Emily. "Miss Wallace," he repeated. This time he said it differently. Emily coughed into her fist and sat back down.

"You've been through a lot today, Miss Wallace, and you have my sympathies. But Will is Miss Heller's son, as you've just said your-self, and I think it's safe to say she's suffering, too." He took in a con-ciliatory breath. "Would you agree with that?"

Emily said nothing.

"Why don't we all have a seat, Miss Heller."

Violet did as she was told, feeling more detached than ever. She hadn't been aware that she was standing. She'd had the identical feeling at the end of Will's trial, and again when she'd visited him at Bellavista: the sense that disaster had missed her by inches. Some-how the feeling failed to comfort her.

"All right, Miss Wallace. Do you feel as though you could answer a few questions?" Lateef pulled open a drawer and rummaged through it, exactly as he'd have done in his own office. "The truth is that we really need your help."

"Don't talk down to me, then. And don't say 'we.'"

Lateef smiled at her patiently. "I'll try my best."

She narrowed her eyes at Violet. "I'm not going to talk with her around."

The smile faded. Violet thought he might glance at her but he did no such thing. He simply let them both watch the benevolence drain from his face.

"You broke the law today, Miss Wallace, and whether or not you regret it now doesn't especially matter. You seem like a decent girl to me, but sometimes I'm not the best judge of these things. Am I wrong this time?"

Emily shrugged and stared up at the ceiling.

"No, I don't think I'm wrong." He looked at Violet now—perhaps for Emily's benefit—then sighed and leaned soberly forward. "I'm told that your parents are on their way, Emily. I'd like to give them some good news when they arrive." There was a trace of appeal in his expression now, almost of vulnerability. Violet couldn't help but admire his technique.

"What do you say, Emily?" He glanced at his watch. "Can we work out a deal, the two of us?"

Emily slouched farther down in her seat. "What kind of a deal?"

"Did Will talk to you about what his plans might be?"

She frowned at him. "Plans?"

"Did he say anything about where he might go next?" Violet said before she could stop herself. "Did he say whether he was—"

"I'm not talking to you, liar." She kept her eyes on Lateef. "Tell her to go away."

Lateef took the watch from his wrist and laid it deliberately across the desktop. "You've got a quarter of an hour until your folks get here, Miss Wallace, and about seven seconds before I ask Sergeant Cruz to keep you overnight." He let his eyes linger on the watchface. "Should I call the sergeant over?"

"I don't give a shit."

"Did Will ask you to go somewhere with him? Somewhere after the station?"

She shook her head stiffly.

"Why did he want to have sex with you, Emily?"

"To save the world." She leered at Violet. "But you knew that already."

Lateef looked up from his watch. *And still he doesn't ask*, Violet thought. The fact that she'd won him over so completely almost sickened her. *It's for Will*, she reminded herself. *It's for his sake, not mine*. But still it was easier not to watch it happen.

Lateef rapped against the desk with his knuckles. "Look at *me*, Emily, not at Miss Heller. Where did Will want to go?"

She shrugged again. "Anywhere I wanted. He had money."

"What money?"

"Six hundred something dollars. He stole it out of a suitcase."

"Wasn't there some place you talked about? There must have been."

She gave the same laugh as before. "He only really ever talked about one place. But I shut him up about that."

"Why?"

She looked past them both as though the answer were obvious. "It was Union Square Station, that's why. He said it was the best place in the world."

S he called out his name and he came through the window in the glory and fulfillment of his calling. Not Lowboy's or any other's but his own. A cardoor slammed shut and the curtains blew open and he came through the window as magnificent and silent as a god. His gold satin jacket hissed as he spread his arms and fell in elegant bright folds against his ribs. *NINJAZ 3:10* was written across the back of it like a psalm. He moved in arabesques and loops like a bird or a deer and hit Secretary across the face before his heels had landed on the floor. He took Lowboy by the hair and threw him up against the dresser. He was a vision to behold and Lowboy shivered just to see him. As yet he hadn't even made a fist.

He let his weight come down on Lowboy's back and asked a simple question. Lowboy turned his head to answer and saw nothing but a rippling in the air. The question was repeated like a punchline. Sometimes one voice asked sometimes another. His beautiful sad voice mellow and endlessly patient. Her thin panicked screeching. The question was simple but where could the answer be found. Lowboy made wellmeaning mindless noises. He wept and he babbled and he made every face that he knew. Where was the answer.

A drawer of the dresser was closed and his hand was inside it. He rolled his eyes back in his head and felt a coolness.

"Look at me motherfucker." His eyes inclined toward the mirror but he saw nothing worth seeing. "Look at me." The voice low and calm and the others behind it. A whirlpool of rabid hysterical hisses and his own voice lost among them like a pigeon locked inside a tabernacle. I'm writing my own psalm, Lowboy said to himself. The drawer was closed again where were his fingers. A face was in the mirror now he shrieked a question at it. A boneless ugly face and very white. Retching and weeping and asking somebody's forgiveness.

How can this face exist in this my world.

In the blink of an eye it was some later hour and he was being pulled along a hallway by his shins. His arms were crossed at his chest and his right hand was wrapped in a blue football jersey. He recognized the hallway: he was traveling backward in time. The lobby came next and the entryway and the pitted green steps. A palm cupped his head as he went down the steps and he looked up and saw Secretary's fat inconsolable face. It was night now or something like night and her hair glowed blue and silver in the backlight. He saw his breath and her breath high above it. The poodle lay flat on the fire escape with its bonnet caught between two of the bars.

They stretched him out against the curb and left him. The voices were even louder now if such a thing was possible. Bickering, wheedling, gibbering at each other and at him. Issuing instructions without number. He shut his eyes and turned his face into the wind. He felt no cold. What time is it, he wondered.

"What time is it?" he said into the air.

He knew better than to hope for a reply. He was leaking from his eyeholes and his ears. The voices were more urgent than he remembered them ever being and he frowned and held his breath and listened closely. Apparently there was something left to do.

• • • •

Soon after that he got onto his feet. What time is it, he said again. Why is it so dark. He stuck his hand inside his shirt and started walking. The street was as dry and lifeless as the moon. Here and there a window flickered bluely. Had they waited until nighttime had they thought that he was dead. He walked with his head down and followed the scuts in the pavement. He passed a window with a TV on behind it and the weatherman waved at him and wished him well. The clock on the livingroom wall said 4:15.

Four fifteen in the morning, Lowboy said to himself. Forty-five minutes to five.

A thought hit him then and the massed voices scattered. It hit him like lightning. 4:15 in the morning. The appointed hour long since come and gone. It was black and cold and lifeless on the street but he saw no sign that there had been a fire.

"Nothing happened," said Lowboy. He said it out loud so that he could believe it. "No fire." He waited for the voices to deny it or to change his mind for him but they kept still. How can they deny it, he thought. They can't. His mouth went dry with victory. What can anyone say. Not a thing in the world. It's 4:17 in the morning.

He thought about all kinds of people as the shock of it passed through him but the one he thought of most was Violet. A song came to him as he thought about her: "I'm a Little Blackbird" by Clarence Williams. Also "Goose Pimples" by Bix Beiderbecke. Also "Do Nothin' Till You Hear from Me."

I'm coming Violet, he said. I'm on my way. Do nothing until you hear from me. He saw her sitting tiredly on the black lacquered couch with the red wall behind it, then jumping up when he walked through the door, then swooning when he told her what he'd done. No one swooned anymore but she would if he asked her. People always did in the old songs. He thought of her on the couch again because it made him happy. I did it Violet, he was saying. I made the world stop ending. She called him her little professor and he was. A policeman was with her but it didn't matter. The policeman got up and reached for his gun but Violet pulled the rug from underneath him. He tried to get up but she hit him with a frying pan. He started singing "You'll Wish You'd Never Been Born" and Violet started singing "Black & Blue." The policeman switched over to "Leavenworth Strut" but Lowboy cut him off with "Sunny Disposish" and Violet was dancing on a stool.

In an alley by the station he saw Quick & Painless and told them the news. He held his broken right hand up as proof and they stood motionless and watched him without blinking. Only the white of the socks on their hands showed in the shadow of the houses and from time to time the glittering of their eyes. When he was a few steps from the alley he stopped and made his presidential face. I did it boys, he said to them. I did it. *Nothing happened.*

At the station he told everyone he saw. They gawked at him in simple disbelief. He walked up the row of turnstiles and picked up farecards from the ground and slid them through the slots and no one stopped him. The station was brighter and more beautiful than he remembered. Argon tubelights palpitated coldly. His skin felt hot against his clothes and when he brought a hand to his eyes his fingerbones clacked in their sockets. Nothing took him by surprise or made him worry. He was moving through a world transfigured and redeemed by sacrifice and it was only right that what he saw seemed foreign. He saw the world the way a headless saint would see it.

The fourteenth farecard was good and he went through the turnstile sideways, breathing very slowly, keeping his right hand pressed against his ribs. There was no pain. The 6 train arrived and he sat down inside it. The station fell away and there was no one on the train but a smell in the air like sheets of almonds baking. Night outside or could it be the tunnel. Stars passed by like tracklights. The inside of the car was clean and gray and free of any shadows. His hands were on the crosspole and his feet were close together and his voice was like a locust in the air. William of Orange is my name, he shouted. Can I please have a smoke. Sometimes it happened that he spoke very clearly. The car was arranged not with L-shaped seatblocks but with ashcolored benches running the length of each wall. A dentist's office or a jailcell or a courtroom. The headmaster's office at the Bellavista Clinic. The smoking lounge with its patterned plastic stools.

Everything else that happened happened softly. In the glass he saw his sly white face reflected. His face made faces at him while he watched it. The stars and struts and guttered bedrock passing. The steady sloughing of the rails and wheels. The train eased into the tunnel like a hand into a pocket and closed over Lowboy's body and held him still.

What time is it now? someone asked. It was 4:27. The train banked through a curve and straightened itself and gave a kind of cough and lost its power. The tubelights flared and flickered and expired. Lowboy opened his eyes as wide as he could and pressed his ghostly face against the glass. He saw colossal shapes and glyphs and signatures. Damp concrete slathered in ciphers. Turquoise and orange and silver and platinum blond. Bleeding heartwrenching letters. Tags the kids called them. Glorious and shrill and wet and horrifying. A righteous text set down for his eyes only.

He sat on the bench and watched the great words passing. They oozed and writhed and chirruped and collapsed. No use trying to decode them. They dripped against the window like tattoos. He made a frightened sound and shut his eyes and the tags made words and signs behind his eyelids. They issued decrees. The almond smell was sharper and he knew that if his eyes came open the unthinkable thing he'd thought of would have happened. It was happening now. He pressed his hands against his face and tried to listen. Something in the car was moving. The tags were coming clear to him or was the cipher broken. Yes he had broken it. They weren't words at all but pictures. Each letter its own heaving organism. They shuddered together like bees in a hive, dancing out messages and swallowing one another and making a history and fucking. When he opened his eyes he understood them perfectly.

Violet and Lateef sat on the 4 train in the early morning, an empty seat between them for propriety, studying the backlit ads across the aisle. NEW CAREERS IN COMPUTING and CAPTAIN MORGAN SPICED RUM and THE INSTITUTE FOR PRACTICAL PHILOSOPHY and JONATHAN ZIZMOR'S FACIAL FRUIT PEELS. From a police recruitment poster a grayscaled woman of no particular age or ethnicity beamed at them like a televangelist: IMAGINE A MOTHER THANKING YOU FOR FINDING HER MISSING SON. Lateef glanced furtively at Violet. They'd spent the last three hours doing next to nothing and the wait seemed to have affected her. She was sitting up straight with her hands in her lap, moving her lips very subtly, like someone just learning to read. She seemed more foreign to him at that moment than at any time since he'd first seen her. She hadn't said a word to him since they'd left the Second Precinct.

"Two more stops," Lateef heard himself saying, as he might have to a tourist or a child. She nodded almost imperceptibly.

"We might not find Will there, you know. He might be gone already."

She said nothing.

"He might not be coming to Union Square at all."

"I know, Detective." She shook her head. "We shouldn't count our blessings."

He smiled and nodded. "That's right. Or our chickens, either."

She didn't answer.

"If you see your son, Miss Heller—this is important—point him out to me right away." He cleared his throat. "Don't pursue him yourself. Can we agree on that?"

She said something too quietly to hear.

"What was that?"

"I hate trains." She took a breath and held it. "I hate them."

"Just two more stops," he repeated lamely, glancing at his watch. "We're in good shape, Miss Heller. It's been less than fifteen minutes since the sighting."

"What sighting?"

He watched her without answering, waiting for her to acknowledge him, but no acknowledgment came. It was impossible that she'd forgotten the last quarter hour—the call, the positive ID, the frantic rush to the 4—but no other explanation came to him. Her expression was the same as when she'd first come to his office: the same spiritless dullness, the same defeat. What's changed in her, he wondered. What pills did she take. What is it that I'm not seeing clearly.

Stop asking questions, he told himself tiredly. Stop playing detective. You've been asking questions all day and they've been the wrong ones and you've been too stupid to answer even those. Too stupid or too self-satisfied or too smitten. You're going to sit here quietly now and get off at Union Square and wait for the boy to come out of the 6. If he doesn't come out you'll have to start over from nothing, which wouldn't be a bad idea at all. Pretend you've never seen her and begin at the beginning. Good morning, Miss Heller. I'm Detective Lateef. Imagine yourself thanking me for finding your missing son.

After a time she seemed to recollect him. Her eyes came slowly into focus and she leaned away from him and licked her lips. "Detective," she said, still not turning her head. "I want you to do something for me."

"That doesn't surprise me, Miss Heller." He managed a smile. "You usually do."

"You'd know my son, wouldn't you? You'd know him if you saw him." She took in another slow breath. "You'd recognize him, I mean."

"If I didn't, I'd just—"

"I want to know what you'll do when you find him. Will you tell me that?"

He waited to answer until she'd looked at him. "I hope you're not planning on leaving me, Miss Heller."

She blushed as though he'd asked her something shameful. "I'll be there," she murmured.

"Then why ask me that question?"

It took her a long time to answer and when she did the words came out awkwardly, tentatively, as though she'd already forgotten what he'd asked. "Just tell me what will happen when you find him."

He was about to repeat his question when he saw that she was looking at the poster. He pressed the heels of both his palms against his eyes. "I'm going to approach him very slowly, with my hands away from my body, so that he can see he's not in any danger. I'm going to talk to him. I'm going to make sure that no one else comes within fifteen feet. I'm going to keep all weapons holstered. And I'm also going to keep you close at hand." He leaned toward her then like the host of a talk show, arranging his hands in his lap. "I'll have to judge his state of mind, to start with, and you know your son best. That's why I need you to stay right with me, Miss Heller."

She closed her eyes and sat up straight and nodded. A few hours earlier she'd have laughed at his manner but now she barely seemed to be listening.

"You won't need me for the rest of it, will you? You won't need me really."

He took her arm and gripped it. "What's the matter with you, Miss Heller? How many of your pick-me-ups did you take?"

She smiled at him or at something just behind him. "I don't have any pick-me-ups, Detective."

"You listen now, Miss Heller. Look at me. I don't pretend to know what's wrong with you and I don't want to know. But whatever it is, you'd better fix it fast. I have no intention of missing your son again—none whatsoever. Do I make myself clear?"

"Yes, Detective. Yes, you do. I'm sorry." But the smile and the diffidence behind the smile were clearer to see than ever.

The train banked hard to the left and the local track met them, flickering behind a row of I beams like a dragon in a black-and-white cartoon. Lateef watched it in the feeble hope that it might calm him. He remembered what Violet had said about trains and he found himself studying the car and the passengers, asking himself what it was about them that she hated. As he looked out the window he began to feel the tunnel's hold, its inescapable authority, the unconditional order it imposed. He wondered whether that might be the reason. We have no say, he thought. None whatsoever. We can't affect the speed or the direction or the order of the stations. The only choice is whether to get off. His thoughts embarrassed him and he recognized their simplicity but he couldn't bring himself to part with them. They brought him nearer to her, possibly even nearer to the boy. They hid a promise of a kind in their simplicity.

"Ali," she said suddenly, putting her hand over his. Her eyes were clearer now than he had ever seen them. She was looking where Lateef had been looking before, through the line of I beams at the local track. They were passing a 6 train, passing it at the slowest possible crawl, their twinned lights coloring the air between the cars. The 6 looked full to overflowing. A delay uptown, Lateef thought, not quite sure what he was meant to be looking for. Then she took his hand in hers and it dawned on him that she'd called him by his first name and that she was touching him willingly for the first time since they'd been in her apartment.

"What is it, Miss Heller?"

"Halfway down the car." Her hand gave a twitch. "Do you see him?"

"I'm not—hold on a minute—"

"Do you see the man in the fur hat?"

He shaded his eyes. "The Hasid?"

"Look past his left shoulder. Right now there's a woman in the way." She got to her feet and crossed the aisle as though the train were standing still. Lateef got up more cautiously and followed. He picked out the Hasid again and took stock of the woman beside him, a fortyish commuter in a nondescript brown coat. There was no one behind her. He wondered almost idly whether the woman was the Hasid's wife, whether she was wearing a wig like some Hasidim did, and why the car should be so crowded at that hour. He made an effort not to wonder about Violet. He'd just decided that the woman wasn't Hasidic at all when he saw the boy behind her clear as day.

"You see him now," said Violet. She said it kindly. "He'll turn this way soon. He always likes to look out on both sides."

A man in sunglasses pushed past the Hasid, hiding the boy again. Lateef cursed him silently. "You're sure that's your son? Did you get a good look?"

He expected her to ignore him and she did. She rested her forehead against the scuffed glass and stared across the flickering divide. Her mouth hung slightly open. He put his hand on her shoulder and she gave a groan and slid out of his grasp.

"We should sit down, Miss Heller. We don't want him to see us."

She turned away at once and clutched at the crosspole. I've frightened her, Lateef thought. Maybe that's for the best. He held his arm out and she took it gratefully.

"You could watch," she said. "He doesn't know you."

"You're forgetting I chased him through half the West Village." He smiled. "I wouldn't mind forgetting that myself."

"That's right," she said quickly. "You did that. I forgot."

"We can see him from here," Lateef said, helping her to sit. He kept an empty seat between them as before. Two girls in matching turquoise parkas gawked at her, not sure whether to laugh, but she looked past them as if they were made of wax. She hasn't even noticed them, he thought. She barely seems aware of where she is. The boy was still facing away from them, his head tipped to one side, swaying lightly with the canting of the train. Lateef appraised his features point by point. The flat blond hair, the boyish stoop, the shapeless thriftstore sweater. It had to be the same boy. He looks relaxed, Lateef thought. Thank the Lord for small mercies.

As he had that thought the local started braking. No sense keeping him in sight, Lateef said to himself. Let him go and get ready. Get off the train at Union Square and wait. The feeling of entrapment broke over him again and he felt his palms and underarms go damp. The local was falling back silently and smoothly and the boy was already drifting out of view. He waited for Violet to react but she did nothing. He kept his eyes on the 6 and when the boy was finally gone he willed himself to turn and look at her. He was sweating freely now. Her head was propped against the wall and her eyes were partly closed. She's sleeping, Lateef thought. How can she be sleeping. But she didn't look asleep so much as dead.

"Miss Heller," he said. The name stuck in his throat.

"Yes?"

"Here's what's going to happen, Miss Heller. We'll get off at the next stop and wait for the local. I'll put everyone up the line on track alert." When she said nothing to that he shook her shoulder gently. "Wake up, Miss Heller. Stay with me now. If he doesn't get off the local, we'll have to get on it ourselves. Some men from my department should be at Union Square already. We'll leave them there in case we somehow miss him."

"All right, Ali," she said. There was an appeal behind her use of his name, a warning of some kind, but it thrilled him regardless. She let him carry her weight as if it were the most natural thing in the world. This will be over within the hour, he reminded himself. A few more hours at the most. He studied their conjoined reflection in the window, a middle-aged black man and a semiconscious foreigner, trying to picture what might happen then. He couldn't picture anything.

When they were almost at the station it occurred to him that his backup would be waiting on the platform and he shifted away from her and sat up straight. She slid farther down against him without opening her eyes. He stared at his reflection helplessly.

At last the station came. "Violet," he said, more sharply than he'd intended. She sat up grudgingly and fixed her hair. The girls in the parkas were giggling openly now. He got to his feet and reached behind him and guided her up.

"Is this it?" she said, passing a hand over her face. The gesture was familiar to Lateef but for a time he couldn't place it. Finally he recognized it as his own.

"Is this it?" she repeated. She seemed not to expect an answer. What's wrong with me, he wondered. Why can't I picture either of us tomorrow. The train came to a stop and the doors slid smoothly open and he led her slowly to the nearest bench, making an effort to keep himself from trembling. I'm frightened of her, he said to himself. Frightened of her and for her. He felt no surprise at the thought.

Before they reached the bench her eyes had closed again. He stared at her the way the girls on the train had been staring and as he did so he remembered what had happened the last time she'd seen her son. Why didn't that put me on my guard, he thought. God knows that should have been enough. But of course he knew why. He sat down next to her and took her hand.

"Violet," he said. "Listen to me, Violet. I want you to open your eyes."

She opened them at once and looked toward him. Toward him but not at him. "Go on ahead," she said steadily. "This is just something that happens."

"There's nowhere to go, Violet. We have to wait here for the local."

She nodded. "When it comes, go ahead."

"He's supposed to get off here, remember? You have to be ready. You have to wake up."

"Where are the men you said would be here? The men from your department?"

"I don't know." He hadn't thought of them until that instant. "Most likely they're waiting for us upstairs."

She looked past him with what might have been concern. The local track was half a step behind her. A quivering started up along its rails.

"Here it comes," said Lateef.

She met his eyes now. "What do we do? Do we get up?"

"We stay right here until it comes to a full stop. We don't turn around. As soon as it's stopped we get up and we go."

She smoothed down the creases in her jeans and said nothing.

"If for any reason he doesn't get off, we get on. We wait until the doors start to close and then we move. Can you do that with me?"

She closed her eyes tightly, as though the question itself was too much for her, then opened them and took hold of his sleeve. The quivering turned to screeching as the local's airbrakes hit. He watched the train arrive on other people's faces. A man in a transparent raincoat turned his head from left to right like a video camera, eyeballs ticking back and forth grotesquely.

"Can we turn around yet?" Violet said through her teeth. "Should we be getting up?"

"Hold on," he told her. "A few seconds more."

He stood without turning and helped her get up and kept her close to him until the doors opened. She'll be all right, he told himself. Just keep her moving. He turned her around by the shoulders, perhaps a little roughly, then stepped forward to look up and down the platform. Its curve was in his favor and the whole train was in view. He counted under his breath from one to nine, ticking his head from side to side as the man in the raincoat had done. No one got off who looked anything like the boy.

"Not here," Violet said behind him. "Some other place." It sounded as though the words were meant for someone else.

"He's on this train," Lateef said under his breath. "You saw—" But the door-closing theme cut him off. Assuming that he's spotted us, he thought. If he's spotted us how much time do we have left. Maybe a minute. He kept the doors of the car from shutting with the heel of his right foot and reached for the standpole to keep from falling over. "Come on, Violet," he said. "Let's not give him the time to change his mind." But when he looked back at the platform she was gone.

Over the next three stations Lateef searched the train from back to front and checked the platform every time it stopped. The cars seemed more crowded than was usual for that hour of the morning but he'd long since lost all confidence in his judgment. At Grand Central he put in a call to Lieutenant Bjornstrand, then switched to the downtown express, still not thinking about Violet at all. The boy was distracting him nicely. He got off somewhere, Lateef said to himself. He must have. Bleecker Street or Astor Place. When the express started to move he sat down heavily on the bench and dug the knuckles of his thumbs into his temples. It hadn't occurred to him to question the other riders—there'd been no time to question them— but as soon as he'd left the local he'd regretted it. He still regretted it. The back of his head was throbbing where his skull had hit the asphalt and his heart was spasming sickly in his chest. He thought about Emily's deposition and her torn and filthy jacket and suddenly he was thinking about Violet. I'll have nothing to tell her, he thought. Not a trace of the boy. She'll think she was seeing things again. He brought his hands forward to cover his face and rolled them evenly from side to side. Maybe she *is* seeing things, he said to himself. Maybe both of us are. He tried to recollect what he'd seen with his own eyes but he seemed to have misplaced the memory. I saw what she told me, he thought, taking his hands from his face. I saw what she told me to see. The possibility occurred to him that he might have been tricked, deliberately misled, made use of in some way he couldn't name. But when he tried to guess at her reason for abandoning him his thoughts went dim or shut down altogether.

He got out at Union Square and went back to the bench and sat where she'd been sitting. The wood felt warm against his back, as if she'd only just left, but he didn't believe it. He sat there silently and stiffly. At one point he'd felt able: he remembered that much. He'd felt confident in his abilities, even proud. It might in fact have been that very day.

I remember now, he thought suddenly. I remember when the feeling left me. I was sitting at my desk looking at the boy's note, the one written in cipher, and I guessed that the keyword was "Violet" and it was. I decoded it and wrote it out in big block letters and appreciated it. Then I stood up and went to the door and saw her waiting for me in the hall.

Lateef sat for a time with his hands in his pockets, tapping his shoetips together, watching the trains come and go. They were nearly full now but the platform was empty and he couldn't understand why that should be. Passengers got on and off but none of them seemed to linger. No one sat on the bench. After what might have been half an hour he got heavily to his feet and walked toward the stairs leading up to the exit and that was when he noticed Violet.

She stood bent to one side in the shadow of the stairs and seeing her there answered his last questions. Her face was tipped sideways and her pale mouth hung open and she moved her eyes as though a train were passing. She flinched as he approached her and from that he judged that she could see him coming. Otherwise he might have thought that she'd gone blind.

"Miss Heller," he said, holding his hand out as if to an infant. But in reality she was prematurely aged, aged almost past recognition. He'd meant to say "Violet" but the name no longer represented her. "Miss Heller," he repeated. She gave no sign of hearing him. He opened his mouth a third time but he couldn't seem to make the slightest sound.

"It's gone bright," she said. "Please turn it off." Her mouth snapped shut after each word like the hinged jaw of a puppet.

"Don't worry, Miss Heller." He took a step toward her. "It's Detective Lateef. It's Ali." He'd seen people in that state before or in something very like it and he knew there was no sense in moving quickly. The current running through her body was so enormous that she barely seemed to have the strength to breathe. He'd seen it times without number, in suicides and barricades and addicts of all kinds, but he had no way of knowing which she was. That wasn't true of course: he knew perfectly well. The fact of it hovered in the air between them, buzzing almost inaudibly, waiting to be given its due. It had been waiting since sometime that afternoon. Lateef looked at Violet and cleared his throat to hear the noise it made. He heard the noise clearly and he was grateful to hear it. He bent over to make himself seem smaller.

"What was in those pills, Miss Heller?"

She ducked as though he'd thrown something at her. "A thing's going to happen," she said, running her tongue over her lips.

"Is that right?" he said. He took another step.

"Very soon. It's happening already."

"Can you hear me, Miss Heller? Do you know who this is?"

He waited a long time for her to answer. When at last she closed her mouth and covered her face with her hands he allowed himself to look over his shoulder. A few steps behind him was a payphone with a yellow receiver. He backed toward it cautiously, forcing his eyes not to stray, and reached it without once losing sight of her. He thanked God that no one else was on the platform. When he put the receiver to his ear the dial tone came through dimly but clearly and he sucked in a breath and thanked God for that also. He dialed Lieutenant Bjornstrand's number and was told that his support was waiting for him up at Thirty-fourth Street. He asked for no explanation and none was offered. He set the receiver back in its cradle, closed his eyes for a moment, then called Ulysses S. Kopeck, MD. Even as he dialed he knew what Kopeck would tell him but he needed to hear the words spoken. He might not pick up the phone, Lateef thought. If he doesn't what then. But Kopeck answered on the second ring.

"Sorry to call you at this hour, Dr. Kopeck. This is Detective—"

"I recognize your voice, Ali. I've been wondering when you might call."

Lateef kept silent for a moment. "You knew what was wrong with her," he said. "You knew exactly what the problem was."

A pause for effect as in a theater. The pause before the punchline. "Of course I did, Detective. Didn't you?"

"Are you trying to tell me, Doctor—" He stopped to take another breath. "Do you mean to tell me that we talked for half an hour in your office, with her waiting right outside, and you never once saw fit to let me know?"

"I have a confidentiality agreement with my patients, Ali. I like to honor that agreement." Kopeck cleared his throat mildly. "In any event, I assumed that her condition was self-evident."

"Not to me it wasn't. Not to me."

"I'm surprised by that, Detective. I'd been told you dealt with cases of this nature regularly. After all, you've been with Miss Heller for the better part of—"

"Just tell me what's wrong with her, you fucker. Give me her diagnosis."

"Since you put it that way, Detective, Miss Heller is a paranoid schizophrenic." He could hear Kopeck's lips smack together as each word was expelled. "Can I help you with anything further?"

The 4 came in behind him and a napkin pirouetted at his feet. He wasn't looking at Violet anymore. He wasn't looking at the train. "I've been with her since this morning, like you said. I've seen my share of schizophrenics. I never would have guessed—"

"Miss Heller has what psychiatrists call a high degree of insight into her disorder, unlike her son. When I was seeing her, she took two hundred milligrams of Clozapine daily, in tablet form, and forty milligrams of Celexa."

"She never told me that. None of it. I asked her—"

"You asked her directly?"

Lateef didn't answer. The 4 had pulled up and its doors had opened. He studied the motionless car packed with commuters. They seemed to be under the impression that they were moving. None of them so much as glanced at Violet.

"She didn't want me to know," Lateef said. "She was right not to tell me. I'd never have taken her with me if I'd known."

"I'll have to take your word for that, Ali."

Lateef looked down at the receiver for a time, weighing it in his palm, then dropped it lightly back into its cradle. The 4 had rolled away without his noticing. He turned his head unwillingly toward the stairs, half expecting to find her gone, wishing to find her gone with all his might. She was in much the same position as before, perhaps drawn farther back into the dark, perhaps bent slightly nearer to the floor. Muttering and working her jaws as though she had something between her teeth. As he came forward he wondered whether she had been listening. No matter now. She was standing with her chin wedged against her left shoulder, cursing everything she saw, but she quieted when he said her name and drew her gently toward him.

At 116th Street the train came to a regretful stop and a man slipped sideways through the doors and sat down across from Lowboy. No one else was in sight. Thirty-seven seats to choose from not counting those reserved for cripples but the man sat down without a moment's doubt. A storklike man with crimped orange hair and the righteous eyes and bearing of a prophet. He stared up and down the aisle as though to quiet his many accusers and when he was finished he turned and smiled out of the side of his mouth at Lowboy. The waitingroom smile of an insurance claims adjuster or a dentist. Can a dentist be a prophet, Lowboy wondered. Can an insurance claims adjuster. He was about to ask when the man held up a finger.

"No laces," the man said, pointing at Lowboy's shoes.

Lowboy stuck out his feet. "Velcro," he said softly. That was the term. He waited for the man to go on talking.

In place of an answer the man raised his finger again. His Adam's apple quivered on his flushed and wattled neck. A moment later he lowered his finger like a dowser's wand until it was pointing down at his own shoes. They were wrapped in silver duct tape from the laces to the shins. The tape looked new and heavy and expensive. It made Lowboy suspicious.

"Where are your socks," Lowboy whispered.

"Where are yours," said the man.

Lowboy looked down and saw the man was right. Who could have taken them, he said to himself. Secretary most likely. That reminded him of something.

"I saved the world," he said.

The man shrugged his shoulders. They rode on in silence as the train made its rounds and the man sucked his teeth and repeated every one of Lowboy's movements. When he pitched the man pitched. When he jerked the man jerked. There was something behind it. At each stop he made a wish that someone else would get on but when the doors opened he always changed his mind. Ninety-sixth Street now. Eighty-sixth Street presently. The man jerking left and right and mimicking him like a monkey at the zoo. Sucking on his teeth and bobbing his head and tapping his heels together to make music. A territorial display or could it be a courtship. The skin on Lowboy's face began to itch.

"What's under the duct tape," he said. "What's behind it."

The man grinned and snorted and got to his feet. "Nike cross trainers," he said. He reclined from the crosspole. "There's a Dumpster at the Foot Locker on Broadway and Eighteenth—"

"Get away from me," said Lowboy.

To his surprise the man sat down at once. "You're one of us," he said. "You're a colleague."

Lowboy looked past the man and said nothing.

The man stretched his legs out and arched both his feet like a dancer. "I take them off sometimes," he said. "On certain occasions. For example when I cross the Musaquontas."

"The Musaquontas," said Lowboy. His throat tightened. "The Quiet River."

"That's the one."

"You must be the Dutchman."

The Dutchman took a comb from his pocket and ran it elegantly through his hair.

"I'm Will," Lowboy offered. "William Heller. Heather Covington said—"

"All right, Will. Good enough. Let's say that you were going to buy a house." He pointed the comb at Lowboy. "Would you sleep in it first?"

"A house?" Lowboy said. It made him think of his sketches of Emily.

The Dutchman nodded. "Would you sleep in it or buy it right away?"

Lowboy shook his head dumbly. Was it really the Dutchman. He looked outside for an answer but there was nothing to see but the sweating walls and weepholes of the tunnel. No ciphers or bar codes or graffiti. The message was gone could he still recollect it.

"Would I sleep in the house," said Lowboy. He considered the question. Emily's face had turned into a house. "Yes," he said. "I'd sleep in it."

"Good boy." The Dutchman's head slid toward him. "Spend the whole goddamn night there. Check it for ectoplasmic activity."

"My mother was a house. So was Emily. I was a piece of paper or a cigarette or a bed."

The Dutchman clucked thoughtfully. "How's Rafa been?"

"Heather Covington," said Lowboy. "She called me 'little baby.' She took me down the tunnel to the bottom of the world and the quilt and the little blue suitcase. I couldn't do it, Dutchman. There was a little white girl in her passport. Her name was Heather Covington. Dr. Zizmor was the one who made her black."

"Covington," said the Dutchman. "Good enough."

"That's what she called herself," said Lowboy. "I called her that. I told her about me and Skull and Bones—"

The Dutchman sat up straight. "What do you know about Skull and Bones?"

"I told Heather Covington," Lowboy said, stammering. "I told Rafa—"

"Shut your mouth," said the Dutchman. "I was a member of that dread society."

"Bones is a milkfaced man," said Lowboy. "Not much to look at. Skull is the size of a—"

"They manage the planet," the Dutchman said, nodding. "They make it *productive*. They're the ones making things hot."

A curtain opened as the Dutchman was talking and Lowboy understood the world completely. He remembered a platform, the back of a train, the cool air growing warmer on a curve. Without Skull & Bones he might never have gotten his calling. He'd recognized them as his enemies and had run up the platform's yellow lip and the doors of the train had opened when he kicked them. He couldn't help but take that as a sign. From the moment he'd entered the train he'd been hallowed and exalted and beloved. He'd disappeared into the tunnel like a plug into a socket and the tunnel had given him everything.

"Things aren't getting hotter," said Lowboy. "Not anymore." He pressed his hands against his stomach. "See that, Dutchman? Nothing there. I've had my sex."

The Dutchman blinked at him. "You've had your sex," he said.

Lowboy bobbed his head. "My calling said to let my insides out. An offering it told me or a sacrifice. It happened just this morning. The world was inside me and I was inside of—"

"Jesus *Christ*," said the Dutchman. He let his head fall back against the window. "Who cares what you've been inside of, little boy?"

A keening came up off the rails or a voice raised in outrage. He made a fist and the train passed Eighty-sixth Street. He made two and it passed Seventy-seventh. "Tell the truth," he said. "That's not right." His voice was no louder than the keening but he could feel it pushing up out of his throat. "Tell the truth Dutchman. I was in a burned car and a woman walked past me. She told me I was out of gas and I was. She called me her doggy. She took me to a five-cornered room."

"Not enough," said the Dutchman. His lips barely fluttered. "Not enough." It rang out in the dead air like a bell.

"It was enough," Lowboy said carefully. "It was." They were passing Sixty-eighth Street. "I had my sex with her. Later when I woke up it was cold."

"It's six o'clock now," said the Dutchman. He said it without opening his mouth. "You didn't stop anything, William."

"I didn't want things to stop," Lowboy shouted. "Just the temperature games. I wanted to keep things from getting hotter. I wanted to keep the end of the world away."

"It goes on and on," said the Dutchman. He tipped over and his face went sad and soft. "It's too painful."

"It's painful," Lowboy said, nodding. He stopped to catch his breath. "It hurts very much. But it's possible—"

"It's *impossible*," said the Dutchman. "One day your body understands that. Then you die."

Lowboy watched as the Dutchman got smaller and smaller. He was lying on his side now humming quietly to himself. Is he dying, Lowboy wondered. Is he falling asleep. The train pulled into Forty-second Street and the C# and A sounded and no one got on.

"You're wrong," Lowboy said to him. "I disagree."

The train bucked forward suddenly and the tunnel fell back and the express track came and kissed the track beneath them. The keening filled the car like a fog or a color but also like the first note of an opera. Lowboy went to the doors and looked out at the tracks and saw the glittering waterway between them. A river whose name he'd long since forgotten. An express train went by with a person at each window and none of them seemed to be dying. I disagree, Lowboy thought. It's not impossible. For the first time since the world hadn't ended he tried to imagine Violet and the trains waiting to take him to her house. Not impossible, he said under his breath. At Bleecker Street I can switch to the uptown F. He bent down to tell the Dutchman but the Dutchman was the size of a receipt. The train shot through Twenty-third Street without stopping. People rolled their eyes and shivered and made faces. People shrieked and laughed and stepped out of their clothes.

At Union Square the Dutchman left the train. He dropped to the floor and glanced over his shoulder and skittered up the aisle like a mouse. He's not dead, Lowboy thought. He's not dead and it's not impossible. He sat on the bench with his face to the window and watched the Dutchman disappear into the crowd. The keening had stopped and he felt almost hopeful. The crowd on the platform surprised him a little but he reminded himself that it was six a.m. Violet would be getting up soon unless he'd made some sort of error or she'd died. Maybe she hadn't ever gone to bed. He pictured her in the kitchenette, hair sticking up like a schoolboy's, frying onions and garlic in butter. Her face was the color of soap but that was perfectly all right. It was always that color first thing in the morning. "Transfer at Fulton Street," he said out loud. "Switch to the uptown platform, then five stops close together on the C." That's all it was.

· · ·

Would she be getting up now, would she be taking her meds, would she be sliding her legs out from under her rustcolored sheets. Would she be muttering to herself, would she slip sideways out of bed, would she throw open the curtains and pick out one of his father's records, would she put it on carefully and smile for a minute and make Turkish coffee in the blue enamel pot. Would she make scrambled eggs and bacon and rye toast. Would she hum out of key to the music, would she change clothes in the hallway or the kitchenette or the bathroom, would she make a face at herself in the mirror as she went by. Would she tap at his door lightly with two fingers, would she come in a moment later, would she choose clothes for him to wear and lay them out across his bed, boxers socks T-shirt button-down corduroys sweater, would she squint at them for a while then change her mind. Would she lay a palm against his forehead to wake him. Would she give him a moment then tug gently on his ear. Would she laugh at him then. Would she call him Professor. Would she seem sorry to have woken him at all.

When he opened his eyes the train still hadn't left. There were people in the car now and some of them were close enough to touch. That was no problem either. He was about to let his eyes shut to make time go faster when he saw Heather Covington shuffling down the uptown platform like someone searching for a missing pet.

The doors slid closed a moment later but by then he was halfway up the stairs. He had news for Heather Covington she'd be very glad to hear it. Union Square Station, he said under his breath. It had always been his favorite on the line. There were too many people on the stairs and when he looked back at the platform Heather Covington was gone. Once he would have been careful not to touch anyone but now it couldn't be helped there were so many of them scratching and stumbling and rushing to get to the train. He remembered at

Columbus Circle how the crowd had spun him slowly clockwise. So much simpler and more beautiful than deciding. I'll go back there, he thought. I'll take Violet tomorrow. Then the last man pushed past him and he came to the top of the stairs.

When he reached the uptown platform Heather Covington was there. The curving track conjoined them like a carousel. The rails clacked and whistled: a flat childish music as if from a calliope. She was at the far end of the platform making for the uptown tunnel. Her feet were bare her shirt was bunched and tattered. Miss Covington, he shouted. He ran up the platform's corrugated lip. Rafa, he called to her. Listen to me Rafa. I've had my sex.

The tunnel puckered like a mouth as she came near it and Lowboy started to worry. People were in his way but he ignored them. I did a good job Rafa, he shouted. The tags told me so. Slow down Miss Covington. The world can stop ending. But then he ran right into Skull & Bones.

He ran into them from behind and he was past them before he saw what he had done. They blinked sleepily at him as he went by, stupid and unsurprised, and caught up with him in three unhurried steps. Have they been expecting me, he wondered. Have they been waiting all this time. They were dressed in tight black uniforms like Nazis and their silent movie softshoe had been neatly put aside. Their names suited them now. They wore their names like hats. They circled him like two cats around a bird, heavy and lazy and indifferent, never coming close enough to touch him. He couldn't explain it. He felt the old fear climbing saplike through his body from the soles of his feet where it had long been stockpiled and he opened his mouth and gave a little cough. He stopped and retched and

Skull & Bones kept circling. His fear made the world happen slowly. The crowd behind him rustled like a sheet. As he looked up the platform he heard his name said in a whisper. Is that you William Heller. Is that William. Is that Will.

It's me, he said. Yes. Is that you Emily. He spun around in a circle and picked her face out of the crowd. It was easy to find her. She wasn't the new Emily or the old Emily either but the one that he'd drawn pictures of at school. A circle with two lines on top of it. A house with a hairy roof. Come here to me, he said. We're not done talking. She took three steps and stopped at the edge of the crowd. He smiled at her and tried to see her better. I'm sorry Emily, he said. Next time I'll do my best to draw you better.

I thought there was a calling Emily. I thought there had to be. Why else was I born if not for that. Dutchman said life is impossible but not if there's a reason. There has to be a reason Emily. Otherwise why this sickness. Without it there's only running away and kissing you and pushing you downstairs. There's only poor sick Will gone up to heaven. Thank God there was a calling Emily. Thank God about the air. There was a reason and I asked you to help me with my body and you tried. I tried with you. You kissed me on the mouth to make it colder. Thank you Emily. Please don't go flat. If not a calling then at least there was your name.

After she was gone he walked into the crowd without bothering to look for Skull & Bones. The fear was sputtering and screaming in his ears but he made up his mind not to pay attention. Most faces in the crowd were strange to him and badly drawn but many more were known to him by sight. Dr. Fleisig was there with Dr. Prekopp beside him and Baby and the laughing brownskinned nurses from the school: Officer Martinez and the sad-eyed dandy from St. Jeb's Buy & Barter and Jonathan Zizmor and the man with the Jamaican beef patty and the women from the dirty magazine. Quick & Painless and Secretary and the man in the gold satin jacket. A flatness over everything like a blacklight. No one answered his greeting. On a bench by a payphone his grandfather sat reading the New York *Daily News*. Air was mustering on the platform and the paper snapped and buckled. The tracks on Lowboy's left began to sigh. He looked back the way he'd come and every face that he saw was familiar. All of them waiting for the ghost train to arrive. Everyone was there but Violet.

Where's Violet, Lowboy shouted. No one moved or breathed or said a word. Where's Violet, he mumbled. Expecting no answer. But a voice rang out behind him and the crowd fell back like crabs before a wave. That voice alone had not been improvised.

"Violet's here," the voice said. "She's upstairs." Lowboy followed the sound to an old black man talking. A schoolteacherly man in a herringbone jacket. Skull & Bones behind him sharpening their teeth.

"Give her a message," said Lowboy. "Tell her something from me." He held his hands out like a prisoner. "I figured out the reason I was born."

"You can tell her yourself," said the man. The air pulled back from him as he stepped forward. "Come upstairs with me, Will. Your mother's sick."

"I know what my mother is." He craned his neck to watch the ghost train coming. He thought about Violet and her sickness and her accent and her orthopedic shoes. He thought about her apartment with its bright red walls and Chinatown lamps and pictures from *Interview* and *National Geographic* and *Vogue*. He remembered her impatience and her dirty mouth and the way she had of misremembering sayings. He remembered *We don't have all the tea in China*.

"I'll tell her," he mumbled, putting his hands down. "I'll tell her something." Then the man bent over and took him in his arms.

The ghost train came up behind them. "Easy," the man said in his kindly black voice. "Nice and easy," he said. He said it kindly and blackly. Was he talking to Lowboy now or to himself. Lowboy let his arms hang and flutter and his feet followed sorrowfully behind. Emily had held him there and kissed him. Where is Violet, he shouted. No one answered. He remembered what Emily had whispered to him on that last unforgivable afternoon.

It's got to happen sometime, Will. It happens to every person in the world.

The noise of the express train blew out of the tunnel as Lowboy brought his mouth to the man's cheek and bit it. There was no hearing anything else. He tasted blood on his teeth and the arms let him loose and his shoeheels hit the platform's slotted edge. The man's hands clutched his sleeves but he slipped out of his sweater like a fish. The man looked down at him in awe. His thin red mouth opened and shut. Skull & Bones came past him then but the express came past him faster. It came in as fast as the ghost train before it and made every living creature catch its breath. Why was I born, Lowboy thought. I know why. He made a face and took a slow step backward. On November 12 the world ended by fire.

ACKNOWLEDGMENTS

Jin Auh, Eric Chinski, Brooke Costello, *Cop Talk* by E. W. Count, *Crazy All the Time* by Frederick L. Covan, MD, *Tell Me I'm Here* by Anne Deveson, Matt Dojny, Doug Dibbern, Eli Greenberg, MD, *The Diagnostic Statistical Manual of Mental Disorders IV*, *Subway Lives* by Jim Dwyer, *Jazz in the Sixties* by Leonard Feather, *Stranger to the System* by Jim Flynn and Nelson Hall, Alex Halberstadt, William Hall, Shirley Hazzard, Edward Henderson, MD, Corin Hewitt, Chloe Hooper, Cheryl Huber, *The Encyclopedia of New York City* by Kenneth T. Jackson, Kirsten Kearse, Peter Knecht, Jay Ko, MD, Steven Koch, William Lubart, PhD, *The Psychiatric Interview in Clinical Practice* by Roger MacKinnon, Haruki Murakami, *Children with Emerald Eyes* by Mira Rothenburg, *Memoirs of My Nervous Illness* by Daniel Paul Schreber, *Autobiography of a Schizophrenic Girl* by Marguerite Sechehaye, Akhil Sharma, *The Code Book* by Simon Singh, *Transit Talk* by Robert W. Snyder, Adrian Tomine, *Surviving Schizophrenia* and *Nowhere to Go* by E. Fuller Torrey, MD, Jared Whitham, *This Stranger, My Son* by Louise Wilson, Barbara Wünschmann-Henderson, PhD, Peter Wünschmann, Andrew Wylie.

THE DEATH OF BUNNY MUNRO

NICK CAVE

I AM DAMNED
thinks Bunny Munro, in a sudden moment of self-awareness
reserved for those who are soon to die . . .

Struggling to keep a grip on reality after his wife's sudden death,
Bunny Munro does the only thing he can think of. With his young
son in tow, he hits the road. An epic chronicle of one man's
judgement and death, *The Death of Bunny Munro* is also an achingly
tender portrait of the relationship between father and son.

'Funny, horrifying and moving, and wrapped up in rich and
restless prose.' *The Times*

'A lyrical end-of-the-pier morality tale . . . A grotesque delight.' *GQ*

'A modern-day parable, illuminated with raw lyricism, scraps of
tenderness and dark phantasmagoria. Accessible, thrilling and
gloriously impolite.' *Sunday Telegraph*

£7.99

ISBN 978 1 84767 378 7

www.meetatthegate.com

UNDER THE SKIN

MICHEL FABER

SHORTLISTED FOR THE WHITBREAD PRIZE

Isserley spends most of her time driving. But why is she so interested in picking up hitchhikers? And why are they always male, well-built and alone?

An utterly unpredictable and macabre mystery, Michel Faber's debut novel is an outstanding piece of fiction that will stay with you long after you have turned the final page.

'A wonderful book. Painful, lyrical, frightening, brilliant . . . I couldn't put it down.' Kate Atkinson

'It'll get to you, one way or another. Of that there is no doubt.' *Observer*

'Strange, adept, original . . . Would that more first novels were as adventurous or as funky and daring in their conception.' *Independent on Sunday*

£7.99

ISBN 978 1 84767 892 8

www.meetatthegate.com

NO ONE BELONGS HERE
MORE THAN YOU

MIRANDA JULY

WINNER OF THE 2007 FRANK O'CONNOR
INTERNATIONAL SHORT STORY AWARD

In her remarkable stories of seemingly ordinary people living
extraordinary lives, Miranda July reveals how a single moment can
change everything.

Whether writing about a middle-aged woman's obsession with
Prince William, or an aging factory worker who has never been in
love, the result is startling, sexy and tender by turns. One of the
most acclaimed debuts of the year, Miranda July is a brilliant new
voice in fiction.

'Blisteringly good.' *Guardian*

'These stories are incredibly charming, beautifully written,
frequently laugh-out-loud funny, and even, a dozen or so times,
profound.' Dave Eggers

'A magically oddball study of depression, repression, envy,
loneliness and aimlessness – and rarely has such a thing been so
entertaining.' *Time Out*

£7.99

ISBN 978 1 84767 116 5

PRETTY MONSTERS

KELLY LINK

Weird, wicked, spooky and delicious, *Pretty Monsters* is a book of tall tales to keep you up all night. Kelly Link creates a world like no other, where ghosts of girlfriends past rub up against Scrabble-loving grandmothers with terrifying magic handbags, wizards sit alongside morbid babysitters, and we encounter a people-eating monster who claims to have a sense of humour.

'Link's stories play in a place few writers go, a netherworld between literature and fantasy, Alice Munro and JK Rowling.' *Time*

'Wonderfully odd and original [and] very scary indeed.'
Sarah Waters

'Funny, moving, tender, brave and dangerous. She is unique, and should be declared a national treasure, and possibly surrounded at all times by a cordon of armed marines.' Neil Gaiman

£8.99

ISBN 978 1 84767 784 6

www.meetatthegate.com